Forever After

A NOVEL BY

KATE LAZLO

THE DIAL PRESS

NEW YORK

Published by
The Dial Press
1 Dag Hammarskjold Plaza
New York, New York 10017

Lines from "Do Not Go Gentle Into That Good
Night" from *The Poems* of Dylan Thomas. Copyright
1952 by Dylan Thomas. Reprinted by permission of
New Directions, The Trustees for the copyright for the
late Dylan Thomas, and David Higham Associates
Limited.

Copyright © 1981 by Kate Lazlo

Manufactured in the United States of America
First printing
Design by Francesca Belanger

Library of Congress Cataloging in Publication Data

Lazlo, Kate.
  Forever after.

  I. Title.
PS3562.A99F6   813'.54   80-26881
ISBN 0-8037-2679-1

*To my loving
and much-loved family*

Forever After

head of Dr. Darvey in the corridor a man lay waiting outside the X-ray department. He was bald, with the long scar of a craniotomy stitched across his skull. Surgery not more than a week ago. He was old. Maybe eighty, from the wrinkled gray of his hands. But there were ten like him in this corridor every day, waiting for orderlies to take them back to their rooms, so why see this one so specially? Maybe because it was six o'clock, the dead end of the hospital day. Maybe it was that he hadn't eaten since breakfast. Maybe it was because this man looked like his own father just before his death. The man lay with eyes at half-mast, in a kind of torpor, uncomplaining. Why didn't he complain? Why the hell *didn't* he? A line of poetry he had once liked swam through Jason Darvey's head: "Do not go gentle into that good night.

Rage, *rage* against the dying of the light!" Oh, my father, he thought. Yes. My father, and someday myself.

He stopped beside the wheeled bed. "Are you all right?"

The wrinkled, blue-veined lids twitched and opened. Pale blue moist eyes stared at him.

"I want to go back to my room," he whispered. "I'm tired. Can you take me back? Please?"

Now he'd done it. He was late already. He looked quickly up and down the hall, but no orderly was in sight.

"I'll see to it," he said, and patted the shrunken shoulder through the washed-out cotton gown.

He went quickly into X-ray. "Hey, Georgina," he said with relief, recognizing the girl at the desk. "Get on the phone, will you, and get an orderly down here fast. That old fellow outside is about to pass out."

"Sure, Dr. Darvey," she smiled, simpered really. Most of the secretaries and receptionists simpered at the doctors . . . simpered but kept tight asses. Or so they complained, the young studs of medicine. He was past all that. Maybe had never been there at all. A pretty tight-assed type himself, probably. Well, there was not much incentive in his specialty. Most of his patients were elderly . . . or children. You don't get cancer much in the nubile young. The gynecologists had the edge on him there. And the orthopedic boys. All those ski accidents . . . nothing wrong with those healthy girls but their broken wrists and ankles.

He stopped briefly at the old man's side. "Somebody will be right along for you. Okay?"

A bubble of saliva broke from the man's mouth and his eyes closed wearily. "Thanks."

He went on down B corridor and pushed open the

swinging doors of the seminar room. Everyone else seemed to be there.

"Sorry to be late. Make me up an excuse, will you?" The nurses laughed and relaxed a little. One of them took a sip of coffee and fingered the cigarette she knew enough not to light in his presence. Wouldn't you think oncology nurses would be scared off *that* particular habit?

Young Badurie, Falk, and Mallows leaned against the wall nonchalantly. They were here for the seminar but not worried about it. It wasn't the sort of stuff they needed to learn for their exams. It just happened to be crucially important, that's all.

"What do you think patients want most?" he started off, glancing around the room. Most of the nurses had notebooks. The young residents rather ostentatiously had none. "We're here to discuss that," he said, "so I'll start by asking for your opinions."

"To get out of our clutches and go home," a nurse said. She was pert Miss Crowell, her smile conspiratorial and a little sly.

"Yes, of course. Nobody wants to stay sick and be stuck in a hospital. That's understandable. But why, in particular, do they find hospitals unattractive? *This* one, for instance."

"Lousy food?" ventured another nurse.

"All right. That's always a big gripe in institutions. What else?"

There was a blank silence. "It's the doctors," said a pale, earnest-looking girl. "They are always complaining about the doctors."

"Oh?" he said. "You residents take note, please."

The three young men sat up a bit starchily. "What *about* the doctors?"

"You're not around enough," the earnest one went on bluntly. "They never get to ask all they want, and we're not supposed to tell them."

He was startled. "What do you mean, you're not supposed to tell them? You're not supposed to tell them they're dying. But what else?"

"Oh, *you* know. We don't even tell them their temperatures. You'd think they were a state secret. They're always interested in knowing their blood pressure and their temperature. And we're not supposed to say. And they're always full of questions about their diseases, and we're not supposed to tell them anything. It makes us feel like dummies . . . and they think we're keeping terrible secrets from them!" She was flushed and embattled, but firm.

He looked at the others. Several of the girls were nodding vigorously, glad to abet little Miss Whiteface even if they wouldn't speak up themselves.

"Well," he said defensively . . . it was not what he had expected. . . . "You know the principle involved. If they know their temperatures or blood pressure, they get all worked up about it without knowing what it means."

Miss Whiteface shook her head till her silly white cap tilted sideways. St. Catherine's, where she had come from, had the silliest caps in America, all puffy and accordion-pleated in front, and with two flying wings in back. He felt his hackles rise. He wasn't used to real opposition. Particularly from nurses in silly caps.

"That makes sense, doesn't it?" he asked her coldly.

"I don't think so," she said positively but with a faint quaver in her voice. It was dangerous to argue with the brass.

He dropped his tense shoulders suddenly. He'd asked for opinions, hadn't he? Well, then, there was no point in playing God and refusing them.

"Why not, then?" he asked gently.

"I think we can tell them their temperatures and tell them what it means, and then they wouldn't be scared. You see, it's not knowing that frightens people." She wasn't pale now. Her face was flushed, nervous.

Yes. Of course she was right. His father had died here, and had never known he was going to, never known he had cancer. Had it been cruel or kind? The question still haunted him. He could remember his father's eyes—washed-out blue, faded denim eyes like those of the old man in the corridor—looking at him and asking, "What is it? Is it cancer?" and his answer, lying, hearty, comforting, "Of course not. It's that arthritis acting up again."

"You may be right," he said slowly. There was a sudden outlet of air as if all those nurses had been holding their breath. "But if you *do* answer questions, you've got to know the answers, and when to give them. And that means you have to be trained to know what to say, and how much, and when." He looked at their watchful faces. The young residents were leaning forward at last, like hunting dogs. Were their special prerogatives to be lost? Their special privilege of *telling* patients while mere nurses stood by in silence?

"Let me think about this for a bit," he said, and smiled at the girl—the courageous one.

The corridor was empty when he came out. The old man was gone. The nurses and the residents streamed away. It was time for his rounds.

He liked evening rounds. In the morning he was followed by three residents and a nurse or two, and everything that happened had to be explained. He was maestro, show-and-tell teacher. They carried notebooks and *wrote* in them. He had them feel here and there, palpate, listen to tumorous lungs, recognize symptoms. It was a grand processional. But at night it was different. He went alone, and by choice. Not many of the other doctors made evening rounds at all. Strictly, it wasn't necessary. But he liked to see his patients before they were put down for the night.

He took the elevator and got out on his floor, 8. It was all freshly painted, chrome yellow for cheer. Not bad, and it *was* startling how they could drum up cheer around here. He stopped at the central desk, where Rose was eating a very fattening jelly donut.

"Anything, Rose?"

She made a slight, ineffectual motion toward concealing the donut, and gave up with a rueful look at him. She was always telling him what she was going to do when she was *Vogue*-model slim, but now—and probably forever—she was plump and full-breasted as a robin. "Oh, hi, Dr. Darvey. Not much action. Old Mr. Bailer says he needs more sleeping pills. I think he may be saving them."

"All right. I'll talk to him. Anything else?"

"One new one. A Mrs. McFarland in room six. She's just out of surgery. Dr. Kimutu. A pin in her femur. Metastatic breast to bone."

"Right. Yes, he told me."

The rooms were in a circle around a central desk and nurses' station. He made it a point to take each room as it came, playing no favorites. Mrs. Croghan was in 801,

a huge fat woman with jowls on her jowls and a sweet temper. Her husband was still there, the last to go, as usual. Why did big women so often marry little, active, rabbity men? He could imagine Mr. Croghan climbing all over that soft mountain of a wife like a bighorn sheep. Mrs. Croghan's radiation was halfway through. He wished he could tell them something hopeful, but it was too soon to know if the tumor could be stopped. He looked at the chart. She'd been vomiting all day. She looked exhausted, but she smiled back at him. Stomach radiation was no fun. He had only once in his life been really nauseated—in Mexico . . . awful! Women were tougher about that than men. If men had to go through the nausea of pregnancy, the population problem would be solved. That was the trouble with most of his bag of tricks. So often the side effects were nausea so bad the patient wanted to die. *Asked* to die.

"Feeling lousy?" he asked. Her chin wobbled in agreement.

"I know it's awful," he said, "but you'll be over the worst of it pretty soon now. Hang on. Have you taken your pills?"

It was the husband who answered. "Yeah, Doc, I been in here all along, and she's took them—at least *tried* to—but they don't do nothing that I can see!" The little man looked at him, his eyes sparking with anger. He had been there all day and his poor wife was *sick*. What kind of a hospital was this?

A good question. What kind of a hospital was it that couldn't cure people? He wanted to say, as helplessly as he felt, "I wish I knew the answer. We're trying." But you didn't fall apart like that, or what did they have to hang on to? You had to be strong and sure, or there was

no strength or sureness anywhere. Mrs. Croghan was frowning at her husband. She didn't want him to complain. She knew—she thought she knew—that they were doing all they could. She, at least, had faith in them . . . in *him*.

"Yes, I know," he said quietly. "But she'll feel better pretty soon. The first few days are the worst. Her body is taking in a lot of radiation. It's not used to it, and it's fighting back. But she'll adapt to it soon, and the nausea won't be so bad." He paused, because what he was saying might well be a lie. It *could* get worse. Some patients couldn't stand the radiation. "If it doesn't improve, we'll have to cut down the dosage and stretch out the treatments a little longer. Okay?"

He was talking to her, but he could see that she was afraid to answer, afraid she would throw up all over him as she had the day before.

It was the husband who answered. "Yeah, but how long would that take? We ain't made of money, ya know, Doc."

"I know. Do you have hospitalization?"

The little man showed his rabbit teeth in a painful grimace. "Nah. We don't get that where I work. I'm just part-time. The rest of the time I do my own business. I do trucking." He glanced at his wife's face. "Never mind, Doc," he said quickly, "the money ain't anything. Just you cure her, Doc, and lemme get her home. Okay?"

Mrs. Croghan's plump hand reached out and clutched at her husband's. Her face grew red with the effort of control, but it was no good. Her great chest began to heave and a wild light came into her eyes.

"Nurse!" Dr. Darvey called sharply. Joanna hurried

in, took one look, swooped up a pan and a towel, and stood beside the bed, holding on to Mrs. Croghan's shuddering shoulders while she retched. Mr. Croghan stared miserably at his wife.

"I'll be back soon," Dr. Darvey said. There was nothing he could do for her right now. She couldn't even hold down the antinausea pills. If she kept on like this, they'd have to put her back on intravenous feeding before she dehydrated. He hoped not. How she had hated that!

The next room was dim and silent. The woman in the bed was asleep. The new one, Mrs. McFarland. The anesthesia hadn't worn off. Her arm lay beside her like a block of wood, with the dextrose solution feeding into her. She shouldn't be here alone. Where was the nurse? He was angry for a moment. No patient just out of surgery should be left alone. And then, hearing voices next door, he realized that Joanna had rushed in when he had called her.

He sat down by the bed, studying the chart. Then he looked at the pale face on the pillow, framed in a soft cloud of brown hair. Astonishing. The chart told him she was in her forties, but the face was the face of a younger woman, broad-cheeked, almost Asiatic, with a softly rounded but strong jawline, quite at odds with the mouth, for there were tiny laughter curls at the corners which even pain had not erased. It was a lovely face. What excellent bones, he mused, and looked again at the chart. Left mastectomy, metastases to bone, ovarectomy to reduce hormones, CMF injections for eight months, then a spread to the hip and femur, and now surgery to insert a strengthening pin in the femur. There wasn't much left to do for her. Maybe radiation

to stop the bone spread. They weren't such good bones after all. He looked up from the chart, depressed, to find her brown eyes looking at him. They didn't seem confused or dull. They stared at him clearly, questioningly.

"Ah, you're awake," he said. "You're just out of the anesthetic. The operation is all over. How do you feel?"

Her eyes flickered away from his and took in the room, the bottle, and her immobile arm. "Magnificent," she whispered, and there was an ironic quiver to the corners of her bloodless lips.

"Well, we don't often get *that* reaction." He smiled faintly. "We may use you to propagandize on the joys of surgery."

Her lips shook as if they intended to smile, but they were taken over by something beyond her volition. He was just in time with the pan. This *was* a vomitous evening he was having.

"Here, I'll do that," said Joanna, coming in. She looked as if it were indecent for him to do it. This was nurse's work. He relinquished the pan reluctantly. There was no part of the body he felt was alien to him. Maybe that was why he had become a doctor. It was as if every pore, every smell, every excreted juice had a special reality he couldn't find in books or in ordinary conversation. As if he could hear and smell blood flowing and could recognize life. Nothing physical offended him. It never had. He remembered that when he was a boy he had sat in the bathtub enjoying the smell of his knees. But it *did* sound odd. He didn't, after all, love disease. He fought it every moment of his life. But he was not offended or disgusted by it. He would fight whatever form it offered to his weapons.

Mrs. McFarland was finished now. She lay back, exhausted, and looked at him. "Will this do it, do you think?" Her voice was still remote, a whisper.

"Do it?" He was puzzled.

She made a face, a grimace of irony. "Cure it, I guess I mean." She looked at her arm and moved it slightly, experimentally. The sheet rolled up and settled back, sagging down so that he could see the bump of one breast and the flat absence of the other.

"It should help."

"Sorry," she whispered. "I know you never use the word 'cure.' If I'm lucky, it may remit. Is that it?"

"Yes. You know what we're trying to do. This pin will protect your femur from breaking and the bone will be strengthened by it. . . ."

"Yes," she said, with a small impatient movement of her head. "I know the principle. Does it work?" Her voice was husky but cultivated.

He shrugged. He had been about to say, as he usually did, that they had had very good luck with this operation. But her large brown eyes stared so calmly at him that he didn't. "It's one of the tools in the arsenal," he said instead. "And we have quite a few now, so the chances are much better than they were even five years ago." He smiled now at her attentive face. "I'll take you to dinner five years from today," he said. He had made that offer before and once, happily, had been taken up on it.

A small bubble of a laugh came from her. "My tastes are expensive." And then her face darkened. "Who *are* you?" she asked abruptly.

"Oh, sorry. I'm Dr. Darvey." He looked around and laughed. "I come with the furniture."

"He does, too," said Joanna briskly, settling the bed and Mrs. McFarland's arm more firmly. "Dr. Darvey is chief of oncology here. Now you just go on back to sleep and in no time it will be morning and we'll get you some breakfast."

"Yes. All right." Her eyes closed as though the suggestion had done it. Probably in the morning she would remember nothing of this first waking.

He finished his rounds. Mr. Margolese was unhappy about his catheter, but there was nothing to be done about it. Prostate was a messy business. Mrs. Snow wanted to know if she could go home tomorrow. She couldn't. Mr. Reynolds asked to be moved because he couldn't stand the snoring of his roommate, Mr. Rosen, whose tongue had been removed, leaving a flap which quivered noisily when he slept.

It was not an unusual night. On his way out he glanced in once more at Mrs. McFarland. She was asleep.

hen she woke
it was with the sense of being tied to something rough,
like a tree whose bark bruised her when she moved.
Maybe she was lying facedown with her hands against
beach shingle. Something was wrong with her hands
and she couldn't seem to move. She could feel the rise
of water in her body that always accompanied panic.
She was going to scream. Her mouth opened and her
eyes shot apart at the same time. She could hear a great,
windy shriek, and it took a minute to recognize her own
voice.

"There, now, it's all right." A fruity voice came out
of a white, billowy figure like a windblown sheet.

"No," she said. "No, it's not!"

"You'll feel fine in a few minutes," the tutti-frutti
voice continued. Her eyes began to focus. It was the

largest nurse she had ever seen, fat rolls exploding from her tight white uniform, a jowly face all stretched and red with effort to contain itself. How could a nurse be so fat? Wasn't it like soldiers? If you were too tall or too fat they wouldn't take you . . . you wouldn't fit the uniforms. Where had she heard that?

"What's wrong with my hands?" she asked, and was surprised that her shrieking voice had gone and she was whispering.

"It's just your intravenous, dearie. It's to feed you up after your operation. Never you mind it."

She looked down the length of the bed toward her hands and tried, experimentally, to move one. Long threads of pain shot through her as though a parade of nerves had been jostled. There were needles in the back of her hand. The needles were attached to a long tube that was attached to a bottle that hung near her head. She was being fed?

"What's for dinner?" she asked, staring at her hand.

"What? Oh, I don't know yet, dearie. Probably you'll have some nice fish and creamed potatoes."

Yes, but what was she being fed through her arm? She had a vision of nice bits of fish sliding into her, accompanied by soft, milky mashed potatoes. And then she threw up. It happened too fast for her to call out for a basin, but miraculously the fat nurse pressed one to her lips and held her head. She must have known what to expect.

Everything hurt. She wanted to move, to get out of this numbing position on her back, to reach up to her nose, to scratch her neck, but she couldn't move. The slightest motion shifted the needle in her hand. Why in the back of her hand? There was no meat there to ac-

commodate a needle. Why not in her vein . . . the good vein in her right elbow, the one she saved for the endless chain of girls having a go at her with hypos and bottles?

There was something wrong with her leg, too. The left leg was either paralyzed or cut off. It didn't move when she told it to.

"What's the matter with my leg?" she whispered fearfully.

"Why, that's where you had your operation, dearie. It's in a cast so you won't move it. Remember, you had a pin put in your leg? Does it all come back to you, dearie?"

Why did she hate being called "dearie"? It was just a pleasantry, like any other, like being told by every clerk to "have a good day." She'd never minded it in English pubs, where the choice was being called "dearie" or "luv." There it was a word so full of robust cheekiness; it went with the cockney voice, the bar full of regulars. She had never got to be a regular, so they had to call her something—"dearie" or "luv." And it had seemed warm and amusing. But here it was like "honey," a cold, meaningless endearment that was no endearment.

"Do I have to stay here like this long?" she asked, the panic rising again. She had never been able to endure being held. One of the boys she had thought she'd loved in college—Martin—had tried to hold her hands once, in fun, so she couldn't escape. It was, she knew now, a boyish display of strength. But she had refused to see him again. Poor Martin had never understood why. She hadn't herself, except to know she wasn't going to be immobilized again, ever, except by her own will. A kind of claustrophobia, her friend Helen had called it.

Helen was full of definitions. It came of being a clinical
psychologist. Tell her anything and she could name it.
But naming wasn't explaining. She had claustrophobia,
all right—in elevators, in subways, in small, win-
dowless rooms. When she wanted to feel real horror she
didn't have to go to a vampire movie. All she had to do
was to imagine being buried alive. It was easier and
cheaper than *Psycho*.

"Till the doctor says, honey. He'll be in to see you
soon."

She nodded and tried to look away, around the room,
to distract herself from what she could see of her hand,
that tube. There was nothing to hold or engage the
mind. Why didn't they ever realize that patients needed
THINGS to distract them? The room was purely func-
tional, all white, venetian blinds, a bed, two chairs, a
bedside table, a yellow curtain, and, hung up at an
angle near the ceiling, the only nonfunctional item in
the room, the TV set. Nonfunctioning, too, she remembered from her last time. Unless you paid. But
there it hung, a blank-faced, menacing presence which
could be lit only when silver crossed some girl's palm
but then would show you the whole world, as dreamed
up in some executive suite of Madison Avenue: the
working girls who lived rich, full, funny lives in apart-
ment houses janitored by lovable eccentrics; the
classrooms where the teacher was beloved by a horde of
lumbering jocks and retarded cases, all lovable; the hospitals where all the doctors were WISE beyond God and
would do anything for their patients—even, if need be,
taking days off to fly to Paris to tell their daughters why
they should see their mothers again; the talk shows
where Johnny or Merv or Mike chatted with an endless

but repetitive chain of artistes who were only too happy
to tell all about their marriages and their new shows; the
quiz shows where women in their forties squealed and
screamed with joy over a year's supply of Oxydol; the
soap operas one could tune in at any time and hear some
haggard woman saying, "But what will he do when he
knows the child isn't his?" or "We've had to keep him
away from the stuff all week!"

But there was nothing else in the room, nothing with
any connection with the real world, just white furniture
and fantasyland. Why not a shelf of seashells? Why
couldn't there be some pictures, a Brueghel one could
look at for hours, always finding something new? Why
not some bits of sculpture? Why not a bookcase with
some choice of reading other than the mysteries that
filled the library wagon's cart every other day? Why not
a plant or two? Something had been catching at the pe-
riphery of her eyes, and she turned her head slightly,
cautiously. There *was* a plant, a pot of yellow chrysan-
themums. The yellow went through her like a wave of
heat.

"Where did the flowers come from?" she asked the fat
lady, who was still fussing away in the corner at something.

"Your husband, I think." She smiled kindly. She
liked for there to be loving relatives. "Here's the card."

So it wasn't what *everyone* might expect. It was what
Harry had thought of specifically for her. Chrysan-
themums. A lovely color but basically an uninterest-
ing flower. Carp, carp, carp. Shut off that beastly
carping. Read the note held out by that fat hand.

For my girl, with all my love. See you soon. Harry.

My girl. Always the possessive case. Was it just a conventional remark, or did he really feel that she was *his*? Either answer was unsatisfactory. The only good thing was that he had thought to do it at all, and that this room could stand a jolt of yellow to pick up the curtain.

"How do you feel?"

She jumped, and a streak of pain ran up her arm. Dr. Kimutu—looking at her out of black, inscrutable oriental eyes. Were they really inscrutable, or were they just black and hard to see into?

"Well, I can't really say fine, can I? Do I have to have this needle in my hand?" Her voice sounded whining, even to herself.

"Just for another two hours and then you'll be free of it. All right?" He smiled, his large front teeth a little like the caricatures of the Japanese during the war. But he was a nice man. He had taken the time and trouble to explain everything to her before the operation.

She smiled back. "Yes. I don't have a wide choice, do I? How did the operation go?"

"It went fine. The pin is in place and the cast will keep things quiet for a while. I don't want the cast on for very long, not like a fracture cast. Just a few days."

"And then?"

"Out of the cast and beginning to take exercises on your bed. And then up and walking with a walker. And then . . ."

"Stop, stop. That all seems years away. How long will it all take?"

"Not so long. Ten days or so."

"And then I can go home?"

To sit by the fire in her living room as she had last

year after the ovarectomy, with a book and some music and the snow drifting down outside. But his expression had changed, stiffened a little.

"Unless there is some radiotherapy to do," he said.

"*Is* there?"

"It is under discussion. I'll let you know as soon as we have made a decision."

"Who makes the decision?" she asked. God, did patients have nothing whatever to say anymore? *She* wanted to make a decision. She felt just like deciding something. "Will you pass me that orange juice, please?" she said firmly to Dr. Kimutu.

"Of course." And he did. "The decision will be made after we look at your X-rays and do some blood tests. We are a team here, you know."

"Yes, I know. That's why I came here." She smiled at him suddenly, broadly. "I'm just a bossy type. I warn you I will want to know everything that happens. Agreed?"

He was a nice young fellow . . . didn't look more than thirty. He couldn't be thirty. College, then about eight or ten years of medical school and interning and specializing, and then enough more years to be what she had been told was a top-flight surgeon. My God, the man must be forty-five, almost as old as she was.

He smiled too. "We'll keep you fully informed, Mrs. McFarland."

"Wait," she said as he turned to go. There was no one else in the room for the moment. "Will you tell me something now?"

"Of course."

"How do you feel about euthanasia?" It was the question she had never quite dared to bring up, but of

course it was central to her existence these days. Did he blanch? Hard to tell. He was silent a moment.

"That is not in question here, Mrs. McFarland," he said, his voice gone formal.

"I know," she went on quickly because he looked as if he might run at any moment, "and I'm not at all a suicidal type. But I don't at all intend to die by painful inches either. When it comes to that, I shall remove myself." She looked at him thoughtfully. "You are Japanese," she said. "You belong to a culture which understands suicide."

He was quiet for so long that she thought she had lost him. "Yes. Mrs. McFarland, it is certainly an impulse I understand. I don't think there is any such need in your case, but I *do* understand your feeling."

"Oh, thank goodness," she cried in relief. "I am so tired of pussyfooting around the subject. What I want to know," she smiled conspiratorially, "is how many Nembutals are enough? People always seem to take too few or too many and spit them up. Couldn't you just tell me that?"

"Why Nembutals?" He was hedging. Was this terrible woman going to ask him for them next? She could see the question in his face.

"Because that's what I've got!" she said triumphantly. "I've got lots, saved up and hidden for when and if I need them. But I do wish you'd tell me how many. Why can't doctors get off their Hippocratic oath and be *useful* to patients—to people—this way? All the little manuals, the drug books, just tell you not to do this or that because it will kill you. They don't tell you what to do in *order* to kill you when it is necessary."

The fat nurse and a young resident came in, and she

knew it was all up. He'd never answer now. The doctors were all so frightened. They dealt with prolonging life, but why not tell them that they had a duty to death, too? And to the people who needed it?

"I'll be back later, Mrs. McFarland, when I've made my rounds. Thirty minutes or so." He put a peculiar, special emphasis on the word "thirty," and the epicanthic fold of his left lid slid down over his eyes. A wink! Thirty! That had to be his answer.

She smiled radiantly. He had given her a gift. There was no way to thank him now except to smile.

r. Darvey was angry, so angry that his eyes felt hot and dry with it and his chest burned as though he had eaten hot chili. And there was nothing he could do anymore. Tony Qual was going to pump his damned, untried poison into Laura and write down her statistics and probably kill her. And then she would be part of an important new experiment but she would be dead, glorious only as a number in Qual's medical journal article.

The worst of it was that he knew it was necessary. Why could he not stand it? He wasn't one of these bleeding hearts who screamed about animals used for medical experiments. He had seen too many people die. Nobody could survive in oncology without developing a hide like a rhinoceros. They'd never get this rotten disease without endless trials, and a lot of people were

going to have to be guinea pigs, and there was no other way that he knew. He would certainly make a lousy research man. He couldn't detach himself enough from the patients to say, "Okay, let's try NCS-forty-two thousand nine hundred and sixty-eight on the odd numbers in corridor B." Not and go home to dinner. Not without remembering that corridor B, room 11, held a girl named Laura, seventeen, with a boyfriend named Toby who sat there every day after school till dark and a widower father who had to leave the room every few minutes so Laura wouldn't see him cry.

She wasn't responding to CMF or to nitrogen mustard, but there was still a chance that Adriamycin would do it. A better chance, probably, than that NCS-42968 would do it. He'd take that chance first. That made him a reactionary, he supposed, wanting to try the sure and the known before the unknown. At least that's what Tony liked to imply, lifting those Latin-lover eyebrows and smiling around the table as if to say, "What can we do with these old fuddy-duddies?"

And worst of all, she'd be given a chance to say yes or no. Tony would go in with the form and ask if she would agree to be part of this important new experiment, and, of course, she would agree, because what did the patients know, anyhow? And so they would inject it, and maybe it would help, but quite surely it would do other things. Her hair would fall out, naturally. Or unnaturally. Her liver would kick up and she would be deathly sick. Her temperature might rise to feverish new heights. She would be nauseated all the time. On the Adriamycin, on the other hand, she would be a little nauseated for a day after each shot, and she should lose some hair, but there would be nothing else.

And they *knew* it was a specific. It had already been tested a thousand times. Jorgenson, for instance, was back at work and doing fine. Driving a truck, at that! Maybe for months yet. Damn Qual. Damn the whole blasted profession. Damn the disease!

He glared so viciously at Maxie, his appointments secretary, that she winced. "My God, what did I do *now?*" she demanded.

"Sorry, Maxie, it's not you. I shouldn't have gotten up this morning. What's new?"

"Dr. Britton says can you come talk to him about a Mrs. McFarland?"

"When did he call?"

"Just ten minutes ago."

"All right. I'll stop in there now." He gave her a bleak, placatory smile and went out. Without her, he would be in a state of total chaos, since he never remembered where he was to be when.

Brit was down the blue corridor, through the green one and into the muddy yellow of the old building. His machinery was too big to move, so he had to stay in the building with the peeling paint and the falling plaster. Tough, but that's what he got for talking them into the new accelerator. He had become immobile. He himself was glad he dealt in smaller things—like drugs—instead of those mechanical monsters.

The swing doors said Radiotherapy and Push Slowly. Brit's office was at the end of the hall. It was full of flowerpots and abstract pictures. A nice office, always sunny, if you ignored the table which was so piled with paper that it had been invisible for years.

"Okay, Brit, what's the problem?"

"Who's got problems?" Brit sounded indignant. He

was a small gnome of a man with a frizz of white hair and a chin too big for his round face. "I have no problems. I just like conversation on a case sometimes. It's nourishing."

"All right, all right. I looked at Mrs. McFarland's chart last night. Seemed okay as far as the surgery went. What about her?"

"She needs radiotherapy. *I* think she shouldn't have had that ovarectomy. *I* would have tried cobalt first. Might have stopped it cold. Too damned much cutting, if you ask me."

"Well, it's too late to worry about that now. Anyway, she's Kimutu's patient now, and his treatment is perfectly sound."

"Ahh-ah, you *are* an old fogey, Jason. *I* know the ovarectomy was logical. I've been around awhile, you know. But now the woman's sterile. *I* know the pin was standard, but now she'll probably always have a stiff leg. But *I* might have done the job without those results. A few thousand rads do wonders for bone, you know!"

"Look, Brit, Kimutu was absolutely sound. You know perfectly well that that pin was the indicated method. As for the past, she's forty-seven, so sterility is hardly a major loss. Anyhow, they're both surgeries over the dam, as you might say. So I suppose what you want now is that she come to you for radiation."

"Damn right. I want her before you get your needle into her."

"It's the left femur, isn't it?"

"Yes. The pin will strengthen the bone, but forty thousand rads would heal it so she could walk easily again. Our last tests showed better than fifty percent

remission on a pin *and* radiation, less than twenty on the pin alone."

"I know. I read the report." He looked at Brit curiously. "You seem very involved, I must say." It wasn't like Brit to think much about sterility or, for that matter, about ease of motion. What he usually talked about was "stopping the bastard." And the bastard was the bug. There wasn't usually much to do with the patient's comfort.

"I knew her brother," Brit said. "Went to school with him. But, anyway, she's quite a woman."

"Oh?"

"She's a writer, did you know that? And very smart. I had a talk with her before Kimutu horned in."

"I see." But he didn't see. They all had what he had heard the nurses call their "purple" patients, patients they felt personally involved with for whatever reason. But Brit was generally more committed to his machines than to people. He noticed people mainly when they responded well to his big guns. Then they were "good" patients.

"Well, what do you want *me* for?"

"Consultation, you mutt!" Brit's shaggy white brows met sharply over his nose. "You're supposed to coordinate treatment, right? So coordinate! I want her first. Here!" He thrust Mrs. McFarland's folder at him. "Read it and weep!"

He knew some of it, but he read anyway. Radical mastectomy four years ago. Local surgeon in her hometown. Cranbrook. Never heard of it. Recovered well. No nodal involvement. Seemed home free, but in two years she got a painful spot on the hip. Thought it was a bruise. Didn't improve. Doctor's X-rays looked suspi-

cious. More tests. Metastasis to the bone. He remembered suddenly the little refrain he had used as a student to memorize the sequence: breast moves to bone, liver, lung; breast moves to bone, liver, lung. Well, so her cancer had gone to bone. Not as bad as primary bone, but not good. She'd done the smart thing. Left her hometown G.P. and gone to Yale Medical. They did the ovarectomy and, later, started her on the CMF. When the femur spread came up, they'd recommended Kimutu, nearer to her home. A mere two hundred miles instead of five. Came to them and checked in with Kimutu. So now she had a pin in her femur.

He looked up. "Well, it seems plain enough. Do you think we might leave her for a few months to see what the pin will do, or do you want to start radiation now?"

Brit's eyebrows worked up and down rapidly. "Now. I'll need her for two weeks. As soon as the surgery calms down. Kimutu says I can start in about five days. Okay?"

"Well, I'm inclined to let it wait a little longer. . . ."

"I know. I expected you'd say that. You always want to do less instead of more, right?"

He smiled. "All right," he admitted. "You've got my number, Brit. With me, sometimes less is more."

"Except with your damn poisons. All *I* want to do is give some nice clean rads. *You* want to poison them!"

"Okay, Brit. I know you think of us as the Borgia boys. But my poisons have saved a lot of people."

Brit waved a plump, pink hand. "So you say, so you say. So I've got Mrs. McFarland for two weeks, right?"

"Yes. That seems all right to me. But have you talked to *her*?"

"Of course not. Until I talked to *you*. So now I'll talk. She can stay as an inpatient and Blue Cross will cover."

"Yes. All right. I'll stop in later and see her."

"Good. Good-bye."

He laughed. "No more to say than that? How's your fishing?"

"Not worth talking about—certainly not to a man who only likes to play tennis!"

"Okay. I'm through." He walked back through the peeling yellow hall smiling a little. He was fond of Brit, thorny as he liked to appear. Back through the green corridor and the blue corridor to his own office. It was not till evening rounds that he got to stop in again at Mrs. McFarland's room.

She was half sitting up, the hospital gown sliding off one shoulder and her short curly brown hair standing out in flattened wisps. Her bedside table was full of books, but she was watching the television set up near the ceiling.

"Hello, Mrs. McFarland," he said. "How are you feeling?"

She looked at him absently. "Oh, not too bad. Do you know that there are four doctor programs on daytime television and no doctor ever makes a mistake? No *star* doctor, anyway. Can I count on that? Do *you* ever make mistakes?" Her brown eyes turned more fully on him and there was a laughing light in them quite unlike the heavy appeal in the eyes of most of his patients. She didn't expect a serious answer, obviously.

"Never," he said gravely. "The only one I ever made was when I was a student. They wanted me to graduate, so they hushed it up and buried it at midnight."

She laughed, a remarkably gay sound in this dooms-

day world. It was not what they call "a brave little laugh." He always stopped reading a book that described that kind of laugh. He preferred people who ranted and yelled to those brave laughers. But Mrs. McFarland laughed normally, happily, like someone being amused at a cocktail party. Refreshing. She clearly didn't remember seeing him before.

"I take it Dr. Britton has told you about his agenda for you?"

"Yes. It's bad for me to take off so much time now." She frowned, then smiled ruefully. "I guess my notions of what's important don't take precedence these days."

"What *is* important?"

"Oh . . ." She waved a hand with a sort of embarrassment. "I'm supposed to be finishing some writing by a deadline. . . ."

Why should she be embarrassed? He was always aware of a stab of envy when he met people who wrote. In high school he had been editor of the paper. In college he had written stories and edited the literary magazine. He had somehow always thought he would end up as the great American novelist. It was a thwarted ambition he never mentioned. Certainly there was little time for self-expression in his work. Whenever he wrote something, it was either a medical article or a prescription, both illegible to laymen. Laymen! A stupid word. Everyone is a layman in *some* field. It just meant ordinary people, nonspecialists, but it always sounded so sneeringly superior.

He looked around her room, suddenly uncomfortable. It was as attractive as flowers, books, and a pretty robe on a chair could make it.

"Well," he said, and his voice was too brisk, "I think

since you're here we might as well do all we can for you this trip. How is your incision?"

"Uncomfortable. But I guess it's supposed to be." She looked at him curiously. "Why do you look so familiar to me? Have we met somewhere?"

He laughed. She didn't remember that he had held her head while she had vomited. "In another life, perhaps."

She laughed, too. "How nice to think. What were you there? A bird? A panther?"

"Oh, no," he protested. "I was already past the animal stuff. I was human." He smiled slyly at her. "I was a writer."

She grinned. "Well, almost human. I'm so glad for you that you behaved and got to be a doctor this time around."

"The reward of virtue?"

"Clearly."

"Oh, Dr. Darvey!" The door opened a delicate crack.

"Yes, Merla, I'm coming." And he left quickly, with a small wave and a smile.

*A*t home
two weeks later, and at last alone, she went to the old
filing cabinet, long too full to be of any more use. But
she knew just where to look—under N. And there they
were, the two pictures of Harry and herself naked, on
their honeymoon. They stood, self-consciously posed,
he like a Pan and she, arms raised, like a wood nymph.
How beautiful she had been! For there was no doubt in
her mind that it was herself she had come to see. Long,
dark hair, a dark brown pubic brush, and those round,
uplifted breasts. The face was young, round, and shy:
Naked Girl Having Her Picture Taken. She looked for a
long time.

The house was very quiet. Harry was at the office,
and the children, of course, had gone and left their
empty rooms—or rather full rooms, full of their junk

which mustn't be thrown out. She was alone. She crutched into her bedroom at last and began to take off her clothes. The pants. She always wore pants now that one leg was slightly plumper than the other. That was the radiation, they had warned her, messing up the drainage of her lymph glands. Then her underpants. She looked at herself, half-naked, in the long hall mirror. The old ovarectomy scar ran straight up from the Venus mound almost to her navel. It had faded, but it was still faintly pink. She hadn't much hair down there now. The radiation had done that, too. She looked like a plump little girl down there, or like those Turkish women who shaved every week in the baths. Harry had once said he'd like to see her shaved and she'd just laughed. But now that she was almost bare, he didn't look there very often. He looked at the *Playboy* girls with their legs open and their hair exposed.

How carelessly happy they had been when they took these pictures! And how difficult it had been to get them printed! Kodak wouldn't touch them. Absurd to remember now, when every other magazine featured nudes, how sexy those embarrassed photos had seemed. She gave a little jump, to put herself in the attitude of the picture, and landed on her left leg. A fierce twinge shot up her thigh and she caught hold of the mirror, frightened. Dr. Britton was right. Her leg and her pelvis were fragile. They wouldn't be strong for a year. If ever, he hadn't said, but implied. She was not to do anything that would make her fall. No rides on her bicycle. No tennis. Not even running. Nothing that would jar.

"You'll be all right if you're careful," he'd said.

"You mean, I guess, that if I'm not, I'll be a basket case?"

His white brows were fierce. "I didn't say that, but maybe we should scare you like that! Your bones are fragile, do you understand? Until the tumor is reduced and the bone hardened, your femur and pelvis are weak. And that pelvic rack holds you up. Do you see?"

"Yes. All right. I'll be careful."

"Come back in two months and we'll look at you again. Make an appointment for a bone scan before you leave. Yes?"

"Yes." She was meek with him for some reason. He looked so domineering, so sure of what he was doing. He was like her father, except that he seemed to have no humor. He didn't respond to her joking.

Joking. That was the facade she wore with doctors. Always had. Maybe because she was afraid. Maybe because they seemed so earnest. Maybe because what they said was so important. Maybe because they often seemed so humorless. When she'd been hit in the eye as a young girl and detached her retina, there had been a ghastly few weeks when she thought she'd be blind. At sixteen! She lay awake nights in the hospital, listening to other people breathe, her eyes bandaged, her head between sandbags, trying to imagine not seeing again. She'd been so eager when a therapist had brought her some braille cards. So interested. And then that solemn surgeon had seen her at it and laced into her and the nurses for letting her try braille. He'd thought it showed a poor psychological attitude when really, she'd been fascinated, and simply wanted to learn braille, as she might have wanted to study Greek.

"I'd love to able to read in the dark," she'd protested, laughing. "Then I wouldn't bother anyone who wanted the light out!" How useful the gift would have been in her marriage!

But he was not amused, and took the cards away from her. Silly man. Why were doctors so often silly in just this way? They always seemed to expect their patients to be terrified morons, and so, of course, they often got what they expected. But if you listened to sick people, really *listened*, you found they often had a pretty clear picture of what was going on. They could, after all, listen to their own bodies. And what did any man know about what a woman's body told her?

She reached up, undid her blouse, and pulled it off. Her white brassiere made her look almost like anyone. Almost. But in the vee of the neck there was a telltale bit of white scar tissue, and her flesh dipped in at the armhole, where it puffed out a little on the other side. She unfastened the bra and it fell to the floor like a weighted beanbag. There she was. The single-breasted Crashaw. A most unusual bird. One breast full and pink-nippled as ever. The other side flat, slightly dug out, with a white scar that ran horizontally across it. No nipple. If she had only known in time that it was possible to save the skin and the nipple and later to get a silicone implant! But her surgeon had never mentioned such a possibility and she'd been too numb with terror to think of it. So here she was, one-breasted, lopsided, with a scar running down her belly, and one arm and one leg slightly larger than the other. If she could cut off her left side, she'd look normal. Everything wrong was on the left! Odd. The hall light was dim, but it was light enough. She looked and looked and then, with a shiver of chill, wiped her eyes fiercely on her arm, leaving a long, wet smear. She mustn't cry. What was the good of it, and Harry would soon be home for lunch, and her eyes always grew red so fast and her

head ached when she cried. No. She pulled on a robe quickly, and hopped over to close the closet door. Better to be like one of those grand dames, like Edith Sitwell, for instance, who swept about in long robes and managed, despite her ugliness, to look at least *interesting*.

But every now and then the thought that she would *always—forever*—have only one breast and be this distorted creature came down on her like the weight of the world and her whole head filled with tears of anger and protest.

She remembered the first doctor she had gone to about the lump. Whatshisname—she had forgotten it, from sheer fury.

"Well, it's just a breast, Mrs. McFarland, not such an essential piece of equipment. After all, you're in your forties. . . ."

She was outraged. In her forties, no longer a sex object, so it was not important.

"You, Dr. Whoeveryouare, are in your forties too," she'd said, dripping ice. "How do you feel about losing your testicles and growing breasts?"

And she'd walked out of there, angrier than she could ever remember, and found another doctor, a surgeon who said the breast had to come off but who at least didn't suggest that it was a minor matter. What man could know how terribly important to her sense of herself her breasts were to a woman? Especially in this breast-ridden age and country where so much of a woman's value was tied up with her looks, her body. Where could one find a man who could think her beautiful—or at least desirable—again? When she'd first had the operation, while she was still invisibly wrapped in

bandages, she'd made laughing fun of her new condition, saying for Harry and the children that she'd be the sexiest single-breasted woman in the state, an Amazon. She'd learn archery, since single-breastedness would make it her natural sport. And, after all, as her dear cleaning woman Maureen had said, "What's a tit?"

Oh God, what *wasn't* a tit! It was herself as a female, a lover, a free spirit who could run naked in the fields, swim naked and free, it was something she'd never be again, tied into clothes, weighted brassieres, cover-ups.

Maybe she should advertise in one of those magazines that offered almost every variety of sexual encounter: "Wanted, one-armed man who would like a one-breasted woman." Maybe she should say "right-handed man." She'd never seen that particular ad. Odd, since there must be thousands of such women roaming the streets.

Well. She put her bra back on, settling the fake breast in its place like a package. Harry would be home soon and he'd be annoyed if she was up. He would make lunch and feed her in front of the fire.

He had been so terribly concerned and good to her. The only thing he had not been was aroused. Poor dear. With the best will in the world, a man cannot respond if he *doesn't* respond. They had had almost no sex since her mastectomy, at first because he had had to be so careful, and then out of habit and the fact that she couldn't bring herself to undress before him, so if there was anything left to arouse a man, she didn't show it. She had slid into bed in a nightgown every night and they had held each other briefly. Harry had kissed and patted her. And they had slept. Harry was sixty, of course, and that made a sort of excuse, but it was

clearly not that. Well, a woman had to be desirable or provocative or why the devil *should* a man be aroused? If she had been able to be blasé, to say with Maureen, "What's a tit?" and *mean* it, to dance and dangle before him as she had once done, perhaps he would have responded in spite of her mutilation? Audacity can do everything. But she couldn't. Too much vanity, that was her trouble. And now the pattern was established so firmly that she couldn't break it, not without a lot of liquor. And Harry didn't drink.

She was back again. The great metal eye stared down at her for a moment, then rattled sideways along its grid, stopped, coughed, and ground back, stared, and went on. Like a typewriter. Like that great scene in *Modern Times* where Charlie Chaplin is fed, without leaving the assembly line, by a giant typewriter that pushed an ear of corn back and forth against his mouth. Only this typewriter did nothing so clear and obvious. It just stared at her, inch by inch, searching out the hot spots in her bones. Bone scans took an hour, and there was nothing to do. "Why don't you run a movie—or even slides—on the ceiling?" she asked the technician. The girl laughed. "Good idea." But she didn't mean it. Just a pleasantry. The sort of answer people are always giving to intelligent ideas that are for comfort rather than function or profit. Like books. There were magazines every-

where, magazines like *Arizona Highways* and *People* and *Reader's Digest*, but there were no books. And when she asked, someone told her there *was* a library down-stairs—which the patients couldn't get to—and then, to be helpful, they'd shown her a small stack on a table at the end of a corridor, all mysteries. Something to di-vert, not depress, the patients. Funny idea, that serious books would necessarily depress. When nothing, really, was more depressing than endless, meaningless "adven-tures," a vision of the need to kill time. Whenever Harry said that, she winced. You can't kill time. Time is what kills *you*.

Back and forth. Zing. Clatter. Pause. Back and forth. Looking. And what there is to see is deep in the bones, out of sight of any but that staring eye. When the eye has done seeing, it spits out its news onto a piece of paper, a film that looks like a fuzzy X-ray except for odd whitish spots, like water drops. She knew because she had asked the girl to show it to her last time. The way the girl had stood in front of the pictures, defen-sively, like a child hiding a cookie, was absurd. "Oh come," she'd said impatiently, "I can't read them any-way. I just want to *see* them." She'd moved aside grudg-ingly, so much a part of the whole system of medical secrecy that she had left the world, the human, sen-sible, humorous world where it seemed natural to tell people the truth that mattered most to *them*, not to the technicians or the nurses or the doctors. What were they always so afraid of? Surely more people wanted to know the truth than wanted to be mollified and fed lies they didn't believe anyway. Why, then, do what most people *don't* want? Why did the system say, "Lie! Smile and smile!" (And be a sinner all the while!)

These girls. They were always so young. Where did they come from, all these twenty-year-old children, so brisk and knowing, pushing the great machines around, saying, "Hold your breath" and "Now breathe," as if they were tuned in to the universe? Heaven help us all if they once forgot to say "now breathe" again. All over the world people on X-ray tables would turn blue in the face and die!

She laughed suddenly. "What?" the girl said, startled.

"Nothing. Will you be here when it gets to my face?" That always frightened her a little, the old claustrophobia that made her knuckles white in elevators. Here, at last, the great steel eye would stare down into her face from inches above it. She would have to lie quite still while the monster passed back and forth over her head.

"Sure. Don't worry about a thing." The voice was as cool and untouched as God. It had heard everything by now. What went on inside that child's head, with its sleek brown hair twisted high on top of her head, the white coat just showing a tiny gold cross at her throat? Didn't she have a mother? A boyfriend who took her to the beach and lay on her in the hollow of a sand dune? What did she sound like away from here where she had to say other things than "Don't worry." "Hold still." "Now breathe." Did she giggle? Did she say, "Oh, hell, you've torn my last pair of pantyhose!" Did she cry when her father died?

The eye lifted suddenly, just in time so it didn't smash her nose. Then it clicked and rattled just a foot either way instead of running out along the whole metal groove. Just a foot—the width of her head plus a few

inches either side. Back and forth, back and forth. Then the eye was above her eyebrows, searching her skull. Looking for . . . what? A tiny, concentrated spot of radioactive light that would tell them. Tell *them*. And when would they tell *her*? When and who would come to her and say, "There is this little spot, and we'll try, but we can't be sure we can burn it out so that it stops whatever it is doing, whatever is making it grow and spread and rot the bones so that they will break and crumble and you will die screaming." No. No one would ever say that to her. She clenched her fingers. It was all right to do that now. The metal eye was finished with them. It was playing over her skull now, those thin, bony ridges so unlike the Neanderthal's but just as vulnerable.

"Just a few minutes more now." The crisp, impersonal voice. The girl's eyes, she could see now, since the machine had moved on, were blue. Crisp eyes. Too bad. She liked dark eyes best. They *looked* warm even if they weren't.

"That's good. It's getting terribly boring." And a laugh. Why did she always do that, say stupid things, pleasantries to mollify people who didn't care who or what she was? She hated that manner she had, of always seeming to placate people, of trying too hard to be friendly, to make an impression, to become *human* and real to these people.

"There. You're done. That wasn't so bad, was it?" The girl's eyes crinkled a bit at their smooth corners, but there was no recognition in the mouth. It was a job to be done before she got off for lunch.

When she swung her feet down off the table and stood, she was a little dizzy. The hard young arm

steadied her. "You'll be okay in a minute. It's the lying down so long does it."

"Yes. Well, thank you. What do I do next?"

"I don't know. Why don't you ask the girl at the desk in the hall. She'll tell you."

"All right. Thanks again." Thanks again? Why? What has she done but her job? Why am I so cranky? I might just as well, for all she cares, be a side fender of a new Ford moving down the assembly line. And next, here comes a chassis! Or perhaps, first, lunch!

riving to the hospital was always a good part of his day. For eight miles he drove almost automatically, sometimes taking notes into his cassette recorder, his head full of the problems waiting. Only, today's drive was different. Beth had been suddenly full of bile, and at such a trifle, that Ellen should go with him on a canoe trip over the weekend. The weather was so fine it would be wonderful to spend it outdoors paddling a river with Ellen. And why get so angry? *She* didn't want to go. She hated doing active things, especially outdoor things that messed up her hairdo. So it wasn't that she felt left out. They had *asked* her. It was something she *chose* not to do. "Why can't we ever do something *I* want to do?" she demanded. And she was so bitter that he was startled.

"What do *you* want to do for two days?"

"I want to go to a good hotel and let somebody else feed me and coddle me and amuse me!"

How strange! On their honeymoon they'd camped out at Bar Harbor and swum in icy water and made love in a tent. She'd loved it. At least she'd seemed to. Now all she ever wanted to do was to get out of the house routines to some big, plush place where a master of ceremonies helped you to play silly games. He hated that kind of thing and she knew it. Last year when they'd gone to Hawaii she'd had her heart's desire and he had been bored to death. Was it always going to be like this, either one or the other of them to be discontented? Ellen, bless her, loved to go with him, camping or canoeing. It was hard to realize she was in college and just back for a weekend. How dumb and still the house seemed without her, especially with Beth alone so much and itching to be off doing something. It couldn't be much fun being a doctor's wife. Husband never at home. No escort service you could count on. Not much fathering service. She was pretty good about it all. She'd managed to make a sort of bachelor girl life out of it: ceramics classes, garden club, bridge afternoons, teaching reading to illiterates, keeping a house and a child going. Lots of friends out there in the suburbs. Not so bad perhaps, except that she rarely had a man around. Gardeners, maybe, or TV repairmen. He had a sudden image of their big bed—king-sized so he wouldn't wake her with night calls, king-sized too for their love life. But not too often these days. He was forty-three now and always tired. The thought of another man bouncing around on their bed did nothing to him. He tried to visualize a big, hairy, virile stud lying with Beth. Nothing. God, what was wrong with him?

Wasn't he even capable of jealousy anymore? He still loved her. She was still highly desirable, a little plump now, but almost as smooth-limbed as the girl he had married.

The trouble wasn't sex. It was talking. They didn't get time to talk much. Sad. There was so much to say at first, so much to find out. And then, somehow, it was all said.

He drew a long, sharp breath, came back into his eyes, and looked at the road. Only a few more blocks and he would be in his office, where his wishes were king and everything was organized for his convenience. He rarely even wanted a vacation. Was he, as Beth said, "a typical coddled tin God over there?" And did he always get his own way? Not medically, that was certain. He'd lost out on Laura, hadn't he? She was still alive, but what a mess! Bald as a golf ball, sick all the time, and with a pressure on her kidneys that just might be the last straw. Her eyes looked like a sick animal's. And then there was Bailer. He *had* been collecting sleeping pills. The nurse had found his cache and taken them away. Perfectly right, except for his nagging doubt that they had the right to keep people alive who didn't want to be. The Hippocratic oath seemed to apply less and less these days when every decision was at war with the ethics of the new world. After all, who, now, should have the right to judge such things as pulling the plug on the old or the comatose? Whose decision should it be whether people should have male or female children? Why should it be a *legal* matter to have an abortion? Did people, or didn't they, have the right to their own bodies? Wasn't that between themselves and whatever God they worshipped? Why should *doctors*

have the right to make such personal decisions? It wasn't a question he'd ever thought much about before. Certainly it wasn't raised in medical school in his day, and not much today. But old Mr. Bailer surely seemed a logical candidate for choosing his own death. First, prostate, and now liver, and he knew there wasn't much to be done for him except to keep him sedated. Why *not* take his pills? In Ed Bailer's place, seventy-nine years old, with no place to go but down, wouldn't *he* take those pills? Doctors were lucky. They could give themselves one quick shot and get it over. Maybe that's why the medical suicide rate was so much higher than that of the rest of the population. Poor mutts out of the profession had to find ways to die without help, and they were usually pretty painful. Why should only doctors have the chance to kill themselves easily while ordinary people had to blow their brains out or dive out of windows—or painfully save up sleeping pills as though they were thieves in the night?

What the devil was wrong with him today? He pulled his blue Dodge into his parking space and sat there a moment, staring out at the little metal placket on the post that said Only Dr. Darvey. What a big shot he was! Beth was right after all. Not about what they liked to do, but about his life. He *was* a coddled man, and that did tend to make you a self-righteous slob. It was all very well to remember that it had taken ten years of work after college to get here, years of never getting enough sleep, of never having any money, and of owing everybody in creation. He'd been young and tough enough to take it. But that was all ten, twelve years back, and it had been all his way ever since, hadn't it? Whatever he needed, he got. Money was no problem.

And he got all the yessirring he could take. And, in addition to all that, he loved what he was doing. So wasn't Beth right after all? Shouldn't he make a special effort to go her way, do her thing? He had the big thing, the job that absorbed his whole existence. And all she had was a nice house and a bunch of time fillers. My God, how did she make it through her days?

"Hi, Doc! Nice morning!"

"Yes, but rain's coming. I can smell it."

"Ah, you're a pessimist." Bill, the big cop posted at the door, grinned and waved a relaxed wrist at him. "It ain't going to rain. The radio *said*." Bill's mother had died of cancer right here in this hospital, but he hadn't held it against the place. A good, hearty fellow.

"Well, we'll see whether to believe the radio or my hunches."

The doors opened automatically before him and he walked into the great lobby. Two floors high, and already full of bustle. He stopped at the pharmacy to jot down the prescription for Mrs. Moseley.

"You look pretty mournful, Bob. What's up?"

The pharmacist compressed his already thin lips. "Jim's sick and I've been done out of my day off. I was going fishing. Da-aam!"

"Too bad. But it's going to rain anyway."

"Huh! That makes it worse. Fish *bite* in the rain!" The pharmacist looked at him as at a sewer of ignorance. Which, of course, he was. He'd last gone fishing when he was fourteen, with a man who'd felt himself to be a humanitarian because he caught fish and then threw them back! They'd kept a few trout for dinner, but they must have tossed back twenty more: it was a stocked lake. And all the way home, with the creel of

fish at his feet, he had kept thinking of that lake—a beautiful, blue sapphire set in piny woods—full of trout with torn, bleeding mouths. And that was called "sport" and fun, a good day of fishing. He hadn't fished since. Tony was right about him, maybe. He *was* a bleeding heart!

He reached his office with a sigh of relief. It was all as it had been yesterday: his white coat on a hanger, the table full of case folders, the coffee urn on its table, already hot, Maxie looking up from her glass cage at one end. There was no problem for *him* of what to do with his day. It was an endless rope of activity that carried on from day to day, with no end in sight. And he wanted no end. He wanted to be carried out of this place in a box! Beth was right. To do what you want, to love doing it, and to know you were useful was the greatest luck of all, far more, even, than temporary things like travel, or good sex, or free time.

"Dr. D., Mrs. Croghan died about an hour ago." Maxie's mouth pulled down mournfully, even though she didn't know Mrs. Croghan or, for that matter, any of his inpatients. She was his office girl.

He stopped, one arm through the sleeve of his white coat. At last. She had hung on for two months, getting worse in spite of anything he had been able to do. The liver section hadn't helped. And now it was over. He swallowed the cud of frustration and it was bitter. He had liked Mrs. Croghan. It had been one of the low spots in his days to see that great bulk getting thinner and more feeble, her smile always there for him, but getting, at last, threadlike, ghostly. And her husband.

He put his other arm in his sleeve. "Does her husband know?"

"Yes. He was there." Maxie looked at him thought-

fully. "You know, I think he knew it would be today. He stayed home from work and came early this morning. Duncan said he's never done that before."

"Is he still here?" How he hoped not!

"Yes. Duncan made him have some coffee at the nurses' station, and I think he's waiting for you in the lounge."

"Yes. Well, I'll go there first. Tell Harrigan I'll be late for morning rounds."

This was the worst part of his job. Her death was a relief, really, but that poor little rabbit of a husband was another matter. He went down the hall and up to 8, making up speeches for him, but when he walked into the lounge and saw him, his mind went blank and empty as a sieve. Mr. Croghan had always been small and wiry, but he had shrunken suddenly into a little old man. Even his mouth, with all those rabbity teeth, looked shriveled, and his eyes were bloodshot blue, unbelieving.

"I'm so sorry," he said, and he found his voice was unsteady. He gripped the little man's shoulder. "I liked your wife. I would have given a lot to be able to save her."

Mr. Croghan's incredulous eyes suddenly filled with tears. "I didn't think it would be this way," he said in a voice cracked and trembling. "I always thought she'd be here to see *me* out." His eyes blinked, blinked. "It ain't fair, Doc. She was eight years younger than me. Did you know that? She was *young!*"

"I know. There's no accounting for this lousy disease," he said, and he felt the hate rising in his throat. "We'll get it licked someday, but that doesn't help right now, does it?"

Mr. Croghan shook his head like a blind worm.

"What'll I do, Doc? I can't think what I ought to do. And what about *her*? The funeral"—he winced—"and all that?"

"We'll help you with all that. Miss Parish will talk to you about funeral arrangements whenever you're ready."

"Where did they . . . where *is* she?" A good question. What happened to people who died in hospitals? Well, he knew the answer to that. They got whisked away at the speed of light, down to the hospital morgue, pending removal. But it sounded so fast, so brutal.

"She'll be moved downstairs until you've decided what arrangements you want to make. I think you should go home now, maybe, before you decide anything. Talk to your family, and then come back later, or call Miss Parish."

"Yeah, yeah." He looked confused, a sad little man with the wind knocked out of him. But there was sudden anger in his mashed face when he looked up. "There wasn't *nothing* you could do, huh?"

"We did everything we could. Believe me, Mr. Croghan, we did all there was to do. We just don't know enough." But maybe there had been something more to do. Maybe Tony Qual had something in his bag of tricks that might have worked. Even the placebo effect might have helped. Even Laetrile! He shook himself. When an oncologist turns witch doctor, he's through. Might as well get that Brazilian herb doctor to prescribe. After all, he'd saved a few in his time. Who knew how? But that way lay madness. Either you believe in science and follow its dictates, or you go down the path that leads to superstition, faith healing, chanting, and prayer. He wasn't going guru yet!

He walked Mr. Croghan to the hospital door and saw
him into a bus, when he'd refused a cab. It was late. He
hurried back up to 8 to do his rounds. They were all
waiting for him, clustered around the nurses' station,
drinking coffee, his three first-year residents and a couple of nurses, including Ann, Miss Whiteface. Ever
since he'd set up that course, she'd followed him around
whenever she could like a devoted dog. Embarrassing,
and out of character for her. She was white-faced and
blunt as a sledgehammer. Devotion sat painfully on her.
And, God knew, on him.

They got started. Mrs. Croghan's bed was empty, the
room cleared, the flowers gone. Only a suitcase still
stood in one corner. They all paused for a moment,
looking in.

"Mr. Croghan will come back later and pick it up,"
he said, and walked on without further comment. The
residents glanced at each other but said nothing. Probably thought him a cold bastard. Well, they'd learn you
had to be.

It was a bad morning. Laura died shortly before
noon. He felt as though he had kept her alive through
sheer will, but of course he hadn't. Nothing had worked
on her. And then Tony Qual had used NCS-42968 on
her, and she'd sunk and sunk. He felt all puckered and
wan when he heard she was dead, as though his stomach had collapsed and the blood run away from his
limbs. Laura was dead. Mrs. Croghan had been bad
enough, but she was a woman in her fifties. She'd lived
and had a husband and children. Not like Laura, just a
kid really, with her first boyfriend and everything waiting in the wings to happen to her. And now it was over
and nothing would ever happen again. He came upstairs
when he heard, and looked at her. Her poor wigged

head lay sideways on the pillow, and her face was ashen white, the features all suddenly smaller and as fine as though they had been cut sharp out of a block of ice. He hadn't been there when she'd died. Nobody had. Her boyfriend didn't visit till after school. Her father hadn't arrived yet.

"Was *anyone* here when it happened?" he asked.

The nurse looked a bit indignant at his tone.

"Well, I'm afraid not," she said defensively. "I was doing beds, and when I came in it was all over."

"I see," he said. And he did. People were always dying here. You couldn't expect to catch the exact moment. And anyway, she had been comatose for two days now. It was nobody's fault. But he wanted to blame someone. Or something. He wanted to hate something. Maybe God. God would do.

She'd been waiting
for well over an hour now, half an hour outside in the big clinic waiting room and three quarters of an hour in this tiny examining cubicle, dressed only in a thin hospital gown and without anything to read. She wished she were in the waiting room again. At least there were magazines. She had limped around the little white cage on her rubber-tipped cane looking for something to keep her head occupied. There was a sign that told her that Munk and Schirmer had made the examining table in Hoboken, New Jersey, and she read that two cardboard boxes contained plastic throwaway hypodermics and Q-tips. There was a small sink with a mirror over it in which she saw a face she had to believe was hers. It wasn't the face she remembered. Someone had been scribbling on her forehead; there were tiny lines above

her mouth; a little brownish spot on one cheek didn't go away anymore; her hair looked as though it had died, not like those great manes of shiny stuff on TV models. She looked closely, one ear on the door. It was awful to get caught staring at yourself, as bad as to be seen picking your nose or squeezing a pimple or any of the unlovely things we do in secret, the burps, fartings, stomach noises, crotch scratchings. But the door didn't open. She went back and sat down, swearing at her stupidity in getting caught like this again. She *knew* she must not go anywhere in this place without a book, or at least a magazine! She went through her purse. She read the back of her electric bill and the names in her address book. There was a clipping from the *National Enquirer* on a new cancer cure. The *Enquirer* was a joke. You always knew that there would be in every issue a great breakthrough on cancer, a new heart treatment, a diet that required nothing of you, an article on Jackie Onassis and another on Farrah Fawcett-Majors, a piece on ESP, somebody's true story about the power of prayer, somebody else's declaration that she had seen life after death and it was great. She knew it all exactly, and in fact had done her spoof of it for the *Saturday Review*. But still, whenever she saw a banner headline on it about a cancer cure, she bought the damned thing. No-stone-unturned department. This was a fight to the finish. Why had she brought it with her? She knew what doctors thought of such stuff. Dr. Robbins had once told her wearily that if one more patient came in and told him about the newest kidney cure from the *Reader's Digest* he would give up his practice and take up worm farming.

She made another tour of the room and peered out

into the corridor. A nurse and an intern were talking
out there, and a woman in a wheelchair was sitting.
Waiting. All of them endlessly waiting. She didn't even
have a pencil on her. With that she could, at least, write
out her last words. Ever since she'd first known she had
cancer, she'd been working over her last words. So
many of the good ones had already been taken. "More
light!" and "Of *course*" and "If God should take my
hand, I *still* wouldn't believe!" and "Miracle? It is *all*
miracle!" and "I'll keep in touch!" She'd even tried
creeping up on profundity by keeping a journal, called,
obviously, *Journal of the Plague Year*. It had begun to
seem a little silly when she'd lingered on for years and
had to add an *s*. And besides, there were so few things
to say that hadn't been felt or repeated by thousands of
people about to die. But there was such an itch to make
a big last impression, to imprint her existence on the
minds, at least, of her children, and with luck, on their
children. Even though Ann assured her she was not
going to have any children in this terrible world. Why
on earth should it matter to her, this itch for continuity?
Why was she always so depressed by pictures in the
family albums of handsome young people whose names
nobody any longer knew, people who were her *relations*,
let alone all those endless boxes of old photos in flea
markets and auction sales, people who had lived and
been pictured, presumably by someone who cared, and
who were now just faded curiosities? Why did she in-
sist, for instance, that when she died and went to hell,
she wanted a tombstone with a glass photograph enclosed in the stone and a long story of her life and
maybe some poetry—*lots* of stuff, instead of simply her
name and the dates of her birth and death? Damn it,

that wasn't enough to stand for a whole life! She was a great cemetery walker, and nothing was more dreary and anonymous than the acres of stones in new cemeteries with only names and dates. The old cemeteries at least had some verses, some weeping, carved angels. If her family couldn't come up with something more lively than her dates, then they could cremate her in a jolly backyard bonfire and forget the whole thing! She wanted people who strolled through cemeteries to come to *her* grave and find it *interesting*. Maybe they would hum one of her favorite songs—as listed on the stone—or do a little Charleston after learning that she had won the Eagle Theater Charleston contest of 1948, also mentioned on the stone. It would have to be a *large* stone!

She laughed aloud suddenly at the picture of Harry trying to think what to put on it, and just then the door opened at last and Dr. Kimutu and Dr. Darvey came in.

"That's a nice sound to hear," said Dr. Darvey. Dr. Kimutu smiled broadly.

She sat down abruptly, feeling as foolish as if she had been caught plucking her eyebrows. Then she grinned sheepishly at them. "I was composing my tombstone," she said, "and it was getting pretty long."

"Well, don't compose it yet." Dr. Darvey had warm brown eyes and he looked concerned, a little like that eye doctor who had forbidden her to learn braille because it showed negative psychology. Dr. Darvey had a thin face and looked very serious, until his eyes twitched into irony. They were not doing that now.

"Your X-rays look very good. You certainly chose a first-rate surgeon," and he glanced with that twitch of a smile at Dr. Kimutu.

"How was the bone scan?"

"Well, that's pretty good, too. . . ."

She picked him up at once. "You mean not *very* good. What have you found?" She felt her throat drying up, so she smiled brightly. "Are my arms going? Is my liver turning green?"

He didn't smile back, a bad sign, she thought. "No, it just shows some activity in your lower back and we want to get to work on that."

"When you say 'activity,' you mean you've found hot spots, more tumor in my bones?"

"Well, there's something there. Have you felt any pain?"

She thought over the two months she'd just put in at home on her crutches. She'd had some backache, but she'd connected it with the pin in her femur and with weakened nerves from sitting so much. "Yes," she admitted slowly, "a little. But not serious pain. Not like that femur."

"Good." He and Dr. Kimutu glanced at each other again. It was like a violinist looking at his accompanist and knowing without words what was conveyed. "That means we've found it early."

"My back," she said. Oh, God, this was it. When your back went, you were a basket case. "What can you do about a back?" she asked numbly. "It's not something you can cut out."

"We have other tools in the arsenal. Dr. Kimutu can't have it all his own way. Now he's got to give way to *my* stuff. Or perhaps it is time for more radiation." He was quite grave. "You know, you are lucky that it has gone into bone, if it had to go at all. There is a lot we can do for secondary bone tumor."

"But isn't there a limit to how much radiation I can have without turning into Hiroshima? I've had quite a lot already on my leg."

"Yes, but you're nowhere near the limit, and this is quite a different place. We *are* keeping careful track of what you are getting."

She looked at him mutely. His face looked strained. Was there a death sentence in it he was trying to hide? Dr. Kimutu bent down suddenly and moved her leg up and down.

"How does that feel? Any pain?"

"No. Really, the leg feels very well, just a little stiff."

He made her sit on the table and prodded and turned it, but he couldn't make it hurt as it had before the radiation treatment.

"It feels fine," she said. "You must have done *something* right."

"Good." His black eyes looked at her with pleasure and he winked. "All right. I'm glad you're doing so well. I'd like to see you again when you make your next appointment. Two months?"

"I guess so."

Then he was gone and there was just Dr. Darvey.

"Will I last two months?" she heard herself say, and then she was angry because her voice was quavery. She got facetious at once. "I've got to get someone to look after my plants, so I'd like to know."

Dr. Darvey smiled and his face warmed up amazingly. He had good, compassionate eyes. Probably needed them, poor man. What a job, telling people their ends had come! And suddenly the thought boiled up into a project. She scarcely heard his reassurance that she would be there in two months.

"Dr. Darvey, have you ever thought of doing a book on your experiences as an oncologist? It's just occurred to me that patients are forever writing *their* experiences, but nobody ever tells it from the doctor's point of view."

"Why, yes, as a matter of fact, I have thought of it. When I was in college I thought I was going to be a novelist." He laughed, almost shyly.

"Thank goodness you made the right choice! There are millions of novelists and we certainly need more of *you.*" But she looked at him with more attention. How strange that this important, busy man should carry around with him the same ambition that she and half the world seemed to have. To tell it all. To write truth and beauty out of themselves, to express the inexpressible. "It's odd," she said, her eyes held and sliding into his, which didn't blink or turn away. "Why do we all need to write?"

"I don't know . . . and I'm afraid I've rather gotten past it. All I write nowadays are medical articles and prescriptions."

"And they're illegible, I suppose." They smiled at each other. "Well," she went on, "I'd like to do a profile of you first—you know, like a *New Yorker* profile. Would you mind? Would you have time to answer a lot of personal questions about your work?"

His eyes seemed very bright and he sat down and looked at her like a person instead of a doctor. "Sounds very interesting," he said. "I think I'd like to do that."

The door opened, and a nurse came in and handed him a piece of paper.

"Yes. Well," he said, getting up, "we'll have to talk about that further. I'll be back in a few minutes."

But it was almost another hour before he got back, an hour in which she scrounged a pencil and wrote a list of questions that came to her mind, among them, what did he do about terminal patients? Did he ever help terminate a life? How did he feel about it? Tricky. He probably wouldn't answer that. They were all so uptight about euthanasia. Except Dr. Kimutu. Thirty, he'd said. Thirty.

She was all set to start interviewing him when he came back, but it wasn't possible. He arrived with a young resident and the nurse and they got her on the table and examined her. Dr. Darvey pushed her stomach, palpated her breast, felt the glands in her neck as impersonally as though he were doing pushups. And the young doctor with him followed along and did it all over again. Well, she thought, they have to learn somehow, but that didn't keep her from feeling like a lump of meat.

"Thank you," he said at last and, finally, he smiled and looked at her as though she were real again. "Nothing else showing up. What I'd like you to do is start on another course of radiation and then we'll try a hormone suppressant. The radiation will stop the tumor and destroy the cancer cells in the back site. Then the hormone suppressant will come in to knock out the remaining loose cancer cells and hopefully prevent more spread. That's the present plan. I've talked to Dr. Britton, and he can take you for the radiotherapy starting this afternoon."

She was startled. All organized so fast. The speed itself was ominous. She was suddenly angry. She hadn't been consulted. What if it weren't convenient? What if she refused?

"That sounds fine, but I'd like to go home and think about it. What happens if I don't do any of those things you suggest?" She put just the faintest emphasis on the word "suggest."

He looked at her in silence for a minute. "Then I think your back tumor will get worse and perhaps invade other bones or even get into your tissues, which would be much more serious."

"You mean there really isn't any choice, don't you?"

"No, I don't mean that. You can go to other places and they may do different things. Some doctors might favor Adriamycin at this point, or chemotherapy and no radiation, or vice versa. You can get other opinions and choose any doctor you like, but eventually you will have to decide on a program to follow." His voice, which had been a little stiff, suddenly grew human again. "I know it's not an easy choice. You really have to rely on other people's judgment—and I have a feeling you're not used to that."

Wasn't she? "I guess not," she said slowly. "The really bad thing is discovering that all your doctors don't even agree with each other, so how can a wretched patient know what to do? Even here. Dr. Britton doesn't really like me to get chemotherapy. He calls it poison."

He frowned. Oh God, she thought, I shouldn't have said that. They are on this damn team thing and I shouldn't have said that about his colleague.

"Yes, I know. Dr. Britton and I don't always agree, but we are agreed on your case."

There was a pause while he wrote something in her folder. What was he writing? Intransigent patient knows it all?

He looked up, very businesslike now. "Do you want

another opinion? Do you prefer to make your own arrangements?" It didn't sound like something he said
often. He was acknowledging her intelligence and her
freedom of choice. That, at least. He had nice hands,
she noticed, looking down at them, long, thin, nervous-
looking, not blunt and hard like Dr. Kimutu's.

"No," she said. "I'll do what you suggest. As long as
it doesn't cut another chunk out of me right away. On
that, I'd like twelve other opinions so I can take an
average. Since nobody knows all the answers, a median
may be the best I can do."

He laughed, relaxed now. He wasn't used to opposition, she thought. Patients probably always did what he
said without question.

"I can arrange for you to have a room in Chancery
House and you can come over for your radiation treatment every day as an outpatient. You won't have to stay
in the hospital all the time. What do you say?"

"*What* house?"

"Chancery House. God knows why they call it that—
after some philanthropist, I suppose. It's just a sort of
hotel for outpatients, closer by than any of the motels.
And a little cheaper."

"That sounds fine," she said. "I don't move with the
speed of light on this cane yet, so the closer the better."

"The leg looks very good. I think we can do just as
well on your back."

She didn't ask and he didn't offer to answer the big
question: How long, O Lord?

"Thank you," she said. The young doctor in the
room made stirring noises as though he expected them
to leave now that it was all settled.

"Here," she said quickly, "I've made you a list of

questions. What do you think about them?" She pushed the scrap of paper into his hand and then, with a small laugh, the *Enquirer* article. "I'm sure you've heard of this," she said, "but anyway . . ."

"Oh, I may not have," he said. "There's not enough time in the world to keep up on everything. Why don't you get dressed now, and I'll see about your reservation at Chancery?"

The idea appealed to him. Why not an article from the oncologist's point of view? He hadn't time to read many books, but he read reviews in the Sunday *Times* and there *were* numbers of books by patients, all of them, he suspected, angry at the state of their treatment and mad at what was happening to them. And why not? He was mad at it himself. Every time he thought of his father's face . . . and it was strange how often that was, even now, seven years later.

He pushed his lunch tray onto the table in the cafeteria and sat down. He didn't often eat here. The place was huge and noisy. Most days he had a sandwich in his office and coffee out of his own urn. But today he wanted this bustling hive of activity. It was impersonal, except for a few handwavings. He sat in a corner by the

window and pulled out the piece of paper. What kind of questions had she thought up?

Her handwriting was small and flowing but very legible. Too legible.

1. What have been your greatest professional triumphs?
2. What have been your worst traumas?
3. Are men or women better patients?
4. Are you religious? Has your work made you more or less so?
5. How has your work affected your family life?
6. Have you ever felt a case warranted suicide? Have you ever helped a patient who asked to die?

The questions went on, but he stuck at 6. As she must have known he would. She had such bright, intelligent eyes. And of course, the answer was no. He looked blankly at his hand, which was stirring mushroom soup around and around. What did he mean, of course the answer was no? The answer, dammit, was yes and yes and yes. Not the way she meant, probably, not the way most people thought—a shot of cyanide or even air in the vein—but certainly he had aided and abetted, increased the doses of sedation until the patient was comatose and then, once more, until his heart gave out. Every oncologist he knew had done that where it was clearly hopeless. Even to Pop, who never knew what he had but who couldn't be saved, whose pain was unbearable. He raised a spoon of soup to his mouth and poured it in, but didn't even taste it. Unbearable to whom? To Pop or to himself? Oh, God, to both of them! Dammit, to both of them!

He put down the list, feeling like someone in a sauna bath whose pores had been opened. The crackle in his

pocket reminded him that there was something more, her clipping. So what was new in the *Enquirer*? A Dr. Ramsey from Pittsburgh had moved to a Caribbean island and opened a clinic there, using a new treatment he'd been working on. He had gotten tired of waiting for the FDA to pass the drug for general use, and decided to go on his own, testing it somewhere outside the United States. And what was it? A takeoff from maytansin, in a strict pattern of shots, on for five days, off for three, on again, and the results—of course, since this was the *Enquirer*—were miraculous. Of forty-seven patients he'd had, thirty-two cases had remitted, eight had gotten no worse, and only seven had gone downhill. All of them were terminal cases who had had radiation and chemotherapy and been given up. That was certainly a miraculous batting average, but of course he'd only followed them for a year. Still, even for a year that was pretty good. Why didn't he know about this stuff? Maytansin, of course, he knew, but this was something more, some conglomerate Dr. Ramsey had worked out.

He put the clipping down beside his plate and looked at it thoughtfully. Why didn't he know about this stuff? He was supposed to know everything, wasn't he? All about Laetrile. All about Max Gerson. Of course there were probably a thousand of these so-called cures out there in the woods. Most of them were just the placebo effect. Still, if you were dying and the placebo worked, why not? Yes, but they also killed sometimes. Not everyone was so easy to hypnotize into life with a sugar pill. It was not predictable. It was not good medicine. It wasn't science.

He realized that he had opened his crackers. He

never ate the crackers they gave you with soup. Usually
he didn't take them, or he returned them. Waste not,
want not. Pop's favorite dictum as he went through the
house turning off lights. Waste not. He put a cracker
into his mouth, but it was too dry and tasteless to swallow. He *had* to finish his soup, which was equally tasteless. Probably he ought to bring lunch from home. He
smiled a little, thinking of Beth's face if he asked her to
pack him a box lunch. She'd do it, all right, and probably fill it full of fancy doodads: carrot sticks in parsley
and garlic salt, cheese bread, a carton of chili. But she
would be thinking, What does he think I am, a caterer? A
waitress? That would take the flavor out of things. He'd
rather she gave him a bologna sandwich and a banana
but she wouldn't. She did whatever he wanted, but she
bottled up her anger and held onto it till it erupted like
Vesuvius, over something quite different, quite small.
Did Mrs. McFarland do that to her husband? He
thought of her eyes. They had too much humor in
them. She could take a man down all right, but by
laughter rather than by sanctimony. Sanctimony! A
word he hadn't used, or even thought, in years. Was
Beth sanctimonious? A good wife, coping with doctor's
wifedom, but a little self-righteous about it all? Slightly
martyred? Can you be *slightly martyred*, or was that like
being *slightly* pregnant?

He slurped the last spoon of soup a little, and looked
up to see Dr. Teckli bearing down on his table. Dr.
Teckli was from Istanbul and he was anxious to get
back there after his year's residency. That must be why
he was so earnest, so totally literal, so inquiring about
every odd tidbit of technology.

"Oh, Dr. Darvey, please," he said breathlessly. He

seemed always to be a little out of breath. "I'm so glad to see you here. I have a question. Please?"

And so he did. Several. Jason answered them patiently. That was part of his job, and, really, he approved of Dr. Teckli. Too many foreign residents got hooked on American life and American pay scales and stayed on here. That defeated the purpose, which was to train doctors for the countries where they were needed. Dr. Teckli was really very able, and he was going back. Probably a girl back home. Or did they have girls in Turkey nowadays? Didn't parents still arrange matches there?

He picked up his tray at last, nodded at Dr. Teckli, who would gladly have stayed there all day asking questions of what he called "the chief doctor." The horse's mouth. That was him!

Back in the office, Maxie was waiting for him, primed. "The Mayer clinic in New Orleans has been on the line. They want to know if you can give them a date for your lecture. They'd like next Monday if that's possible."

"Oh, no. I can't do it that soon. And never on Monday, Maxie. You know that. Tell them the first time I can get away is in about three weeks." He glanced at the big, scenic New England calendar behind Maxie. "Why don't you tell them three weeks from tomorrow?"

"Okay, but they'll be disappointed!"

He shrugged and went to his desk. In three weeks or so maybe things around here would be cleared up a little. He couldn't leave when Mr. Bailer was so near the end. And there was his seminar in Tate Memorial. And maybe, if he gave her enough time to plan, Beth would go to New Orleans with him. She hated medical

conferences usually, but if she had time to get her clothes together and her hair done, she rather fancied looking gorgeous for those poor young doctors. God, he was acid this afternoon! Anyway, there was no hurry. He had dozens of things to do this week, and there were Mrs. Walsh's X-rays to check right now. He had called Chancery House, but he still had to tell Brit that Mrs. McFarland was coming in this afternoon at four. He supposed she had gone to her room and gotten settled in by now. What had he been thinking of not to tell her she could eat here, in the cafeteria? She was not up to shopping for food, not with that cane, and though there were kitchenettes in Chancery House units, they didn't do much good without food.

He had a meeting with Forester at two. That would just give him time. He left the hospital and walked rapidly to the corner. It was a beautiful day, crisply October, with most of the leaves already on the ground. How good it smelled! It wasn't often he noticed the smell of the hospital; usually it was only when he was outdoors that he recognized a new note in his throat, an absence. Clear, moving air! When he got to the grocery on the next block, he went in. He didn't shop very often, so the immense size of this department store, this food Macy's, rather took him aback. But they were very well organized. The aisles were numbered and there were signs listing what they had. Coffee, of course. And cream. And a one-pound box of sugar. And bread and butter. Terrible bread. Not like Beth's great home-made loaves. But it would have to do. A can of something. What, tuna fish? No, probably still full of mercury. But what wasn't? Sardines? Salmon? Salmon. That would be something useful even for dinner.

And some frozen vegetables. Green beans? Always safe. Everybody ate beans. And maybe a small steak. And perhaps some fruit, a few grapes? What about breakfast? Granola. Well, then, a quart of milk to go with it.

By the time he had gotten to the checkout counter, he had a half-full basket. And when he'd paid and walked out again, he felt, suddenly, like an idiot. It was not his job to take care of patients' food! He stalked up to Chancery House at last, feeling ridiculous. When he got into the lobby, he stopped at the desk.

"Can you tell me what room Mrs. McFarland has?" he asked. He knew the girl at the desk vaguely. At least he had seen her before. She would think he was either crazy or philandering. Well, he was certainly a little crazy today.

"She's got two forty-three, Dr. Darvey. Do you want me to ring her? Her husband could come down, probably."

"Yes. Well, why don't you ring them and tell them there are some groceries here for them?" He tried to smile. "Courtesy of the oncology department."

"Sure, if that's what you want, Doctor. Gee," she looked at the brown paper bag in awe, "you sure do have a good department!"

He walked away, feeling such a fool that he wanted to bloody himself somehow. He banged his hand on a tree as he passed it and a shower of gold leaves fell down on him. Of course her family would be with her. And they probably had done all the shopping they needed. He didn't know Mr. McFarland, but obviously he would be with her, had probably driven her down. He would think the hospital weird, or himself crazy.

Certainly not reassuring. As for Mrs. McFarland, if she got him to answer all the questions on her list, she would know more about him than he knew himself. More than he wanted to know.

 *he groceries*
were incredible. She looked at them as Harry set them
out on the tiny kitchen counter. Nothing like this had
ever happened to her before, that a doctor should buy
her groceries. She felt suffused with warmth, with delight.

"Whatever have you done to him?" Harry asked,
laughing and astonished.

"I don't know. I can't imagine. But isn't it lovely?"
She was sitting in the blue chair, watching what came
out of the bag, trying to fathom Dr. Darvey's character
by what came out of the bag. How strange, she
thought, watching the granola, the milk, the steak
emerge from the sack as Harry pulled them out.
Harry's hair was still up in funny gray spikes from
when he had been sleeping while he waited for her. The

side of his cheek was red from lying on it. He didn't
look properly awake yet, but how glad she was to have
him here. The room was fine, but the whole huge
building pressed down on it in a great silence. Where
was everybody else? There wasn't the sound of a TV
set or a toilet flushing or footsteps along the corridor.
But in every one of these beehive rooms there was
someone, someone sick, someone on crutches or in bandages, someone who couldn't sleep. Why was she so
slow to help anyone? Why not knock on the doors near
her, introduce herself, ask whoever it was in for a cup
of coffee? She shrank from doing that, as she shrank at
home from getting too close to neighbors. Privacy was
so valuable, even when it was so lonely that she hated
it.

"When do you have to leave?" she asked. She
couldn't imagine this termite mound without him.

"I can stay till you're back from your treatment, darling. I'll go over with you. It doesn't take long, does it?"

"Oh, no. I remember from last time. Just a minute.
They zap me on one side and then turn me over on the
other and it's done. I'm like a loaf of bread." She looked
at him. He was so big and warm, so concerned about
her. How could she let him go? "Do you *have* to leave
today?"

He stood up from putting the milk in the refrigerator.
"Well, no, I suppose I could . . ."

"No, of course you must go. I'm perfectly all right. I
just like to see you here." She smiled. "Two weeks isn't
so long. Maybe I'll get some writing done. How can I
be immortal if I don't get some words on paper?" She
laughed. "I hope paper is immortal. Did you bring my
typewriter up from the car?"

"Yes. Everything's out of the car. What time is it?"

She looked at her watch. "Three-thirty."

"Maybe we'd better get started."

He always had to get places early or precisely on the dot. Maybe long years of getting to court on time. Now it was obsessive.

"It's only a three-minute walk," she said.

"Yes, but you've got to walk slowly. I think we'd better go."

She sighed, getting up reluctantly from the deep chair. Because of him, she'd spent years waiting for other people, nice, normal, *late* people. That was what marriage meant, getting used to someone else's patterns. How much she loved to read in bed! And it wasn't possible unless she was sick, because he would come to bed, hump over beside her, and breathe in that special exhausted way that she knew meant "When will you put out the light?" So she put it out. And going anywhere in the car meant her being rushed to get in the car and then waiting endlessly while he did the several things he always remembered at the last minute: locking the porch door, collecting a late library book, going to the toilet. And marriage meant remembering to tighten the jam jars after he'd used them so they wouldn't come apart in her hands and smash jam all over the floor. And not being able to have people in for a casual drink because they "owed" other people a dinner instead. And none of it was important beside what he also was: loving, thoughtful, protective. She never lifted anything anymore if he was near. And she would not soon forget that when she had had her ovarectomy he had walked beside her moving stretcher down the hall to the operating room and said good-bye there because he had to get

back. And then, when she'd come out of the anesthesia, there he was beside the bed in her room, quite unexpectedly.

"Why are you here?" she'd whispered. "I thought you had appointments for today."

He'd shaken his head, embarrassed. "You looked so pathetic on that stretcher," he said . . . and said no more. But she had held his hand very tightly for a long time. So marriage was a crazy mixed bag, and you couldn't have the good parts without making room for the others.

"Okay, I'm ready." She stood by the door with her cane, waiting, as she knew she'd have to.

"Shall I open your window a little?" he asked, and when she nodded, resigned, he also looked around and saw that the heater needed to be turned on so it wouldn't be too cold when she got back.

In the hospital she said good-bye to him and went in for her treatment. It was all just as it had been for her leg. The monster machine, the teen-aged technician. Only this time Dr. Britton came in and drew lines on her back with a soft, cold pencil.

"Do you do tattooing also?" she asked, smiling and trying to see what he was up to.

"As a matter of fact, we do. We make a small tattoo to show us what area has been irradiated so we don't do that place again." Dr. Britton worked his lips up and down like a child chewing gum. "Now don't move till I measure." Something icy cold touched her back and she shivered. "There," he said, pointing to the technician, "take it from there."

The teenybopper took over then, and fiddled her under the right spot on the machine. Then they all

went away. She lay there alone under the monster, while the girl's voice called from the shelter of her lead-shielded control room: "Don't move, Mrs. McFarland."

Sara didn't even breathe. What would happen if this terrific zing of radiation hit the wrong place? Suddenly her kidneys would fall apart or her liver would rot. She was so still that she felt dead already, ready for the hospital morgue. There was a high, humming sound, no sensation at all, and then it went on for what seemed like an eternity. It was only forty seconds, they told her later. The girl came at last to help her off the table.

"That's all for today," she said cheerfully. "We'll see you tomorrow at the same time."

"Couldn't I come in the morning?" she asked. She always woke so early it would be nice to get it over and then have her whole day free to do as she liked.

"Well, I'll see." The girl went away, looked up the book, and came back. "Would you like nine-thirty?"

"Oh, yes. That would be fine."

"Okay. Nine-thirty, then."

Harry was scarcely into his magazine before she came out. She smiled at the nurse behind the counter. Helen. They were friends from last time. She was an old-timer. "Hi, Helen," she said.

"You back so soon? Did we do something wrong?" Helen was round, fat, and jolly. She seemed to spend most of her time watering the plants that took up half the office. This hospital was a great place for plants, though they didn't look exactly healthy.

"You did all right. I just like it here so I'm back."

She smiled and turned away. The waiting room was almost empty. But there was a mother and a small boy who looked perfectly normal, and a young man with a

mustache and a bald head, the kind of scruffy bald head that comes from hair dropping out suddenly, that comes from Adriamycin—and probably other poisons.

Back at Chancery House, Harry put his books and papers back into his briefcase and prepared to leave.

"You sure you'll be all right?"

"Oh, yes. As long as I'm off those crutches, I can maneuver as well as a skier with a broken ankle."

"Lovely image," he said, grimacing. He really hated sickness, she knew, or even joking references to it. "You've got to be very slow and careful when you walk outside. Look *down!*"

"Yes, dear. I will. I'll be fine, really. You'd better be off while it's still light. You've got a long drive."

"I hate to leave you here alone. I'll call when I get home."

She knew what a great concession that was. He still, after all his years as a lawyer, telephoned long distance with a horrified awareness of money dribbling away through the line. He always preferred to write letters.

"Yes, do, darling," she said, and smiled at him affectionately. What a dear he was, and how anxious she was to have him leave, so she could have this room to herself, with her books, her papers, her typewriter, the TV set, and those fantastic groceries in the tiny kitchenette.

 *e wondered often*
that week how Mrs. McFarland was doing. But it was a busy time. Fall always was, for some reason. More new cases came in than at any other time. Maybe the depression that came with winter ahead. He wondered if it were also true in the South. He would have to get some statistics on case loads at different seasons in different climates. If there *were* a difference, it would be one more pointer toward the psychological element in cancer. He hoped it wasn't true. Curious as he was about such matters, he didn't *really* want the psychological factor to loom too large. Because what could you *do* about it? And there was so much phoniness in the field. He had faith in his bottles, his hypos, his chemicals— and, of course, in Brit's machines and Kimutu's knives. Of *their* usefulness, he had *proof.*

On Friday, in a free moment, he went to the patients'

library and looked for one of Mrs. McFarland's books. There weren't any. Not surprising. The shelves held mainly mysteries, travel, and uplift. Not many novels of her sort. He wasn't sure what her sort were, but he had an idea they were sensitive, delicate, ironic. He smiled at that. For all he knew, she wrote spy stories or Westerns. He'd no idea. But just as he was leaving the library, she came in. She looked too pale and drawn.

"How are you doing?" he asked, going to her with a flash of concern.

She smiled that full, radiant, welcoming smile that had so startled him the first time he had seen it. Nothing tentative and polite about it. She *was* glad to see him. "Well, I'm so glad to see you," she said. "I'm awful!"

"Oh? What's the trouble?" She shouldn't be awful. The radiation had just started a few days ago. And before that she had felt so well.

"It's my back. I didn't know I had one till last night. Do you think the radiation could be stirring things up? I couldn't sleep all night it was so achy. I walked around most of the night."

He had a sudden sharp vision of her in that blue and tan room—he knew Chancery—walking around like a creature in a cage. What did her husband do for her? Did he sleep through it all?

"Don't you have those Tylenol pills I gave you?"

"Yes. I took some, but they didn't seem to reach it."

"I'll give you a prescription for some stronger stuff." She looked so wan he decided to do it at once. "Are you in pain right now?"

"Yes, but it's not as bad." She smiled. "Everything is worse in the night, when you're alone. *You* know."

"Has your husband left?"

"Oh, yes. He had to get back to his work. He's a law-yer, you know, and he has cases coming up. He calls every night, but I don't like to . . ." she stopped abruptly, and looked down at the book she had idly picked up. What she didn't say was totally clear to him. She didn't like to tell him how terrible she felt. Why not? He knew the answer to that, too. There were two kinds of patients: the ones who needed sympathy and complained all the time to get it, and the ones who also needed sympathy—as who didn't?—but who never complained because they didn't want to worry anyone else.

"Yes," he said. "I know." And he looked at her so sadly that she flushed a little and looked alarmed. Doc-tors weren't supposed to look sad. It frightened their pa-tients. "Come along," he went on quickly. "The pharmacy is still open. I'll get you something for the pain." He slowed his nervous, rapid stride to stay be-side her limping walk. "I think the pain will go down after a few days," he said. "Radiation *does* sometimes make things worse for a while. It's killing cells, after all. But you get adjusted to it quite soon and it will stop giving you pain. You had no trouble with the femur ra-diation, remember? But backs have more nerve connec-tions. Meanwhile, I'll give you some pills so you can sleep."

She shook her head. "I don't think I'd use them," she said. "I do so hate to take drugs." And then she saw his face and laughed ruefully. "That's pretty silly, isn't it, since I'm taking just about all the drugs in the world! I don't suppose it matters a bit what I take from here on. I could even try heroin. Or marijuana!"

"In that order?"

She positively grinned at that. "I know. I'm probably the only person in the United States who hasn't even *tried* pot. My son thinks I'm a relic of the Dark Ages. I think it's my mother's fault. When I was a child, she always used to warn me not to buy candy from a man outside our grammar school. She was sure he had doped the candies to set us up as addicts. She used to read *True Confessions* and think they were true. And that girl on the front covers, you know, the one with her dress half torn off and a beast of a man slavering over her? That girl was being set up for the white slave trade!" She laughed again, limping along beside him as quickly as she could. "I've never gotten over that fear of drugs. My mother was a powerful woman!"

"She had a powerful imagination, anyway. That's probably where you got *yours*. Is she still alive?"

"No. No, she's not." She glanced up at him quickly, almost with embarrassment. "She died ten years ago. Of lung cancer."

He was silent. Stupid of him. He'd read that in her dossier. It was one of the negative factors in her background. Lots of cancer in the family. Her mother. An aunt. A cousin.

They came to the pharmacy. Use it or not, he'd give her some sleeping pills and some Tylenol with codeine. He stood at the counter and wrote out the prescriptions rapidly. Nembutal should do it, at least for now. And the beefed-up Tylenol. He turned to her. She looked very small, very pale, but her eyes were so bright. So alive. "I want you to take these pills," he said sharply. "There's no point in suffering it out. That's just a delusion. Or maybe pride. But I promise you won't become

a dope addict if you'll take these just when you're really uncomfortable."

Her eyes quirked up humorously. "All right. I'm not in love with pain, exactly. I just don't trust drugs. But I'll take them, I'll take them." She was reassuring him, as if he were her child. Funny. She was older than he, of course. He knew exactly how old. Not old enough to be his mother. Four years older, to be exact. He knew all about her. It was all in the dossier—her age, her height, her weight, her childhood diseases, her family's diseases, her occupation, her children's ages, the history of her cancer, her X-rays, her blood counts, her cortisol levels, her bone scans—everything, and nothing. Nothing that told him as much as what she had just said about her mother—and about drugs.

"You know," he said, as he picked up the drug bottles and offered them to her, "I've been looking at your questions."

"Yes? Were they very impertinent?"

"Well, I'm not sure that's the word. No, of course not. It's just that they cover everything I've ever thought or worried about in my profession."

"Do they? Oh, that's great! I thought they would sound so inept to you. You must have dozens of answers to questions I haven't even thought of. Those were just some I thought would interest people. And you know . . ." she stood at the big outer doors, smiling at him, "that's what sells articles!"

He passed through the electric eye and went out with her. The evening was windy and cool, but the sky was clear. He had been looking at skies lately. Thinking of other places to be. From the back garden at home the stars were a great wheeling march of lights and he felt

as small as you're supposed to feel. It was as if he were suddenly developing all the cliché feelings he had never found time for in his life. Strange.

"What a lovely night," she said, looking up. The trees about the hospital were blowing against the sky, and her hair blew about her face.

"Yes, but we'd better get you home before it starts to rain." He walked beside her slowly. "What questions shall I try to answer for you?"

They walked side by side down the line of creaking elm trees. She was silent for a moment, and he remembered that he had rounds still to do and that he had told Beth he would be home early. He was already late for rounds. But he continued to walk beside her. She was still limping a little, but she had discarded her cane. Brit would be annoyed at that. He thought she should use it for another week.

"How about religion, for starters? Are you religious? Has your work changed that in any way?"

"That's a big one." How could he answer that? He rarely thought about it. "I don't think about it much, I guess," he said slowly. "I've the same religion as my family—they're Presbyterians—but aside from going to church years ago to indoctrinate my daughter, I don't really pay much attention to it. But patients *do* ask me about God sometimes," he laughed dryly, "as if I knew any more about him than they do."

"And what do you say?"

"I say what I think they need to hear. After all, if people need God, who am I to say I doubt his existence?"

"*Do* you doubt it?"

"Yes. Often. Especially when a patient dies." Like

Laura, he thought bitterly. Where was God when Laura was dying?

"I see."

She was only a shadow now, limping beside him in the dusk. What am I talking like this for? he thought angrily. She may be needing God before she's through, and I won't be able to comfort her with him then.

"How do *you* feel about God?" His voice was abrupt. Chancery House loomed before them, most of its windows lit.

"Oh, I don't need time to think. I don't believe in him at all." Her voice was merry and he looked at her in surprise. Even though he didn't really believe, he always felt a little solemn about the subject of God.

"At least not a God of the old man variety, the kind that is watching the swallow fall. Something must have started all this. . . ." She waved her hand at Chancery House and the parking lot, the blowing trees and the stars. "But it's far too big for our conception to make any sense of at all. It's as if an ant tried to figure out what the tree he was on wanted him to *do*. Light candles, perhaps?" She laughed, and he was startled to hear that there was no fear, no caution in her laugh. When *he* spoke negatively about God, he always rather expected a lightning bolt. Ridiculous. He was evidently far more superstitious than she.

"Isn't it absurd to think that whatever made this universe," she looked up at the sky, "should be influenced by whether any one of us swears or fornicates or goes to church? Do we care about an ant's moral condition?"

She clapped her hand over her mouth suddenly, like a child. "Oh, come on now, you're interviewing *me*. You know more about my views on God than I know about yours!"

He laughed, too. She was so spontaneous. Everything she said seemed to come from her with the freshness and enthusiasm of a child. She reminded him of Ellen. He had to push to remember that she was a woman of forty-seven, and that she had crow's feet around her eyes, and scars, and that probably she had not long to live. He was frightened suddenly. She was too young to die. She was like Laura. It wasn't fair. He would have to find the way to keep her alive.

They talked a little longer, standing outside the building under the lights from the windows. And once she stopped in midsentence to exclaim, "I haven't thanked you for my groceries! What a lovely thing that was to do! I haven't gotten over it yet!"

He waved a hand in deprecation, feeling shy as a boy being thanked for a corsage. "It's all right. I was afraid you were too done in to shop that first day. Are you managing all right now?"

Her face was full of mischief. "We-ee-ll," she said doubtfully, "I don't know. Could be I need regular shopping service!" Then she laughed, and he forgot to be embarrassed.

She didn't ask him in, and in any case, he hadn't time, but he went back to the hospital at last, slightly disappointed. He so seldom got to talk to anyone interesting these days. It would have been nice to talk more, to see where she was staying, to sit in her room over a glass of wine—a pleasant, somehow antique thing to do these days. There were lots of things to say to a reporter who wanted to do his profile.

 *e likes me,*
she thought, and was struck at once by how adolescent
that sounded. But he *did* seem to like her, and it certainly did no harm to have your oncologist *care* about
you. At once the mercenary sound of that struck her.
Was she trying to be interesting to him so he would
work harder at keeping her alive? How disgusting! But
it surely wasn't all that. She was obsessively interested
in him, and not all for the article. She didn't know
many doctors, and their world seemed to her as strange
as Saturn. And he was so attractive, too. That thin,
fine-boned face and his warm brown eyes were so
charming that she liked even to see him at the end of a
corridor in the hospital.

She opened the door to her room in Chancery House
and a cloud of silence puffed out at her, silence and the

shut-in smell she always associated with air-conditioned rooms. She put her purse down, turned on the light, and sat down with a sigh of tiredness. She should have turned on the TV when she was up. She didn't want to think about anything, and the TV was a buffer not to be denied. But the stillness, the dry mattress–smelling room was too much. She got up and opened the window, slid the screen open, and breathed in the cold, windy evening air. She felt like Juliet, like all the young women on balconies in all the old love stories. How delightful he was! They had talked about all kinds of things, but what mattered most was the catching of their eyes, the warm interest in his. But of course it was just interest. Why shouldn't he be interested, as he might be in any patient who got up off a bed and turned into a person? Doctors must be such double doers. Schizoid, perhaps. Clear, crisp, helpful, hardheaded on the one hand, and somewhere down inside surely they must be like other people, emotional and vulnerable. It couldn't be only the tough, the killers, who became doctors.

What had he said about that? When she asked what he would consider the chief characteristic of oncologists, he had said "Toughness," and then smiled that wry quirk of a smile.

"But you're not tough," she'd said.

"Not enough." He'd laughed. "There's a spectrum of toughness. I guess I'm at the lower end of it. Unfortunately."

"Why unfortunately? I don't think doctors should be tough."

"They'd better be if they want to be useful," he'd said with a grim edge in his voice.

Of course she could understand that. How awful to work over people and get friendly with them and then lose them! How would he feel when *she* died? And at once her back began to ache. Psychosomatic? Or hadn't she been noticing it while she walked and talked to him? She left the window and sat down again in one of the two comfortable chairs in the room. But that made it worse. That dull ache settled like a slowly filling pitcher of water into one side of her back, and she couldn't sit still. She got up again and turned on the TV set, something to make a cheerful noise. But there were just lines and swiftly roaring lights. Something was wrong with it. In a panic, she went at once to the phone and called maintenance.

"My TV set doesn't work," she told the bored man's voice at the other end.

"Well, I'm sorry, lady. I'll take your room number down but we can't do anything till the repair man gets here tomorrow."

"Oh. Yes, I see. I'm in room two forty-three."

"Okay, ma'am."

So here she was to be, all evening, with no TV set and her back acting up. That pitcher of water settled more solidly and the ache was so severe that she could not stay quiet. She tried lying down on the bed, but that made it worse. It was as if her whole spine were filled with a fluid that tormented the nerves. She got up again as fast as she could. Oh, God. Oh, God. This must be what it's really like. Because she hadn't known before. For all the years since she'd had the mastectomy, she hadn't been in real pain. Even the operation on the femur had been mostly discomfort. Never real pain. Never anything like this. This must have been

what he meant when he kept asking her what she was taking for pain, and she'd said, always, "Nothing," with such an air of bravado. But it hadn't ever hurt like this. This must be what all the books meant, all those stories of screaming people, Ivan Ilyitch, and D. H. Lawrence's mother. *This* was it. And turning to cross the room again, her hands pressed tight around her back, she thought in terror, This probably isn't anything. It will get worse, much worse. My back will begin to disintegrate into powder and I'll not be able to stand it. Oh, God. What shall I do? Is it time to take my pills?

She took up her purse and poured the contents out onto the table. There were her Nembutal pills. She went nowhere without them anymore. A whole full bottle, more than the thirty that Dr. Kimutu had said. Could they really do it? They looked so small, so cheerfully yellow, so innocuous. Why didn't anyone ever tell you *exactly* what happened when you took thirty Nembutals? You fell asleep, obviously, but what happened before and after? Did you vomit? Did you strangle while your body was going into its coma? Did you drown on your own vomit? She had read that somewhere. And what happened inside you? Did your organs explode, or did they just run down and stop? Why wouldn't anyone *tell* you these things? She would use them, all right. But maybe a single cyanide pill would be better, certainly faster. She remembered that woman, Joanna, who had taken cyanide in her hospital bed when she found she had liver cancer and there was nothing to be done. But Joanna had been a chemist. She could get the stuff. God, she was brave! Looking it all up, then taking the stuff to the hospital in her purse,

along with a lemon. First you sucked the lemon to acid-
ify your stomach lining and make it somehow more sus-
ceptible. Then you took the cyanide pill and, in a puff,
it was all over. The nurses found Joanna. She'd rung
her bell just before she took the cyanide. Why did she
want to be found so soon? Or did she still hope they
could save her?

She shivered, and the shiver enveloped her back like a
wet sheet of pain.

Marilyn Monroe died of barbiturates, and so many
others. But the papers never described what they *looked*
like when they were found. An overdose, they merely
said. No use at all to people who wanted to know just
what happened. Because, after all, she could do it another way: she could do carbon monoxide in her car. It
was much more complicated, but she knew how to do
it, and it might be faster. She could just sit there in the
car and read. How long did thirty Nembutals take before you went into a coma? Was it minutes or hours?
Was there time to regret it? Was there time to call up
people and talk to them while you waited? It was so
lonely here.

The sound of the telephone made her jump, and the
streak of pain in her back made her yelp like a kicked
small dog. She went to the phone on the wall, holding
the bottle of Nembutal pills in her hand.

"Hello?"

"How are you, darling? How is the radiation going?"

"Oh, Harry! Oh, darling, I'm so glad you called!"
His voice sounded so near and so worried it was like a
warm bath of comfort.

"Well, how is it?" The legal mind wanted no distrac-
tions from the point. "Ann and Jeff are here with me,
and we're all sitting around talking about you."

"Oh, how lovely. I must talk to them, too. I'm all right. I had my third treatment today . . . and I'm still here. Let me talk to Ann."

"Mom?"

"Yes, love. How are things at home?"

"That's not the point. The point is, how are *you*?" The querulous, anxious tone she knew so well.

"I'm fine. They're shooting all kinds of interesting machines at me, but there's no knowing the effect yet. Still, they seem to know what they're doing. This morning they tattooed me!"

"Tattooed?"

She laughed, and startled herself. "Yes. Nothing exciting, unfortunately. Not a mermaid or a naked gent. Just a little dot so they'd know where *not* to irradiate me again."

"Hmmmn. That's clever."

"Yes. I'm so radiant now I glow in the dark."

"Gee, the energy crisis could use you!"

"Yes. Is Jeff there too? How did he ever get away from school?"

"Huh! That's no problem for his nibs. He just *leaves*!" There was the sound of wrestling and hard breathing, and then Jeff's voice.

"Hi, Mom? Don't believe anything the twerp tells you. I'm on legitimate time off—*reading* days!" He was triumphant. "So how are you doing?"

"How do I sound?"

There was a pause. "A little funny. Are you sure you're all right? Should we come down and keep you company?"

Oh, God, how lovely that would be! But there was that sound in his voice, that faint edge of fright. She had done that to him once when he was little, and now,

whenever she was ill or seemed to be leaving, she could hear it in his voice, a tiny edge of panic, even now when he was eighteen. How could she ever have done such an awful thing? How could she? And Harry, too. Surely one of them should have known better! It came back to her with a rush: they had been driving somewhere and the two children in the back seat had quarreled and scuffled until she was almost frantic. Suddenly, she had stopped the car. "Get out!" she'd told them in a positive shout of rage. They'd tumbled out in fright at her furious face. "Stay there!" she'd yelled, and clashed the gears and driven off down the strange country road, leaving the two figures growing tinier and tinier in the rearview mirror. Harry had looked shocked—she didn't often get so angry—but he had said nothing, and she had driven on in her rage for a whole mile before she stopped the car. Then she'd paused, taken a few deep breaths, and gone back for them. But it must have been ten minutes before she got back. They were still standing where she'd left them, but Ann had her arm around Jeff. Jeff's face was a rain of frightened tears. How could she have done such a thing? He had only been about five, but she was sure it had done something to his psyche. He had always hated being left alone, or even with baby-sitters. Of course now it was so far in the past, it surely had been outgrown, except for that thin, edgy sound in his voice sometimes—like when he first heard she had cancer. It was good, at least, that he and Ann had gotten so close.

"Mom?"

"Yes, darling. I'd love you to come, but where could I put you? I have this nice room, but it's only got my bed, and there's not much point in coming down and

then going off to sleep in the Holiday Inn. I won't be too much longer, Jeff dear. Ten more days. . . ."

"*And* a weekend, don't forget!"

"Yes, well, you'll have to be back at school anyway. What are you reading for your reading days?"

He laughed. "Wa-al, you see, maa-am, it's like this. There's all that deep stuff to plow through, but I just found an old pile of Tarzan comics in the attic and . . ."

"Oh, Jeff!" But she couldn't help laughing. Who wouldn't rather read Tarzan?

"Mom?" Ann again. "I'm sending you some stuff to read. And I want your opinion on the Morrison. Okay?" Ann was a very junior editor, but she took her job very seriously. It was so much what she had always wanted.

"Yes. Good. I need reading stuff. There's nothing here but detective stories and things like *How to Diet and Eat All You Want.*

"How?"

"I don't know. I haven't read it yet. That's for tomorrow."

And then, with thanks and love and kisses all around, and regards to Ann's young husband, the call was over. She could hear Harry's voice in the background, telling everyone it was time to sign off.

"Good-bye." She clicked the phone down slowly, reluctantly. The silence of the room closed over her and the waters in her back began to rise like a tidal wave, engulfing her.

Oh, God. Oh, God. She stared wildly at the telephone. She would call them back. They must *help* her. They were her family and they loved her. But when the

receiver was in her hand, she put it down. She knew she couldn't frighten them like that, not ever again.

She walked around the room, past the bed with its crumpled blue spread, over to the table, to the TV set with its blank gray face, to the closet, to the bathroom, back to the kitchen, clutching the bottle of Nembutals. She stopped at the sink, got a glass of water, and drank it slowly, groaning a little between sips. It felt good to groan, to make a noise. But it didn't really help. Nothing helped. Nothing was any good. Oh, God. Oh, God.

Nothing could help her. Her back was breaking up into shards and there was nothing to do about it. She stopped at the phone and stared at it. Dr. Darvey was out there somewhere! At the other end of the line somewhere!

She dialed the hospital number and waited, breathing stealthily, so the motion would not reach her back. "Oncology, please," she said.

"Oncology department. Miss Croyden speaking."

"Is Doctor Darvey there? Can I speak to him please?" Her voice sounded strange, but not out of control, surely.

"I'm sorry. He's on rounds now. Can I have your name, please?"

"Mrs. McFarland," she said, and tears began to roll down her face. "Tell him Mrs. McFarland."

"May I have your telephone number?"

"It's extension two four three in Chancery House."

She hung up and began to walk again. She scarcely limped now; she'd almost forgotten her leg. Now it was her damned back. Was there no end to this rotten, lousy, fucking disease? Did it go on forever, jumping

from place to place? Everything they did just tried to catch it where it was, after the event, and hold it there. But then it jumped like a Mexican jumping bean and started up somewhere else. They didn't know what they were doing, really. They didn't know any more than witch doctors what to do about this crazy thing. And all this radiation. The monster machine she lay under every morning. That was making it worse. Her back hadn't hurt till she started these radiation treatments. Dr. Britton thought he had the answer, but his monsters didn't help either. It was all just a game of "catch up," only they weren't catching up.

When the phone rang, she jumped again, and yelped. She couldn't talk to anyone again. She almost didn't answer it, but she had never in her life not answered the telephone. It had always seemed that something wonderful and important was coming, something she mustn't miss: a publisher telling her that, yes, yes, he wanted her book, had to have it for a million-dollar advance; or Washington calling to tell them that Harry was needed to be a justice of the Supreme Court; or that they had won the state lottery. So she always answered it, even when she had had to run in from the garden and bark her shins on the furniture in the dim house.

"Hello?"

"Mrs. McFarland? Dr. Darvey. Did you call?"

Oh, thank God. His voice was like the gold ring on the merry-go-round. She grabbed it and held on.

"Yes. Oh, I'm so sorry to bother you. I know you're busy. . . ."

"What's the matter?" His voice was sharp, pushing all the excuses aside.

"It's my back." And suddenly she was crying, hor-

ribly, shamefully, sobbing. And it was wonderful, such a relief that she couldn't stop.

"Did you take your Tylenol?"

"What?" She looked down. The Nembutal was still in her hand, and the two bottles of pills he'd given her were still on the table.

"Oh, I'm so sorry," she said. "I guess I didn't think of it. Shall I take them now?" She could barely control her voice.

"Wait. I'll be over in a few minutes. What room are you?"

"Two four three, but I don't want you to . . ."

"Right." He hung up abruptly, and she stood holding the receiver, awash with relief, her back pounding and retreating as before, but she hardly conscious of it.

She looked around the room. It was messy. She walked, half-bent over, and cleared away a towel on the chair, the slippers on the counter, the newspaper from the floor near her bed. And then she went into the bathroom and washed her face and looked at it in the mirror. She was an old hag. She looked very white, and the lines around her eyes were like crumpled onionskin typing paper. She put on a little rouge, a very little, because it looked too odd against her whiteness, and combed her hair. When the bell rang, she went to the door slowly, delicately, moving like someone with a water jar on her head.

"Oh, God," he said, standing in the doorway and looking at her.

It was so exactly what she'd been repeating all evening that she just stared at him.

"Come in. I'm sorry to have called. . . ."

"Oh, shut up," he said with a vicious note that pushed her back into the room. "Where does it hurt?"

She couldn't smile, not even bravely. "Where doesn't it?" she said, and her voice had gone into a whisper. "Sorry," she said. "It hurts here, and here, and here. . . ." She pointed. "Do you think it's the radiation?"

"Very probably. Is this the third day? It's usually worst in the beginning."

"Yes. The third day." It sounded like a movie title. Her next book, perhaps. If there was one. *The Third Day*.

"All right. Sit down, will you please?" He pointed her to the edge of the bed. Then, without looking at her again, he opened his little bag—he was still in his white hospital coat—took out a hypodermic and a small bottle, and began to fill the needle.

"What *is* it?" she asked suspiciously.

"It's a muscle relaxer and a painkiller in one, and you should be able to sleep after it. Okay?" He glanced down at her just briefly, and smiled his wry twitch of a smile. "Is that okay?"

"Yes. Whatever you say. My God, I sound like Katherine in *The Taming of the Shrew*. I sure feel tamed." She tried to smile, but her face felt too stiff, and the tears of pain and anger still trickled from her eyes against her will.

"All right." He rubbed her arm briskly with alcohol and stuck the needle into her. When she winced, he said, "I'm not too good at this anymore. My nurses do most of it and I get out of practice. Did that hurt?"

"No, not really." Almost at once something began to happen. A faint, warm tide began to creep over her, dulling, dulling the pain in her back. He stood over her, looking at her.

"I think you should get some sleep now," he said.

"You've fixed it so I have to, haven't you?" she said, and suddenly she could smile again. The waters receded from her back like a withdrawing tide. "What *is* that stuff? It feels marvelous. Is it heroin or something?"

"Yes, and you're going to wake up in the white slave trade," he said, smiling back. "Here, I'll help you get into bed."

"Oh, no!" She was startled. "I can do it." But she found her fingers fumbled at her neck, and he took over and unbuttoned her like a child. She scarcely knew how he did it, but he found her nightgown in the closet, slipped it over her head, pulled her pants off, and got her into bed.

"I feel drunk," she said once, smiling foolishly at him.

"Yes. Well, that's not so bad, is it?" And he pulled the covers over her. He had somehow undressed her without ever undressing her all over. There was always a covered part of her. It must, she thought sleepily, be one of those things they taught in medical school, like illegible prescription writing: how to examine a patient while the sheet is always over most of them. How funny that was. How silly.

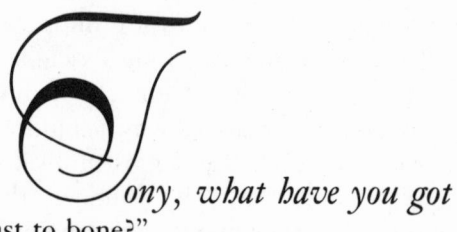ony, *what have you got*
for metastatic breast to bone?"

Tony's Latin lover eyebrows went up slowly. "Oh,
you've tried everything else, have you?"

He wanted to grind his teeth at the man, but it was
too important to fool with. "No, not quite. There's still
Adriamycin, but I want some view ahead. What results
did you get from the NCS-four two nine six eight?"
Besides killing Laura, he longed to say.

"Not too bad, Jase. Come and I'll show you." He
took him back to the tiny study behind his lab where he
kept his records. They were beautifully, surprisingly
neat, not like his own sometimes chaotic, hard-to-find
records. Thank God for Maxie. When Tony began pulling case folders out of his file, he looked out the window onto the roofs below. A whole regiment of chim-

ney pots smoked into the chilly November gloom. Ten o'clock in the morning and all gray, as usual.

Why did anyone live in this vile climate? Why did *he*? It wasn't as if he and Beth were stuck here anymore. He could go almost anywhere now. Even to Hawaii. It had been exciting to be asked to stay last year by the university medical school. Why had he just laughed at the notion?

"Here we are," said Tony, putting a group of folders down on the table. Royal or editorial we, he wondered, but he nodded and sat down before them.

"You see, we took twenty cases and a control group of twenty. Of the control group, eleven are now dead. Of the NCS-four two nine six eight group, only five."

Yes. And one was Laura. Why in God's name Laura? Well, for that matter, why should a child like that get breast cancer? It was a most unlikely age and site. And galloping, at that. The younger, the worse—that was another little mnemonic from medical school.

"How long is it now?"

"Four months. Not conclusive, of course, but interesting. Interesting." His voice went up and he sounded like a man fingering a piece of cloth.

He didn't know why he disliked Tony Qual. He knew his stuff, all right. There was something female— or feline—about him, too smooth, too sure for his own uncertainties. Gay, perhaps. Maybe not. And anyway, he didn't dislike gays particularly. It was just this man.

"What side effects?" he asked shortly.

"Well, there's the rub. Nausea. Depilation. Dehydration. I used a lot of intravenous—both dextrose and saline. Most of them adjusted after a while. All but the five."

Yes. Laura couldn't adjust. She had wasted away into a ghost and died like a whisper.

"But fifteen are still alive?" he persisted. That wasn't bad. "Negative signs on any of them?"

Tony tossed back his well-brushed hair and sighed. "Some. Edema in the legs of one. A suggestion of jaundice in another."

"Oh?"

"He's having a liver scan tomorrow morning. Shall I let you know?"

"Yes, please. What are your dosages?"

"I've had the best luck with forty milligrams for a week, then a week off, then fifty for a week, another week off, then sixty, and so on. The weeks off are time for white cell recovery, of course."

"Where do you stop?"

Tony laughed. "I don't stop. At least I haven't stopped yet. Room seventeen is up to a hundred milligrams a week and doing all right. I'm not sure how long to go on raising the quantity. I'm going to try a cutoff at a hundred and ten to see if that amount contains it. If not, of course, I'll go further."

"Yes, I see. Well, thank you, Tony. Keep me posted, will you? It's hard to keep up with all the research, and I need it, God knows."

He started toward the door and then paused. "Oh, by the way, what's this fellow in the Caribbean up to? The one from Pittsburgh?"

Tony spread his long, acid-stained fingers. "You mean Dr. Ramsey? I don't know. I've seen some of his results, but frankly, they're hard to believe."

"Is he a quack, do you think?"

Tony laughed. "Oh, come on, Jase, you think everyone is a quack. Even me."

He smiled acidly. "Not *you*, Tony, or you wouldn't be here. What about this fellow?"

"Ooops. Well, I don't know too much. He's got *something*, all right. Some maytansin derivative. He's just worked on terminal cases, and so far, according to *him*, he's got eight months on seventy percent of his cases and over a year on ten percent."

"And the rest are dead?"

"Yes, but that's not bad, you know, Jase. Not bad at all."

"No. Why aren't *we* working on his line?"

"Well, you know he left the country because the FDA wouldn't okay his stuff. It makes sense for us to wait a while longer to see what he's got. After all, we've got enough trial runs to keep us busy here for the next fifty years!"

"Don't take fifty, Tony. Don't take fifty!"

He went down the hall and up to his office. There was a residents meeting he had to go to. So there was something, perhaps, coming up in the wings. But so damn slowly! And all Tony could talk about was a few more months, and months of baldness and dehydration and nausea. And then, maybe, liver or lung involvement, and that meant a swat at more surgery. Oh, damn this goddamn thing! He had rarely been so depressed. And actually, the prospects weren't that bad. Look at Mrs. Mortimer, home free six years after her mastectomy. And Abbott Jenkins, half his liver gone, but doing fine. It was just that she looked so pitiful last night, and that she slept at last like someone who had seen God. And *he* was God.

"I'll be back in time," he said suddenly, waving at Maxie. It was nine-thirty. She would be coming over

for her treatment, if she could get up. He hurried down the corridor, through the swinging doors and down the peeling hall of the old building. Brit was not visible; no clinic today. But the waiting room, as always, was full, mostly patients, some relatives. You could always tell the patients. They had a sort of waiting look, and a kind of embarrassed good humor, as if they were apologizing to their families for getting sick.

She was not in the waiting room. He pushed through the inner door to the rabbit warren of examining rooms and the machine rooms. Bettina sat at the control panel, glancing through the small, thick-paned window at the cobalt machine.

"Dr. Britton here?" he asked her, for something to explain himself.

She looked a little surprised. Surely he knew Thursday wasn't his clinic day. "No," she smiled. "Just us chickens doing all the work."

"Oh. Yes. I forgot it was Thursday. Who have you got in there?" He looked through the little window. There she was.

"That's Mrs. McFarland."

"Oh, yes. How's she doing? She had a bad night, I understand. Did she get here on time?"

"Yes. She's always a little early. She didn't *say* anything about feeling bad." She looked down at the folder on her desk. "But I wouldn't be surprised. It's only her fourth day."

She was lying on her face, both arms raised above her head. Above her, what she called "the monster" was aiming something invisible at her back. As he watched, the red light on Bettina's board went off. Mrs. Mc-Farland stirred, pulled her arms down, as if she too had

seen the signal. The humming, he knew, stopped when the red light went out. The treatment was over. She turned her head to the door, waiting, the machine still only a foot above her. She couldn't get up till the technician came in. But she looked toward the window and saw him. Her smile, half hidden in the pillow, was so warm that he stepped back a little, as though she had embraced him. She waved four fingers at him, and then Bettina was inside, moving the machine, helping her to get up. She sat up awkwardly, said something to Bettina, flexed her arms over her head. But she kept her eyes on the little window. He moved away, began to thumb idly through her folder. It was getting pretty thick. Too thick.

"Hello," she said. "How nice to see you. Are you conferring with Dr. Britton about some poor, wretched soul?" She sounded almost gay, not at all the poor creature he had seen last night. He thought, Poor creature, but it was clear to him suddenly that he had gone beyond where those words stood for her, represented a dying patient. She was no longer a "poor creature." She was Sara McFarland, a very specific person. And he was not here to confer with Brit, but solely to see how she was.

"I had to be down this way," he said, "so I thought I'd see how you are this morning."

They were walking down the radiology corridor. "I'm much better," she said. "And I'm really very sorry to have troubled you so much last night. I don't know what you gave me, but if I can have some every time I'm in the doldrums, life will be beautiful."

He frowned. "I understood you were in pain, not in doldrums."

"Yes, of course. But the result was so spectacular. I mean, I could use whatever it was for depression, too. Or is that called drug addiction?" She laughed up at him. "You needn't worry. I'm not at all a drug addict type, if you remember."

"Yes, I do." She looked remarkably well this morning. Even her hair seemed to have come back to life. Dying hair was very obvious. And her skin looked clear. Even her lips had a fuller roundness.

"What do you think of me?" she asked, smiling, and he realized he had been looking at her too pointedly.

"I think you're looking very much better. How many more days do you have?" He knew precisely how many, but he needed to make medical-sounding noises because he felt so uneasy with his· interest in this woman. With this *patient*. She was a purple patient for him as well as for Brit.

"Six more. If I keep getting better at this rate, I'll be leaping out of here straight onto the tennis court!" She looked so happy that his heart sank. This kind of euphoric well-being was so often just a stage, beyond which lay downs he hated to think of.

"Have you looked over the questions for your profile?"

"Yes, but you've asked questions I can hardly answer, certainly not unless I'm anonymous."

"Oh, no! I do hope you don't mean that. I'd like to use your name—*and* all your titles." She smiled wryly. "It's much easier to sell when you've got a real lion by the tail!"

"Am I a real lion?" The notion amused him. He certainly never thought of himself in such terms. What was he in his own mind? A doctor who had had some suc-

cess in his work, whose name was familiar to medical journal readers—a small contingent!—who was called often for consultations and committees. Did that constitute a lion? How strange. He had always wanted to be famous, but he had always thought of fame in quite different ways, as a novelist is famous, or an actor. It was his rather ugly secret to want to be famous—immortal? But doctors didn't get famous like that, not unless they were researchers, discoverers, like Pasteur or Fleming. No. This article would be too uncomfortable if he were honest, and not worth doing if he were not.

He explained that to her. "You know, I couldn't be frank in my answers if my name were used. All my colleagues, and my patients, for that matter, would be hurt or angry. No, I couldn't do that. Don't you have a formula of some sort: the name will be kept back to protect the innocent—or perhaps the guilty?"

She sighed. "Oh, I suppose so, but it won't be as easy to sell. You know yourself how much more likely you are to read an article about someone specific. Well . . ." She looked at him and smiled. "Never mind. I'll take what I can get. But you must understand that it's purely speculation; I may not find a market at all."

"That's all right. I don't mind that. Of course, I'll need some time to think over your questions. And when will I get to answer them?" The loudspeaker, which was never silent, suddenly said his name, and though he had paid no attention to it before, his own name caught his ear. "Dr. Darvey. Dr. Darvey. Please, the nurses' station, eighth floor. Dr. Darvey . . ."

"Well, I'll see you before you go in any case," he said.

She held out her hand. "Thank you so much for last night. That was beyond the call of duty."

Her hand was warm and moist, and her eyes on him quite grave. She was a fine-looking woman for her age, he thought. What a beauty she must have been as a girl!

He squeezed her hand and let it go reluctantly. "Just part of our spectacular service package," he said as lightly as he could, and he went off to answer his call.

It was her next-to-last-day. Tomorrow she would have her last treatment. And she had not seen Dr. Darvey since that day outside the cobalt room. She must stop this ridiculous wash of disappointment she felt every day when he was not there. He was terribly busy, and after all, even if he liked her, she was only one of his patients. There had been nothing more on the article. No messages or thoughts. Silence. And she had gone through the rest of her treatments, feeling much better, but lounging through the rest of her days, a little sleepy, as they said she'd be, without enough initiative to do more than read and fix small, elegant meals on her tiny stove. That, at least, was rather fun. She had been reckless about food, as she never was at home. After all, no one named Mc-Farland could ever be expected to buy lobster tails at

seven dollars a pound, or rib lamb chops at four or good wine at eight-fifty a bottle. But she had done it here and eaten like a gourmet. After all, she kept saying to herself, if you are dying of cancer, you ought to have *some* indulgences. The condemned man ate a hearty dinner.

But really, she thought, and would not allow herself to think, *really*, maybe they had found the answer for her after all. She didn't use the word "cure." *They* never used that word. But even a long remission, while they dreamed up something else, would do. She *did* feel well. She took her clothes off in her room and stood in front of the bathroom door mirror. Not great. The white line still showed from her ovarectomy, and now another scar on her hip from the pin in her femur. But at least you couldn't see both scars at once. And she didn't look as fat as all that food this week should have made her. Odd. She looked fatter in her clothes than without them. Ah, if only she had lived in the seventeenth century when Rubens women were de rigueur! But if she'd lived then, she'd be long dead by now. Like poor Dudley's wife. Or rather Dudley's poor wife. She'd been reading a life of Queen Elizabeth—she always liked history, *distant* history, when she was feeling rotten; it brought her into a long vista, which was cheering somehow—anyway, Elizabeth's lover, Leicester, had a wife he regularly left at home on his estates in the country. And the poor woman got breast cancer. Obviously psychosomatic, no? Anyway, everyone knew about it and just shook their heads. There was nothing to be done for her. Leicester, of course, was too busy at court to get home much, and she just sank and died. Ugh. Leicester was an insensitive clod. Well, maybe not. In those days they were so used to death. There were doc-

tors, but they hadn't the foggiest notion what they were doing most of the time. You were lucky not to be a great man, because if you were you could afford doctors—who would kill you faster. A king was in real trouble. His body couldn't be let alone to cure itself. He was a challenge to the doctors, who tried everything on him from daily bleedings to ground rhinoceros horn to wrappings in hot mixes of horse droppings and goat's blood. If he didn't die at once, he surely wished he *could*.

She limped over to her treatment as fast as she could this morning. It was cold and gray out, and she kept her coat buttoned up to her chin. The hospital seemed warm and welcoming. Was she becoming an eternal patient? One of those people who felt more at home in a hospital than at home? Then it was time she left.

He wasn't there when she got out of the cobalt room. She went through the waiting room and smiled at the bald-headed boy with the mustache. They hadn't spoken, but most of the "regulars" now knew each other by sight, and smiled. She was surprised, in a way, that they talked to each other so little but she knew, herself, that she wouldn't want to discuss her trouble with casual acquaintances. Perhaps they all felt that way. Oh, Lord, I don't want to rehearse my disaster to anyone else! Odd, since most people in trouble liked to talk. Maybe cancer was just too *much* trouble.

This morning she felt so tense and irritable that it was an effort even to smile. The prospect ahead looked so dreary that, all of a sudden, she couldn't contemplate it: the trip home, the solicitousness of Harry and the children, the visits of her good friends, who looked at her with their knowledge in their eyes even when they were being most talkative and jolly.

She had gone up in the elevator and reached the main lobby when she saw him. He was hurrying after her. After *her*? It was ridiculous how her heart lurched when she saw him. He *was* a dear man, of course, but did she have to be quite such an absurd old woman?

"Ah, I thought I'd missed you," he said, coming up to her. He *had* come after her. "I was a little late and Bettina said you'd left. How *are* you?"

They stood in the lobby with people eddying about them as though they were stones in a stream. He looked tired, she thought. His face was almost gaunt, but his eyes were as brown and as caring as always. Wonderful eyes. Compassionate eyes.

"I'm fine," she said. "Should I say that? Will it make you relax your efforts for the 'big breakthrough' if too many of your patients say that?"

He laughed. "No, we'll go right on working at it. Here," he looked around at the heaving life of the lobby, "how about a cup of coffee?"

"Yes. Lovely. I'm terribly bored with my own company." She thought at once that it sounded like a bit of whining, and she felt her face grow hot. It was all ridiculous. She was acting, and *feeling*, like a schoolgirl with her first beau. And really it was the oldest cliché in the world—a patient in love with her doctor. The moment she thought the word "love" she shivered inwardly and glanced sharply at him as though he might have heard. If there was anything more ludicrous than a patient falling for her doctor, it was a middle-aged, single-breasted woman with cancer doing it. She moved slightly away from him as they walked, afraid she might brush against him and he would guess. And what would he do? What would he say? Oh, God, not another one! I've just been decent to this patient, and there she goes. Oh, Lord!

The cafeteria was almost full. It was coffee break time, and everyone was taking advantage of it. They found a table at last, but it was at the end of a long table with three other people. He raised his eyebrows and lifted his shoulders as if in despair.

"This place is a madhouse around ten," he said. "Sorry."

He was wearing his white coat, and his stethoscope stuck out of his pocket.

"Do you always carry a stethoscope?" she asked. Silly question, but she was still so embarrassed by her thoughts that she couldn't think of anything sensible to say.

"Always," he said, and grinned broadly. "How else would they know I was a doctor?"

"Of course. And that *is* of the essence, isn't it?"

"Certainly. If attractive novelists won't write about us, we've got to strut about and show off somehow, don't we? Look at us!" He gestured around the full cafeteria, and it *was* funny how many stethoscopes hung out of how many pockets. He was laughing at her, but it didn't hurt. It was warm laughter.

"I'm *trying* to write about you, but you're a hard man to tie down." Oh, God, she couldn't seem to say anything that wasn't suggestive. She didn't mean "tie down" in the other sense, and he might think . . .

"I know." He was sober again. "Sugar?"

"Yes, thanks."

"I thought, if you aren't too busy, we might have some time to talk later today. I have a meeting this afternoon, but I'll be done around four. I have to be home for dinner, but I'll be back for evening rounds. Would you be free, perhaps, about eight?"

"Where else? The night life in Chancery House isn't really riotous. I'd love a visitor."

He looked suddenly discomfited, and she realized with horror that she had assumed he would come to her, when what he probably meant was that she should come *here* or to his office. Caesar's wife had nothing on doctors for punctilio. And they had to, she thought grimly, with patients like me. She was awash with embarrassment. "I'm sorry," she said, stirring her coffee so rapidly that it roiled over the top into her saucer. "You probably can't leave the hospital. Shall I . . ."

"No, no," he broke in. "Of course I can. I'll be over around eight. I've been thinking over your questions, and I've even thought of some others."

"That's fine," she said coolly. She would have to be very businesslike about this. After all, what she was doing was research for an article. She'd done it dozens of times before. One *needed* some quiet talk time for that. She looked around. The cafeteria was jumping with noise, and she found she had almost been shouting. Her throat felt dry, even a little sore. They would surely have to go someplace quieter to talk.

"Good. Then I'll see you later." He stood up, and then, noticing her cup was half full, sat down again. "I'm sorry," he said ruefully. "I've forgotten how to behave with a lady. I go out so seldom."

"It's all right. I'm finished." She smiled and stood. There was something gentle and old-fashioned about him, and she realized suddenly that, like her, he belonged to a middle-aged generation, not like the brash young residents who slanged about the hospital and joked in all the latest idioms.

Now that she knew she would see him again, she was

anxious to leave him. She shook hands when he reached out, annoyed that her hand was so damp. She still had hot flashes when a flood of moisture washed over her. Hot flashes! What could be more middle-aged than that? It was high time she went home. She was losing, as they said about menopausal women, her marbles.

ow that he knew he would talk to her again, he felt better, quite childishly better. It had been a horrible week. Mr. Bailer had gotten some more sleeping pills, but not enough, and had had to have his stomach pumped out. He had wanted to put the poor old man out of his misery, but instead had had to supervise his return to a world that had nothing for him but pain and degeneration. Then there had been three new admissions under twenty, and he particularly hated to see adolescents come in. They all seemed to have one face and it was Ellen's. Mrs. Starbuck's baby had died after all. And Beth had decided not to go to the meeting in New Orleans next month, so he would have to go alone. "I'm so tired of doctor talk!" she'd said. And why shouldn't she be? It must seem pretty grim stuff if you weren't absorbed in

it. Still, he would have to go alone, and he felt suddenly lonely, isolated from everyone he cared about. Probably Ellen's first real absence from home was making him broody.

A rotten week, all told. And tomorrow Sara Mc-Farland was going home. There was no way of knowing how long the radiation would hold her. She was getting pretty near the edge for any more spinal radiation. After that, they would have to go it on chemo alone. There was still Adriamycin. And maybe, by then, Tony's NCS could have proved itself and been rendered less toxic. She was so fierce about the Adriamycin, it made him smile to recollect. She was one of those patients who read up on her disease and was full of lore, some even he didn't know. Anyway, she knew Adriamycin made your hair drop out. For starters.

"The very idea makes my skin crawl," she'd said, with a little shiver. "You know, it was bad enough taking that stuff they said might grow me a mustache. Luckily it didn't. But it's always easier to take hair away than to add it."

"No, I don't see that," he'd protested. "There are very good wigs now and . . ."

"Oh, God," she'd said. "Wigs! How would you like to lose all your hair and be told that toupees were very good these days?"

She'd been really indignant with him, and after a few defensive moments, he'd seen why. It was so easy for healthy people to make light of the losses of the sick. Then she'd told him about that doctor who'd said her breast didn't much matter because she was forty-three. Her anger still rumbled on that one. Well, why wouldn't it? Once we get them, we keep taking things

away from them, cutting them up, taking out pieces, changing their looks. It had to be psychologically devastating. He must remember that. She had made it suddenly so obvious that he had been ashamed of some of the maundering comforts he had offered other patients. He had to stop talking to patients as if their losses didn't matter, as if they could be made up. There were substitutions, obviously, but they were not the *real thing*. A silicone breast was not the same, no matter how soft. Nor a wig. Nor a urinary bag for a lost bladder. He—they all—had to *admit* the loss, agree with patients that they *were* losing something important, and only then make the point that they had no choice and that a reasonably active life could be lived after all.

It was her anger that had shown him this so clearly, though he had always been dimly aware of it. She was a real help to him. It was good having a patient so intelligent and articulate. He snorted suddenly to himself. Articulate and intelligent! Yes, but that wasn't all. Sara McFarland had become more important than that. He shivered a little, as though a goose had walked over his grave. That was a saying of his mother's. Well, any doctor who got too interested in a patient was sick himself, and if it was a cancer patient, he was sicker, and if it was a cancer patient with metastases, he was crazy!

The day went slowly. By the time he had finished with the afternoon meeting, he was tired. Tired and keyed up, at one time. He went out to the parking lot and stared up at a gray sky that was spitting snow. The beginning of the long, brutal Northern winter. He was getting so he hated winter. In the old days, at college, when he had skied, he had loved it, but now that he was too busy for skiing, winter meant mainly snow

tires, slippery roads, storm windows, a rise in the flu and cold rates dangerous for his patients, gray mornings, and dark evenings. Nothing to be said for it. Maybe it was middle age settling in. At forty-three you were supposed to be in your prime, but how long was a prime? And doctors lived unhealthy lives: long hours, no exercise, plastic cafeteria food, too much coffee. What he would like would be a vacation, not just a weekend planned around a medical conference, but a month—*months*—with nothing to do but loaf, swim, climb mountains, read all the books in the world, listen to music, *breathe*!

The driveway of his house was already a slushy inch deep in snow when he got there. He drove right into the garage so he could get out and go directly into the kitchen.

"Jocko?" Beth stood in the kitchen in an apron, smiling at him. She hadn't called him that for a long time.

"Hi, Beth, what are you so jolly about?" It was the wrong thing to say. It implied she was generally morose, which wasn't true.

"Well," she said with some asperity, "am I that much of a grouch?"

"Sorry, darling. Of course you're not. Though I wouldn't be surprised if you were. I lead you a tough life, don't I?" He bent and kissed her neck, which smelled strongly of White Shoulders, as always. She believed a woman should use one perfume all her life so it was a sort of trademark.

She was smiling again now, twisting away from him a little so she could face him.

"Guess what?"

He backed off to look at her. There was no question that she was particularly radiant tonight.

"I give up. What?"

"Dora has asked me to go to Martinique to help her find a house! She's going to pay my way!"

"Well, that sounds pretty grand, I must say." Her sister, Dora, of course, had all the money in the world and had only last week said she was tired of this wretched climate and wanted to move to the Caribbean. He felt, as always, slightly raw when Dora offered to "pay Beth's way," as she so often did. It seemed to suggest he couldn't. But he knew that when she did, Beth traveled in a style quite out of their range—at least out of his psychological range. He *could*, he supposed, travel in presidential staterooms and live in hotel penthouses, but it never really occurred to him to do it. It always seemed slightly comic and pretentious. But, of course, it was duck soup to Beth.

"Can't I come?" he asked, putting on an injured air.

"Oh, Jocko, I wish you could. *Can* you?" Her eagerness made her look quite girlish, except for that absurd beehive of a hairdo she still insisted on.

He twisted out of his coat, turning away toward the closet. "You know I can't. When are you supposed to be going?"

"Next week! Isn't it marvelous? She's already got our tickets!" Dora loved the fait accompli surprise.

"And how long will you be away?"

"I'm not sure. It depends on how long it takes to find Dor the ultimate house! Two weeks anyway." She looked suddenly concerned, housewifely. "Can you manage, do you think?"

"Of course. I guess I'll eat out mostly. I wish Ellen were here, but I guess that's a fond hope."

"Mmnn. She doesn't get her break till Thanksgiving. Dor wanted her to go, too, but she couldn't, she said."

"Oh? You mean you've called her?"

"Well, of course. What a marvelous holiday it would have been for her!"

"What did she say?"

She shrugged. "Oh, you know Ellen. Too much work to do. She's just like you, really. One of those dedicated types. Now *I'm* different! I might just kick over the traces and fall in love with a native and never come back!" She looked at him brightly, challenge in her eyes, but he didn't take her up on it. She loved to suggest great affairs with other men, but she had never meant it. As far as he knew. But how far did one *know* anyone?

"What's for dinner? Can I ask something so ordinary?" Perhaps, he thought, she did mean it. Maybe it would be good for her. For them both, even. What Margaret Mead called "refreshing infidelities" that kept a marriage alive.

"Pot roast," she said. "Oh, Jocko, do you have to go back for evening rounds tonight?" She eyed him provocatively and slid her hand inside his shirt, a gesture that once used to steam him up immediately. She was so keyed up she was even getting sexy, which didn't happen too often lately.

He backed off a little, trying not to show that he was disentangling himself. Instead, he leaned and kissed her lightly before he spoke. "You're a doctor's wife," he said. "You know better than to ask that."

"Yes, I do." She sighed theatrically. "What a fate!"

And then they had dinner and talked about Martinique and what he should eat while she was away. Casserole talk. And all the time he was thinking, What will we talk about tonight?

hen she opened
the door, she was wearing a long green housecoat or
robe, vaguely Chinese, and she smiled, but she looked
stiff, embarrassed.

"I wasn't sure you'd have time to come," she said
with a kind of humility. He was, after all, such a busy,
important man, but there was a little lift to the corners
of her mouth that said she didn't *really* feel humble, that
they were *two* busy, important people, that they were
equals. "Let me take your coat." She hung it in the
small closet and waved her hand in toward the room. It
was a large room, dominated by her bed, but there were
two comfortable chairs, a table, a TV set.

"You don't look quite real in clothes," she said, and
then put her hand over her mouth in comic alarm. "I
mean without your white coat."

"Well, I hardly have any other clothes," he said, grinning. "It's possible I was born in a white coat."

"That's one of the things I shall want to know," she said. "Do sit down. I thought, if you like it, we might have some white wine?"

"Yes. Fine." He sat down and watched her get the chilled bottle out of the refrigerator. She moved quite easily tonight, or perhaps it was that her robe concealed her limp. Perhaps that was why she'd worn it. "How are you feeling this evening?" he asked in his best hospital manner.

"Me?" She sounded as if it were an absurd question. She was *used* to feeling well. "Oh, I'm really much better." She paused to look at him, her brown eyes quite shining in the lamplight. "I'm so much better it's scary. It's as if all that back pain had washed right out of me. Fantastic. Can radiation really do that?"

"Yes. It often does. Quite remarkable stuff."

"Especially when you remember how deadly it is. I feel as though it's a race between the radiation killing me or curing me!" She laughed, handing him a water glass full of wine. "I'm sorry, but these are all the glasses they have here. They didn't anticipate wine. Or maybe it's forbidden."

He held it up to the light, smiling. "Well, at least we can see through the glass. In the army we drank wine out of celluloid mugs or dusty green bottles. I must say, it lost a little that way."

She sat back and looked at him. "The army. Do you want to tell me about that? I should have some background on you *personally* as well as your opinions about cancer."

He stirred uneasily. He hadn't talked about the army

for years. In fact, he realized suddenly, he hadn't talked about himself in years. Just given medical opinions. As if there were nothing left of him. Perhaps that was why he had risen so eagerly to her questions. To see if there *was* anything left.

She saw at once that he was uncomfortable. It was as if she had radar, for she changed the subject.

"Tell me," she said, "have you always wanted to be a doctor?"

"When I wasn't wanting to be a writer," he said, smiling. And suddenly he stopped smiling and stared into his glass. It was true. Those were the only things he had ever wanted to be. Did that show what Beth acidly called his "dedication" or was it one-sidedness, inertia?

"You're very lucky," she said gravely. "So few people know what they want to be. Now, when they could do anything, *be* anything, they can't find the thing they want. I think my son is a little like that."

"Does it worry you?" he asked, thinking how wonderful it was that Ellen knew exactly what she wanted to be. She was going to be an anthropologist.

"It does a little. He's a dear and I adore him, but he doesn't seem to have any real sense of direction. Lots of interests, but no clear direction."

"Is that so bad? Perhaps what he has is a gift for enjoying life. Our generation was so driven that we still tend to think everyone should get into one job and go on to the top. It's probably the Depression we lived through. We hadn't time to feel around and take our time."

"Yes," she said eagerly, "I think that's true." Then she eyed him mischievously over the rim of her glass.

"But you're too recent for a Depression child. How would you know that?"

He snorted, laughing. She was trying to squeeze his age out of him. Well, why not? It would be one for the profile.

"Okay," he said, "I'll tell you. I'm forty-three." And he grinned back at her.

"Well, I got that bit of information, didn't I?" And she smiled and pretended to write it down. "Now, where were you brought up?"

"Can't you tell from my accent? I'm from the West."

"Mid or far?"

"Far. Oregon. Have I lost all my Western twang?"

"Every bit. Tell me, what kind of childhood did you have?"

And he did tell her. All kinds of silly things, like his wonderful mountain climbing with his uncle, and his disastrous fishing expedition.

"Are you an only child?" she asked. "I'd guess you *are*."

"Oh? Do I seem spoiled?"

"No more than most doctors," she said judicially.

"Well, you're wrong there. I have three sisters."

"Ah. Spoiled as the only boy!"

"Oh, come . . . you win *both* ways, don't you?" And they smiled at each other delightedly, and she went to get more wine.

They went through his childhood and his medical school career, and suddenly he found that he *was* telling her things he'd never told anyone, that he'd buried so deep they were almost forgotten.

He drained his glass suddenly when he realized this. "You're a very good interviewer," he said stiffly. She

was clearly a pro and knew how to get the answers she needed. He felt all at once angry, manipulated.

"Oh, no," she said quickly, "I'm rotten at this usually. I guess it's that I'm so interested in this article—and in you."

They were both silenced by that, staring at each other. My God, he thought, and tried not to go on, not to think what came next. My God, she's a lovely woman. My God, I could love her. My God, I have to get out of here.

He got up clumsily. "I'm sorry," he said. "I have to go. I didn't realize it was so late."

"Oh, I'm sorry if I've kept you too long." Her voice had gone suddenly formal. When she went to the closet for his coat, he saw that she *was* limping a little.

"You'll take those pain pills if you need them," he said, pushed back into his doctoring. "I don't want to think of you being uncomfortable because you're afraid of them." That was true, but what he couldn't say, what he wouldn't think, was that she was probably so close to her death that a little drug addiction could not much matter.

She smiled. It wasn't beauty he saw. She was, after all, not young, and there were signs of her age on her face. But she was so warm, so *engaged*, that she radiated and seemed beautiful. Though he knew quite well what she looked like. He had felt and pounded her body. The thought made him shiver a little. This is ridiculous, was his last clear thought as he let her hold his coat. I'm going mad.

"Shall I see you tomorrow before I leave?"

"Of course. And you'll be back on December twelfth, won't you?"

"That's an awful time to get here, the roads are so bad, but I'll come if I have to swim through the slush." Her smile was a little strained, he thought. Was she wondering why she had to come back so soon?

"We've got to check your back again and do another bone scan to make sure we've got things settled down."

She gave a quick, short sigh, like a child who has just stopped crying. "I know. It seems so endless."

They were standing at the door, and he was trying to think of a good closing line when she leaned over and kissed his cheek.

"Thank you for everything," she said. "You *have* been wonderful to me." And she opened the door and let him go.

 *He drove home*
through the thickening snow in a fine welter of emotions he hadn't known he had. He didn't think words much, hadn't since Cambridge, but he knew he had to find some words to account for what he felt. Words are a balm and a fright and a spelling out. All right, so what had happened? All right, so nothing had happened. He and a patient had had a friendly chat and he'd said good-bye and come on home. That she had kissed him was nothing, obviously just an expression of friendly gratitude. He'd been kissed by women patients before—a few times on the mouth, as he recalled. So it was just her general openness and warmth. So why did the spot on his cheek feel so tingling? He remembered suddenly a wonderful story by Chekhov called "The Kiss" in which a young soldier is kissed by mistake in a dark

room and spends a whole summer building on it, though he had never seen the girl and wouldn't have recognized her if he had.

Here he was, turning into a Chekhov hero, God help him, all delicate sensibility. What nonsense. If there was anything he had told her that was really true about his job it was that you had to be tough. Oncologists and surgeons had to be tough. And he *was* or he wouldn't have survived this long. So knock it off.

He was still saying things like that to himself when he drove into his garage.

Beth was on the living-room floor poring over a map of Martinique when he locked the garage door and went in.

"You're really going, are you?" he asked, stopping in the doorway.

She looked up, smiling. "I've been there, and all over the island, and back home since you left." She looked at the wall clock. "You're late, aren't you? Trouble? You look funny."

God, did all this nothing *show*? "I'm not funny, I'm tired," he said, turning away from her. But he wasn't tired, really. He was all hopped up as if he'd had a sniff of cocaine.

"Oh, poor dear. Come here and let me rub your head." She heaved up onto the couch and patted her lap.

"Oh, I don't really need it tonight, Beth. It's not a headache." But she kept patting her lap and at last he lay down on the couch and let himself be soothed. Beth had kind hands and they always felt cool. He looked up into her face as she pressed his temples. A fine-looking woman—big blue eyes, hair that would be quite lovely if she'd let it loose, just a little crepeyness beginning at

her throat. Beth was thirty-nine, but anyone would guess twenty-nine, or even less.

Suddenly he realized her hands had slid down and were fumbling at his chest. He wanted to move away, but she had already opened his shirt and her fingers were dabbling at his nipples. He could feel them stiffen, and that old, familiar tightening of the groin that always went with it. How well she knew him!

"My, what a sexy kitten you are tonight," he said lightly, but he couldn't move away. It was already too late. She didn't initiate sex very often anymore, so it was not possible to turn it down. It might be just what he needed to quiet him so he could sleep.

"Do you realize," she asked softly, rubbing him, "that we're all alone in the house and that Mother isn't coming in?"

He laughed. Her mother coming in had been the nightmare of their courting days. There was nothing wrong with her mother, except that she was suspicious of their silences and was always walking into rooms to "get her knitting bag."

He reached around her and began to lift her sweater and to undo her bra. She was perfectly still now, waiting for him. When he lifted the sweater over her head, he got her silly beehive of hair caught in it and there was a little tussle to get it through the opening. Then, again, she was absolutely passive while he undid her slacks and pulled them off and pulled her pants down over her feet. She was a beautiful creature still, he thought, looking at her perfect figure with its thick brush of blond hair and its round hips. He felt engorged, tension rising from his cock as he looked at her. His wife was a beauty even now.

When he pulled her down onto the floor and slid over

her, she gave a quick shiver, as she always had. It was an effort, in spite of her readiness. She was always a little tight and dry, and he had to go slowly to make his way in. Slowly and carefully. And she held her face averted, her arms around his neck and her body absolutely still. She *did* respond sometimes, but mostly she was as still as a statue and waited for him to move against her, in her. When he grew warmer and began to drive hard into her, she moaned a little and hid her face in his shoulder. That moan was the only sound she ever made, and he never really knew if it meant she wanted him, too, or was ready, or was playacting to please him, or was in pain. It could have been any of those things— she'd never say—but by now he didn't care which. He needed to be released. He pushed as though he were shouldering through a door, a door never more than half open.

When he had finished and lay, inert, against her, kissing her neck, he thought, Why do I think that *I* am finished; why not that *we* are? Why does it always seem to be something I am doing *to* her, not *with* her? Even tonight, when surely it was her idea? Nothing had changed in all the years of their marriage. It was just as it had been the first time, only now he was perhaps less aware of her than he had been then. The brute thing that assailed him now was that he hadn't been thinking of her at all tonight. Only the perfume of her neck had brought him back to her. He had been thinking of Sara McFarland. He had been fantasizing *her* in his arms, like a schoolboy masturbating over a picture of Betty Grable!

He pulled himself up abruptly. The room looked strange, with the lamplight pouring over Beth's clothes

on the couch and the map of Martinique on the floor. It was like a place he had never seen. His wife, lying naked on the carpet, looked up at him, her legs still slightly parted.

"What's the matter, darling?" she asked. "Wasn't it all right for you?" Coquettish. Strange. She was always sexiest when it was over.

"Yes, of course," he smiled down at her. "You are always all right for me. And what's more, you know it. You can tell. Which is more than *I* always can about *you*."

She reached for her clothes, piled them in her arms, and got up. "It was fine," she said. "Lovely," and she smiled back at him as she started toward the bathroom, her back the color of ivory against the green carpet.

So there it was, just as always, and he didn't *know*. They had never been good at talking about their feelings or reactions. She was, even now, a little shy about that. She couldn't use the words. And he wasn't much better. Fine doctor, he thought wryly. He knew all about human anatomy except how people *felt*. He should have taken more psychology. If that would carry over. But he doubted that anything you could read could tell you in any specific case what people *felt*, unless, as Sara had mentioned last night—no, this evening—unless there was truly in a doctor a kind of mystical relationship to the bodies of patients, like that book she had once read by Wassermann—*Dr. Kirkoven*, was it?—where the doctor looks at his patient and talks to him and *senses* his disease as clearly as if it were his own. What a great method of diagnosis! And he grimaced sardonically at the idea. He *did*, he thought, feel for his patients, but there was nothing mystical about it.

He was not a mystical type. No Maharishi, he! And the words rhymed in his head so he smiled as he lay back on the couch. His eyes drooped and he thought it was time to get to bed. He had morning rounds, a meeting at ten, and clinic all afternoon. And she was going home tomorrow.

hat could have possessed her to do such a thing? He was clearly a rather formal man, maybe even a little nervous about any outside contact with patients. Why had she done such a damned fool, impulsive thing? But, after all, it was so unimportant, she thought at four o'clock in the morning. By four-ten she was sure it had ruined their good, friendly relations. By four-twenty she was wondering what his wife was like, and by four-thirty she lay quivering with shame because obviously such an attractive young doctor must have a lovely wife, perhaps one whom he told about his adventures with patients. By five she was sure he would not talk about it to his wife. He would just be stiff and uncomfortable with her from now on. Maybe he wouldn't let her finish the questioning she needed if she was to do her article. Maybe he would transfer her to another doctor!

She got up at six. It was still dark and the street lamp outside her window was surrounded with a nimbus of foggy light. The building was utterly silent, like a cemetery. No one even running water or turning on a radio. She went to the bathroom. Her face in the mirror looked gray and ancient like that girl in *Lost Horizon* who leaves and turns suddenly into an old crone. Oh, God. Harry was coming around noon, and she had one more session with Jason. She called him Jason in her head, though she had never said anything but Dr. Darvey out loud. What if she had kissed him on the lips and said, "Good night, Jason"?

She turned on the shower and stepped in carefully, holding on to the shower curtain. All the fine, careless recklessness of youth had gone from her. All she did now was think things like, If I slip and fall in the bathtub and break a hip, I shall probably never walk again. It may be hard for me even to get to my purse to get my Nembutal bottle. So she watched her feet all the time, afraid to step off a curb unaware and jar herself into limping for days. She clung to bannisters and tried not to let it show. She let the water purl over her and began to wash. She saved her legs for last, because she had to lean down to do them and that was difficult. They weren't too bad, she thought, looking down at them. She had always had good legs, perhaps a bit too much calf, but her ankles were slim. They didn't look much changed, except that one thigh was slightly larger than the other. And you might not even notice that if you weren't expecting it. The hardest part was her toes. She had trouble bending her back far enough to do her toes. I shall have to soak them, she thought, or I shall always have dirty toes, like Jeff's when he was a little boy and insisted on wearing his torn sneakers.

Jeff. How good it would be to see Jeff again. And
Ann. They had both said they would be home to see
her. Though she didn't quite see how they *could*. Jeff
wasn't supposed to get another break till Thanksgiving,
and Ann couldn't take time off from her job easily.
They shouldn't come, really, she thought. Perhaps I
should call and tell them not to. She always hated to
have them travel home in winter anyway. But why
were they coming? Did they know something *she* didn't
know? Had Jason talked to Harry and the children?
Had he said, "Your mother hasn't got much more
time"? Had he done that? And had he been horrified,
disgusted to have her kiss him? Was she like a whited
sepulcher to him, a leper clinging to him for warmth?

She got out of the tub, shivering. The room was cold.
Too much air conditioning, and she never knew how to
adjust it. Well, if he had told Harry something, she
would know it when he arrived. He had always had
trouble concealing things from her. That time when he
had had an affair with one of his clients. He had been so
awkward and full of revealing hesitations that it had
been almost funny. Almost. She didn't think there had
been any more after that, unless he had grown much
more artful. It was all too difficult to arrange. And anyway, he *did* love her, she thought. He didn't really want
to hurt her. Why had *she* never had an affair? Inertia?
Half her friends were divorced or separated. There had
been lots of chances. But here she was, a bit of an
anomaly nowadays: still married, and even faithful,
after twenty-five years. And now, when she would have
liked to squeeze everything, including love affairs, into
her last few years, now she couldn't do it. Who would
want a cancerous woman with a single breast, scars, and
crow's feet around her eyes? She might, if she dressed

up, and did her hair well, and used enough makeup, still pass for enough of a woman to attract men—old men in St. Petersburg?—but what could she do with them if she *got* any offers? She cringed at the thought of anyone seeing her body. Suppose a man kissed her and then began to touch her breasts, tried to fondle her? The thought gave her cold chills.

She toweled briskly and put her robe on. There was not much to do this morning except have her last zap under the machine and then come back to Chancery to meet Harry. Harry would, maybe, take her somewhere special for lunch. She would come back, see Dr. Darvey at the clinic, and then she would go home.

First of all, breakfast. She particularly liked breakfasts, especially when she could have them alone with a book. She got it all ready—orange juice, eggs and sausage, coffee—and set it all on the little table and sat down with a sigh of pleasure. It had been a harrowing night. There were lots of things she liked to do alone, she thought, slicing the sausage with her fork. Maybe she was really a loner after all. Harry was so self-sufficient that she always felt like the social butterfly of the family. But really, she liked eating alone (but *not* in restaurants), she liked walking alone on beaches and collecting shells, she liked going to movies or the theater alone and not having to make conversation in the intermissions. Curious, though, how seldom she had ever done those things alone. There had always been someone. First high school friends, then college boyfriends, then Harry. Well, now she would get to do something alone, the big thing: DIE. Was it any use to think that everybody had to die? The wise and the silly alike? The brave and the scared stiff? The atheists and the believ-

ers? It *was* some good to read about people like Sam Johnson, so terrified of death, and coming to it at last quite decently. What helped was to think of herself as a tiny mote in a huge, ongoing enterprise, one molecule in a universe of molecules. Her death then seemed to lose importance. It was part of the immense scheme of things, a scheme so vast that nobody understood it. So why worry that Sara McFarland was soon to die? What was Sara McFarland, after all?

Sometimes she could feel that so beautifully, and all the tremors inside her sank into a peaceful, accepting stillness. But not always. Not for long. Other times she would think, How can all the things in my head be wiped out like this? I'm full of quotations that have meant something to me. I'm full of strange bits of information about everything from the emu to estrogen. I've been collecting for forty-seven years, collecting ideas, images, feelings. How can all that be wiped out so simply—like a wet eraser going over a school blackboard? And when she thought this, the tremor came back and the stillness evaporated again.

She remembered coming into her father's room the day after his funeral. It was a small, bright, tidied-up room, but his glasses were still on his desk, his notebooks on the night table. There was even a sheet of paper in the typewriter that said: WHEN I CONSIDER ALL THESE THINGS, I AM IN DESPAIR. She would never know what things, or which particular despair. He was dead, and his old yellow sweater with the buttons off hung there over a chair back just as he had left it, bearing the sagging imprint of his body. How could these *things*, these dead *things*, go on when all the life in his head had just disappeared?

Hell, she thought miserably, I better get out of here before I turn into a drizzling mess. She finished her coffee in two more gulps and washed the dishes. Half an hour with the morning show, and then it was time to go off for her last treatment. After all, who knew? Maybe the big breakthrough would come. There was just no right time to die. There were always so many loose ends. Now, like a flick of darkness, came an image of Ann's face, withdrawn, almost sullen. Whatever it was that was wrong needed time—at least a *little* time—to ferret out. And how could she leave—*forever*—with that unease about Ann hanging over her?

Maybe they could keep her alive another year. If she could have another year feeling this well, *that* would be *something*.

*r. Britton came in*
to see her this morning after her zap. The end of her
treatment probably. He didn't usually see patients on
Tuesdays.

"How do you feel now?" he asked her, his brows
knitted like two furry caterpillars, his face unsmiling.

"I feel wonderful," she said. "At first I had a terrible
backache, but it went away, and I've felt really well for
a week now. Will it last?"

He frowned harder. "You know better than to ask
that question, Mrs. McFarland," and then, somewhere
under his white mustache, there was the start of a
smile. "Why not?" he said. "You've got the right temperament, and I've got the right machines!"

She laughed. He was gruff, but it was a put-on.
Maybe he needed that gruffness to hide behind.

"What's the right temperament?" she asked, just to hear him say again what she had already heard so often before.

"You're cheerful and tough and you don't throw in the towel!" Then he really did smile at her before he made her lie down so he could examine her back.

How wrong he was! How wrong everyone was! What a facade she had evidently built over the years. People always thought she was optimistic, good-tempered, cheerful, and energetic. The facade was too strong now to break. So even now she gave off the same vibes. Even now, when she was frightened so much of the time, she joked with the doctors, made positive comments to the other patients, put on self-possession like a robe so that no one could see her trembling inside it. Why *not* throw in the towel—oughtn't doctors to say "sponge"? Why not let everyone know how scared she was? Maybe they would have some comfort for her. Why always be on the comforting side? It was just dumb pride, wasn't it?

She didn't say any of it, but the inner shiver went on like quivering mercury inside her.

"Are you cold?" Dr. Britton asked once.

"No. It's all right. I just shiver sometimes." Why didn't she tell him she was frightened? Why didn't she ask him what came next? But she knew, really, that she was waiting, waiting to see Jason Darvey. To look at his thin, dark face and to read there both what he thought of her and what the verdict was. She didn't want to go home. She was afraid to be so far away from him and from this great umbilicus of a hospital when something, finally, went wrong. And yet, at the moment, she also longed to get away from this great beehive of woe out

into the free air where people lived and did things and didn't think of illness as a natural state.

"I think," Dr. Britton said, looking at her back as she sat now on the table, "you should be without pain for some time now."

"Well, that's good news," she said cheerfully, and her voice sounded familiar and alien, a sound she kept making that had no relation to her thoughts.

And then they chatted a few minutes about his holiday in Istanbul, her wish to live by the sea, their next appointment. He was always in a hurry—she had seen him in the halls with his white coat almost flying in the still, hospital air—but he gave no sign of impatience. How nice of him!

"Well," he said at last, "I have patients, *sick* people, and your family is maybe waiting for you?"

So she dressed, said good-bye to Bettina, the lab technician, and went back to Chancery House to pack. It was cold, a blowy day with a sky too gray for anything but snow to come from it. Exhilarating, though. It *smelled* real. She breathed deeply, even though a deep breath drew a thin line of pain up her chest and made her cough. The air was too cold even to hold the smell of smog that should have come from the high hospital chimneys. It was only when she went in or came out that she recognized that special hospital smell—clean, medicinal—a mixture of Clorox and decay.

At the house she looked into the parking lot, and there was the car. How good and familiar it looked, the red station wagon with its clutter of glasses and junk on the front window. He was here already. She didn't know why there should be that slight dimming of her spirits, as though a light bulb had lost power for a mo-

ment. But she knew as soon as she had opened the door
to her room. Harry was sitting in the blue chair watching the TV set, and she felt something happen to her
face muscles, a stiffening grimace of pleasure and false-
ness.

"Darling! You're early! But how good to see you!"

He got up at once, smiling, but she felt in his smile
the same stiffness that was in her own. "Oh, I couldn't
wait any longer for my girl to come home." He took her
in his arms a little gingerly, as if she might crack, and
kissed her lightly. She had thought ever since she got
this disease that he had been afraid to kiss her deeply
for fear he would catch it. Even though he surely knew
better. The uneasiness of the healthy with the diseased.
She could understand it quite well, but she drew away
from him quickly, and stood back to look at him. It was
quite marvelous how well he still looked, how young,
even though he was so much older than she. His hair
was a sort of steel and black combination that was very
interesting, and his face was not much lined. Even his
narrow lips had not fallen in as they do on some aging
men. They were much as they had always been when
he had laughingly told her—and proved—that though
they were thin, they were flexible and demanding.

"You need a haircut," she said, not because he did,
but because it was one of the things she always did for
him, and it reminded him of her usefulness. How ridiculous to want to make him remember how important
she was to him! How useful!

He laughed and shook his head so that the part got
lost and the long hairs went awry on the wrong side of
it. "Well, high time you came home and did it! How *are*
you, darling?" He looked at her from gray eyes set so
deep they always looked hooded and inscrutable to her.

"I'm feeling pretty good," she said. "They must know what they're doing. Oh, Harry, let's get out of here fast and have some lunch. I'm starving!"

So they went to lunch at the best place they could find in a hurry. Harry didn't want to drive into the center of the city; he hated traffic. The place was not the posh restaurant she'd hoped for, but it rarely was with Harry. He liked to be fed fast, and he didn't much care for gourmet food. As long as there was lots of it, he was content. That came of being a McFarland, she thought tenderly, and patted his hand across the table.

"You can't imagine how good it is to get out of that hospital," she said.

"Well, you've only been there a half hour a day," he protested.

"No, I mean the whole thing. Chancery House, too. It all smells of sickness. Ugh. You get so you forget *any-one* is healthy."

"It will be good to get you home, Sara," he said, and his face leaned toward her with his bushy eyebrows drawn so she thought he really meant it. And why not? The house must be a shambles and the food a disaster— and his hair uncut. Sometimes she thought she was just a sort of comfortable wind-up toy who did cozy things about the house. Useful, politic, glad to be of use. It wasn't as if they talked much anymore. Oh, no, that wasn't fair. They talked about the children, they discussed their friends, they occasionally talked about the plot of one of her books, they argued about social engagements. He was very proud of her, which was pleasant, because he could have been competitive and jealous over her small successes, and that would have been ghastly. But he was proud because, somehow, he didn't feel threatened. He was so self-contained that whatever

she did could only redound to his prestige. She shook her head and looked down at the menu. Why was she so unfair to him lately? He was so good a husband. Freud was right. What do women want? Dear God, what do they *want*? You get a husband who is good-looking, thoughtful, a good provider, gentle, intelligent, and you complain. Or rather, you don't complain; you just feel a sense of absence. Something is missing that is more important than all the good qualities you *see* are there. You want something else—anger, even—something that touches you sharply where you *feel*, some abrasive desire that wants you even with your warts and your ugliness. She would have preferred often that he shout and hit her than that he compress his lips in silence and walk out of the room, his shoulders high with unspoken irritation.

"Are the kids really at home?" she asked.

"Yes. Jeff's arriving on the afternoon bus, but he should be there before we get back. Ann's home."

"Ah, how nice! How *is* she?"

"Fine. She's dying to see you."

"Is she?" She looked at him thoughtfully. "You know, dear, there's something wrong between Ann and me and I'm not sure what it is."

"Oh? I don't know what it could be. She's very concerned about you, you know."

"I know. But it isn't that. It seems to me that lately—the last six months or so—I can't do anything to suit her. She's so irritable with me. Has she said anything? It's so uncomfortable. I feel sometimes as if she hates me, she can't get away from me fast enough!"

He looked startled and nervous, his lips working in and out in the odd chewing motion he had when he was disturbed.

"I hadn't noticed that! She seems perfectly all right to me. I think you're too sensitive. You imagine things."

She looked at him and a wave of weariness passed over her like a wind off a tomb. He couldn't deal with feelings. Whenever she talked of them, he got worried and tried to turn her off by calling her too imaginative. Sometimes, generously, he even excused her for being imaginative by adding that it was good for her books but she shouldn't let it creep into "real" life.

"Well, never mind. I think it's good of her to come home. Why on earth *did* she? Did she think I would die tomorrow or something?"

She said it purposely, because she knew how any mention of her death upset him. He couldn't deal even with the speculation. So she couldn't talk to him much about her dying, the manner of it, nor the dispositions she wanted made after it. It was hard not to be able to talk about it. All he would say was something high-pitched and nervous about her being around in twenty years still.

"Don't be silly, darling," he said now, and took a sip of his tepid water. "She hadn't been home for quite a while, and she wanted to see you. She really loves you very much, you know."

"I know. At least I hope so, because I sure love *her*." And her eyes filled absurdly with tears, so she took a gulp of water too and coughed. Sentimental old fool, that's what she was!

So then they ate the dreary food, the bowl of Campbell's onion soup, the dry pastrami sandwich, the gelatinous apple pie made, all too clearly, from packaged last year's apples and cornstarch. And the coffee.

"It will be good to get back to your coffee," he said gallantly, making a face over the brown stuff in his cup.

"I've almost forgotten how to make it," she said. "I've been living on instant and hospital coffee."

It wasn't the lunch she had anticipated, but then, it never was. Harry was a dear, good man, but he had little capacity for impulse. In all these years he had never thrown his hat down and said, "Let's go eat the best food in town!" or come home with an armload of roses, or bought tickets for a weekend in Bermuda, or whipped her off to the theater for a surprise. Maybe it came of being poor when young, or maybe it was the Scottish stringency of his upbringing, but it was a loss to her. She felt it so often that she had developed, as a kind of aggression against him, an unnatural impulsiveness of her own. She was always saying, "Let's go down the Nile this winter!" or "Let's have all the lawyers in town over for dinner and watch them fight." Maybe that irritated *him*, but he was good-humored about it. He just laughed and they had the Johnsons over for bridge again.

After lunch, she deposited him in her room and went off for her appointment with Dr. Darvey. Jason, that is.

"Do you want me to come too?" Harry asked.

She was startled, dismayed. "No, of course not. You'd just have to sit around the hospital for God knows how long—and the magazines are all *Field and Stream*! You're better off here with my books and the telly."

"All right. I'll see you later, then."

Then she was walking, half blown by the wind, across the parking lot and down the road to the hospital. She was exhilarated and nervous at the same time. How would he be today, after her foolishness last night? What would he say? Would he mention it in any way?

Would he be distant and cold as ice? Oh, God, why didn't she just tell him that she loved him, was mad about him? She had never said that to anyone but Harry, and that was years ago and in another country. But why not? What was there, these days, to lose? Surely, with so little time left, she should throw out all the inhibitions that made life so dreary?

But suppose he was disgusted? Suppose he tried to be polite, to extricate himself without hurting her feelings? How could she stand that? She'd been, perhaps, spoiled. All her life men had made passes at her, thought her attractive, wanted her. She'd been nobly pure, but it was nice to have desire visible in men's eyes. How could she endure it now, old and ugly and maimed, to make a pass at a man and see him withdraw? Her pride tingled down her back, anticipating, rejecting.

In one of the examining rooms of the long corridor at last, she sat in her clumsy cotton hospital gown, waiting for him to come in. She looked down at her front. One breast poked out the ugly piece of overwashed cotton. The cloth on the other side lay flat against her. Hospital gowns did nothing for the amour propre. Her legs dangled, naked and white. A few hairs stood up below her knee where she had forgotten to shave. Patients should never take their clothes off, she thought for the hundredth time. They turned, if they did, into things, creatures to be manipulated, objects without personality, all of a piece with their cotton gowns. How could any man respond to such a sight?

A discreet knock at last and the door opened. She stiffened, the smile on her face instant but rigid. But it was not Jason. It was a dark, foreign-looking doctor—

she could tell that from the white coat and the stethoscope!—very young and, she thought, a little nervous.

"How do you do?" he said with great formality. She
felt that he was only a plane trip away from salaaming.
"I am Dr. Teckli. I shall examine you, if you please."

"How do you do?" she said with equal gravity, but
her face flamed hot with anxiety. "Isn't Dr. Darvey in
today?" she asked casually as she lay down on the table.
She was afraid that it would sound like a repudiation of
Dr. Teckli's talents, but she had to know that this long
day's wait was not going to be empty after all.

"Oh, yes, indeed," he said, beginning to palpate her
breast. "He will be in shortly to see you." His rather
chilly fingers walked up and down her breast, covering
it inch by inch as though any missing inch must be *the
one* showing disaster. However did doctors get so blasé
about this endless palpating of women's breasts, this
feeling up of necks, this tapping and squeezing of stom-
achs and thighs? It must surely be that patients in these
horrible gowns were just protoplasm. Is that what she
was for Jason? And suddenly, with a flaring of delight
that startled her, she thought she knew why this
young man was examining her. It could be because *he*
didn't want to, because for him, now, it would be too
intimate. On the other hand, the self-denigrating voice
always inside her took over, he may have sent this
young man for quite other reasons: he was too busy, the
young man needed practice, a few solo flights.

He turned her over, stroked her back gently without
any pressure. She could visualize what he was seeing.
Her back descending into those pale green underpants
that Ann had given her for "glamour," her back a little
too solid—about ten pounds too solid. She had always

been a borderline case, about ten pounds overweight, since Jeff had been born. Before, she had been able to diet down in a rigorous week, but since the cancer she would always start and then be tripped up by the question: What the hell, why not enjoy what's left of life? What am I dieting *for*? The question was so unanswerable that she would begin to eat greedily again, great gobs of irresistible chocolate ice cream with maple syrup and nuts, an afternoon vodka and orange juice with cheese tidbits, desserts of pie and ice cream; and then, in three days or so, she would step on the scale or try to pull up a skirt zipper, and look down at herself in disgust. How heavenly to be one of those thin people who ate everything and didn't have to worry about it. Someone ought to write a book about the psychological horror of being overweight, endlessly thinking about it, giving in to greed, hating oneself, trying again. It wasn't too bad for her, because she had always stopped in time—barely—but those poor people thirty, forty, fifty pounds overweight, whose whole lives were a struggle to get thin. Thin people just had no conception of what it was like to think about food all the time, and crave it, and dread it. A grim way to live.

"You look very fine," said Dr. Teckli. He tried to smile, but his young face seemed to have a perpetually anxious expression. Not very reassuring in a doctor, she thought. He took her blood pressure.

"Well, I think *that's* all right," she said cheerfully. "It's my only well-behaving thing. And I think my kidneys. Do you suppose I could give my blood pressure and my kidneys to someone when I die? Nobody seems to want anything else."

"Oh, I don't know, I am sure. Why not? We will

have to see." He was almost babbling, he was so disturbed by her question. He hadn't an idea that she was joking. "But not now, not, certainly, for a very long time."

She was sorry for him. It must be hard to get the nuances of a foreign language, and harder still with sick, frightened people.

"I'm just joking," she said quickly, and smiled widely so he would understand. Why didn't Jason come? *Why* had he sent this poor fellow?

"Dr. Darvey will be in to see you soon," he said solemnly, relieved. "If you would get dressed now?"

"Yes. Thank you."

He all but backed out of the room, nodding at her with as reassuring an air as he could muster.

She dressed quickly, glad to put on herself with her own clothes, afraid he would come in before she was ready, because after she dressed behind the curtain she had to hurry across the room to comb her hair and put on her lipstick before the one small mirror.

She needn't have hurried. She sat there again for half an hour. Once she peered out the door and saw him at the end of the hall talking to a young couple with a baby. He didn't see her, and she ducked back. After a while she thought, rebelliously, that he would have come at once if he really cared about her as much as he seemed to—coffee, groceries, their lovely talk at Chancery House. It was obviously all in her own silly head. She was a patient and he was rather interested in her doing an article about him. It was a pure ego trip for him—he probably didn't get many writer-patients—and she was too fatuous to recognize it. She had worked herself up to a fine, angry self-scorn before he finally came in.

"I'm so sorry to keep you waiting, Mrs. McFarland," he said. His eyes looked crinkled up and so concerned, that the bile washed out of her almost at once. "It's been a terrible morning."

"It's all right," she said. "I know you're busy, and this time I had a book." She didn't mention that she had been too twitchy to read it. That, after all, was her own fault.

He sat down in the chair by the little table. "You're leaving today, aren't you?"

"Yes, I guess I am, unless Dr. Took . . . Turk . . ."

"Teckli," he said, smiling. "He's Turkish."

"I know," she said solemnly, and they both smiled as if she had been very witty.

"He thinks you're in good shape, so what I want is to keep you that way. I shall want you to take this new drug that's just been developed. It's not experimental anymore and it does seem to be working very effectively. . . ."

"What are the side effects?"

He laughed and reached out suddenly to pat her hand. "You *are* suspicious," he said, and drew his hand away as suddenly as he had put it there. "It's only got one side effect that could be at all troublesome. It may make you drowsy occasionally, so you shouldn't drive if you notice that."

"Nothing else? No hair falling out? No nausea?"

"None of those. I promise."

He had a husky voice, she thought irrelevantly, almost a smoker's voice, but she knew he didn't smoke. A good, pleasant, reassuring voice. A perfect doctor's voice.

"All right." She paused and they looked at each other. It was a look as solid as a pyramid, heavy, immu-

table, wordless. It was a look, she thought wildly, that Dante might have turned on Beatrice, that Laura might have returned to Petrarch. She couldn't drop her eyes nor move out of his look, and a wash of heat swept over her and away before she could move or speak. Oh, God, is this true or is it all in me? Am I brutally embarrassing him? Can it be true?

"Sara," he said and turned away, and then repeated, "Sara."

He had never called her that.

She spoke in a rush, frantic to escape, frightened to believe his voice. "Will you send me the answers to my questions? Could you, might you come up sometime, to finish the article? Do you ever have a weekend off? I mean . . ."

He was staring down at his hands, which lay out along his knees, and he seemed not to hear her.

"I know you're busy," she babbled.

"Oh, stop that!" he said in an anger that was like a blast. And then he looked at her, saw the terror in her face, saw something more, and stopped, said calmly, "Of course I'm busy, but of course I'll answer the questions. And I *will* come, if you like."

Her shivering breath quieted a little. "That would be fine," she said quickly. And then, because she couldn't leave it so undecided, "When would be a good weekend for you, Jason?"

The "Jason" hit them both like a hammer, and they were still, absorbing it, when the nurse tapped and came in.

"Dr. Darvey," she said briskly, "Mr. Cardena's X-rays have come down and Dr. Baffara wants to talk to you about them."

"Yes," he said—she thought thankfully—and got up.

"I'll see that you get your prescription, Mrs. Mc-Farland," he said. "If you'll go out to the pharmacy, I'll call them."

"Yes, of course," she said. "And thank you so much." She clenched and opened her fingers like a child saying good-bye.

"I'll be in touch," he said. "And you call if you have any pain."

"Yes, I will." She didn't want him to go, but it was too horribly embarrassing with the nurse waiting; and she wished he *would* go, as long as she knew she would see him again. But he lingered. "You'll take six a day," he said. "They'll put it on the label to remind you." He was very serious, all business, but his eyes looked strange, almost as if they wanted to cry—or laugh, perhaps.

She picked up her purse. "I'll remember. I'm very good about taking medicine when I have to, even when I hate it." And she smiled inclusively at him and at the waiting nurse. "Thanks again." And they all went out the door together, almost jamming it, until he dropped back and let them go ahead of him.

*H*ome *was not the same.*
When she had come home before it was always with a sense of relief. When the car turned the corner and she could see her house was still standing, she took a deep breath of pleasure. Because what she always expected to see was a still-smoking heap of ashes. She had no confidence in things lasting, and she always foresaw disaster. Strange. She was so full of morbid imaginings and people always thought her such an optimist, so *jolly*.

But this time, even the house looked alien. They pulled into the driveway of the big brick house and she looked at it almost without recognition. Had she really lived here for twenty-three years? Was it this place she and Harry had papered and painted themselves, working until late at night in curtainless rooms with hanging, unshaded bulbs glaring over their heads?

It was so different now. There was more money. They had hired a lot done since then—pulled down a porch, added a breezeway, built a new fireplace, redecorated the inside. It was a comfortable, cozy house now. It hadn't changed much in fifteen years. Why not? Had they tired of redoing it? Had they realized at last that the house made no important difference anymore? Watching the pleasure of young friends in reorganizing a living room, changing the curtains, thinking and planning and shopping for weeks for a new carpet, she had understood that none of that mattered to her anymore. Even when she got cross with the shabbiness of a rug or a couch, the prospect of spending weeks shopping, matching, picking, arranging with an upholsterer all seemed such a bore that she let it go. After all, would they really be any happier if they had a new rug? You had to be very young to believe it could be important. And she wasn't young anymore.

Ann and Jeff were at the car door when she opened it. It was like a royal progress. She squirmed out of the door carefully, protecting her back, and then stood and looked at them. Jeff, as always, needed a haircut, not to make him conventional (she liked long-haired men) but to make him as handsome as he could be. Whenever it got too long, his thick hair stuck out in an absurd square about his big, hawk-nosed face. But he looked at her now in such a funny way: anxiously, his smile fixed as though for a photograph. He put his arm around her shoulders and gave her a hug that started to be fierce and suddenly loosened as if he had just remembered about her back.

"Hello, darlings," she said, hugging him back and holding her other arm out for Ann. Ann walked into it

reluctantly. She didn't care for physical contact, but she didn't evade it now. She just looked as if she were doing something a little silly. Her face looked tight and anxious, a little irritable, as it did so often nowadays.

"God, it's good to get home and to find you all here," she said, and the love gushed out of her eyes so nakedly that she embarrassed herself as well as them. "Here, take this bag, Jeff, will you? I can't think why I took so much stuff. I always leave home as if I were going on a world cruise and would need *everything*!" She began to laugh, and it turned into a cough, a tickle that wouldn't stop. They all waited, looking solemn, though she waved her hand negligently to show it was nothing.

Heavens, if everything she did got this much sober attention, she'd go crazy.

Then they went inside. There it was, her house, a nice house, big rooms, a little shabby, but comfortable; remarkably tidy—that would be Ann's doing. But even Ann couldn't keep Jeff from absentmindedly leaving his jacket on a chair and his sneakers under the coffee table.

"Well," said Harry, "glad to be home?"

And, horribly, she wasn't sure! There was an anonymity to the hospital that was a kind of safety. A concentration. She didn't have to do anything except what she was told: "Now breathe," "Turn over, please, Mrs. McFarland," "Now just one more," "Now take these." She could be sick and think about herself and worry and, in the stillness of her room, she could even cry savagely and no one saw or cared. But home, she had to put on her face again. The children were not children anymore. They were quick and perceptive adults, and they were watching her like hawks. And Harry. She couldn't cry in her bed because *he* was there, and there was no point in upsetting him, especially when there

was nothing he could *do*—except, maybe, hold her. She had done that once, burst into tears and clung to him and begged him to hold on to her, hold so fast that she couldn't die, that he mustn't let this happen to her! And he had tried, holding her, murmuring endearments and the lies that were the best he could do, the best anyone could do.

"Darling, don't cry. You're getting better. I'll *see* to it. And you know they've got so many new things now. Don't cry so, darling. It'll be all right. Darling?"

Because of course what she wanted was the impossible. What she wanted was for the clock to turn back to that wonderful time before she'd even thought of a lump in the breast, to the time when she was young and whole and would live forever.

"The house looks so *neat*," she said, looking around at the three of them. They were the people she loved best in the world, but they couldn't help her now, and there was no point in making them miserable. The only one who could help her now was Jason Darvey. Maybe. At least he understood that there was no such thing as a "normal" life for her anymore. He knew, even as he played the reassuring game, that what mattered were those strange cells in her body that clung and divided too fast, and that if he couldn't find a way to stop them, she would soon be dead.

She felt broken in two. All the time she listened to Harry and the children, all the time she peered into the oven and exclaimed over the beef roast that Ann was cooking, all the time she chattered and told them funny stories about her hospital experiences—she somehow managed to make the awful things sound funny, the boy with the shaved head, the "zapping" room and its monster machines, the Turkish doctor—all the time,

like a heartbeat inside her, was the knowledge that it was pretense, that everything was pretense now, and it was almost too exhausting to bear.

But why was Ann so hostile? She *did* everything. She wouldn't let her mother lift a finger, wash a dish, or carry out a plate; but her voice was so sharp, even her smiles so acid, that it was uncomfortable to look at her. What was the matter with her lovely girl? They had always so loved and confided in each other. Why was there such a wall now? What had happened to them?

"Oh, Mom," she'd say angrily, "will you for God's sake leave the dishes alone? I can do them, can't I?"

It wasn't till late, when Harry and Jeff were watching a football game on television, that she was alone with Ann.

"Darling," she said at last, having to clear it up, "what's the matter? Why are you so angry with me?"

"What?" Her huge green eyes looked startled and guilty.

"I don't know, but it seems as if you're mad at me about something. What did I do?"

"You didn't do anything, Mom. I'm not mad at you." But her eyes filled with tears. "Mom," she started to say, and suddenly she burst into tears and buried her face in her mother's shoulder. "I'm not angry with *you*," she said jerkily at last, when she could speak. "I'm just angry, I guess at God." And she smiled forlornly, and then they sat down on the couch and talked. They had the room to themselves, and at last, slowly, there emerged what was really the matter.

"We've always been such good friends, Mom, you know?"

Yes, she did know. It was one of her great prides, that her daughter *talked* to her, told her all kinds of

things, her love affairs, her physical problems, her an-
noyances with people. She had been a real confidante
for Ann, she'd always thought with great complacency,
listening to the litany of her friends about their silent,
uptight children who got in trouble and never told their
parents *anything*. That wouldn't happen to her and *her*
children, she'd thought. But of course it *did*. She was as
much an atheist as a superstitious woman can be, but
she recognized one thing in the Bible as right and appli-
cable to her: pride goeth before a fall, and of all the sins,
the greatest was pride—the greatest because it challenged the basic cussedness of life and/or God. You
were safe as long as you recognized that life was hard,
fiendish, uncaring. Then you couldn't be surprised or
destroyed. It was when you thought you'd licked it,
when you thought you had somehow brought off a coup
against the fates or society or God, it was *then* that a
monster from the Jungian deeps came up and smashed
you into a screaming pulp. And it must always have
been true, and understood, even back when herdsmen
were speaking the truths that would later become a
Bible. The remarkable thing about the Bible was not
that it was the word of God, but just the opposite—that
it was the words of men, and it so often realized the
true condition of people. About some things, we were
always so wise!

And then Ann began to talk, a great spate of words
and hiccupings and jarring sobs, and she wasn't aware
for a long time of what she was saying. But it came to
her at last because she was so bright.

"You know, Mom, what I think it is, really? I can't
forgive you for getting sick and maybe leaving me! Does
that make any sense to you?"

And she looked up with her poor, sweet young face

rivered in tears, but brightening with self-discovery.

"Yes, it makes sense," was all she could say if she was not to crack up and blubber herself.

"We've always been such good friends, that even now, when I'm married—and I *do* love Stan—I feel as if you're somehow doing it on *purpose* to punish me, and that you'll go away and I'll never be safe again. Isn't that crazy?"

It was the car business all over again. That scene so long ago came back to her outlined in fire—those two little figures standing alone by the side of the road as she drove back, waiting, panicked, because she had gone away and maybe she wasn't coming back. And Ann, her arm around her little brother, comforting him, but so frightened herself. What should she do?

"Oh, Ann. Oh, my love," she cried and held her, crooning mindlessly, crying into her daughter's long, silky hair. "I'm so sorry, darling. I won't leave you unless I must. And even if I have to, it won't be to punish you, darling. Not ever. I love you."

And they clung together until they both began to feel a little foolish and Jeff called downstairs to ask if there were any cookies in the house, and they drew apart, red-nosed and teary-eyed and smiling at each other.

e looked up at Chancery House every morning on his way across the parking lot. He thought he knew which was her window, but of course it wasn't her window anymore. Some other patient had moved into it. He arrived at his parking space, Only Dr. Darvey, and walked with his usual briskness into the hospital. It was almost his only exercise these days. Hello to Bill at the door and then a smile at Lottie D., a wave toward the pharmacy, the cocoon of his office with Maxie peering at him through her new contact lenses that still made her eyes water. The smell of the coffee urn pervading the room.

"Good morning, Maxie. What's new? Your eyes feel any better?"

"Hi, Dr. D. Yes, I guess they do." She was doubtful but determined. It was hard for him to remember that

at that age he could have been so ardent to have contacts. Now he wore reading glasses, which he carried in
his breast pocket and left everywhere, and it never occurred to him to wonder if they ruined his looks.
"These damn glasses just *ruin* my face," Maxie had told
him when she decided on contacts. So now she was no
longer ruined, just red-eyed and blinky. A pleasant-
looking girl, Maxie, who was always trying to do something *extra* to herself. Once it was blue eye stuff all over
her lids, once it was pancake makeup so white she
looked like a Charles Addams vampire lady, once it was
green fingernails that made him feel Martian, or sick.
And she was most attractive when she was left alone, a
decent nose, perhaps too small a mouth, nice, dark blue
eyes, now red. How little we know how we look! When
he went into the toilet, he looked curiously at himself.
He was getting on. His thin face was already lined, and
far too pale. His nose was . . . a nose . . . his mouth a
little too large. He couldn't see his eyes, at least not
with any sort of expression that told him anything.
Deepish sockets, but that was all. The windows of the
soul. Could anybody, looking at someone's eyes alone,
tell anything about him? Eyes had no expression. The
expression came from the lines and wrinkles around
them. Sara's eyes were wide and brown, but that said
nothing. The big thing was that they were so luminous,
as if light came *from* them instead of going *to* them. He
couldn't imagine them dead, even though he knew too
well what dead eyes looked like. It was a good idea to
close the eyes of the dead. Otherwise you stared into
drying, glazed eyes like those of a mackerel in the bot-
tom of your boat. Dead eyes said nothing. All that nonsense about the peaceful eyes of the dead was just

that—nonsense. They had no expression at all, and even the skin around them generally lost its lines. That's why relatives so often insisted their dead relatives didn't look like them. They were gone out of their eyes, and when you were gone out of your eyes, you were all gone. Sara wanted to know if he was religious. She wanted to know for the article; but really, he thought, she wanted to know for herself. She'd said she never really "trusted" religious people. They had so easy an out and were so self-deluded. She wanted to know if he was "convinced." What had he said? He had taken Ellen to church years ago, as if he could give her God as a personal gift; but in himself, did he really believe? He stared into his eyes in the glass. How hard it was, if you'd had a conventionally religious upbringing, to realize that you didn't believe in God, or in any of the paraphernalia surrounding God. Two feelings he had: there is no personal God; but if there *were*, I should have to *hate* him. God moves in mysterious ways his wonders to perform. Well, they were *too* mysterious. He had not accepted the death of Laura. The hell with a mystery that would do *that*!

He drew back from the mirror, surprised and uneasy at how far he had come. He had always, when he thought of it at all, considered himself a conventionally decent Christian. A form. A pleasant rite—with music and flowers. A decency, a technique for burials and baptisms and marriages. But really, he didn't believe in the fundament under all that. He didn't believe in God; not even that wonderful one Michelangelo had put on the Sistine ceiling. He believed instead in Michelangelo.

When he came out again into his office he felt strange, almost light-headed, as though a great weight

of confusion had rolled off him. It's no small thing, he
thought wryly, to find, at forty-three, that you don't
believe in God. Maxie, he noticed suddenly, for the
first time, wore a gold and enamel cross over her shirt.
He must have seen it a hundred times and never registered it. What was all this business of wearing crosses,
anyway? What was the point of proclaiming your faith
to the world? If you had it, you had it. You were, presumably, lucky. Why wear it on your person any more
than you would wear a sign saying "I believe in birth
control!" or "Hey, I'm gay!" Were these not all private
matters?

The day was full, but it seemed hollow. Beth had left
yesterday, in a whirl of joyful packing. So much joy for
these weeks away from him! That showed what was
most important in *her* life! At once, the twinge of con-
science hit him. He corrected the sentence in his head.
He was always doing that. Why wouldn't *anyone* be glad
of a delightful change of scene when the home place was
so empty, so dull? So she was gone. Sara had been gone
a week or more, too, and now, now he was all alone
with his house and his office and his forty-six patients.
Not quite alone!

"What's so funny?" asked Maxie, pursing her small
mouth inquiringly.

"Nothing," he said, because he could think of nothing
that would suit. "Was I laughing?"

She looked at him judiciously. "Well, smiling rather
hard!"

"Sorry," he said soberly, and that made her laugh.

"It's all right to smile. Anyone who can smile around
here had *better*," she said darkly.

"Hey! Is it that bad?"

"Well, people are always dying around here, aren't they?"

"They're always dying everywhere. You just don't see them." And that was true. Sara had said that the minute she got out of the hospital, she felt reprieved, as though she were back in a world without death. But of course it was an illusion. Because we hide death so successfully: in hospitals, in nursing homes, in funeral homes organized to cover it over with brisk efficiency. How different death must have been in other times, in Shakespeare's day, for instance, when everyone died at home, right in front of you. You saw it happen day after day, and there was nothing to buffer you against it. He remembered a tombstone he had seen once in Ireland, over a child of six: "Here lyeth the death of all our hopes." And she must have died in her bed of diphtheria or smallpox, with her parents standing by, helpless. He had seen so many deaths; he didn't know why that epitaph had stuck with him so many years.

He looked at his appointments calendar and sighed. Usually he was glad to see it filled, but today he was depressed. He didn't really want to talk to the cancer education group at eleven or the first-year residents at four. He didn't want to ask Shannon to recheck Mrs. Watson's hip X-ray again. He didn't want . . .

"Oh, Dr. D., Mrs. McFarland called this morning."

"What?" Alarm surged through him like an electric shock.

"When?"

"Quite early. I'd just gotten here."

"Did she say what it was?"

"No. She just wanted you to call back when you had time. She left her number."

"All right." He glanced at the clock. It was a quarter past nine—time for his morning rounds. "What's the number?"

He sat back in his chair after he'd dialed, consciously relaxing his rigidity. The phone rang only once, and she was there.

"Hello?" Her voice sounded strange, instantly recognizable, but strained. She must have been sitting there, waiting.

"It's Jason Darvey. What's the matter?"

"I'm so sorry . . ." she began, but he broke in.

"Never mind. It's all right. What's the matter?"

And then her voice, scarcely audible, whispering, "It's my chest," she said. "It's so sore I can hardly breathe."

Oh, God. "How long has this been going on?"

"For a couple of days. I thought at first I was catching a cold. I kept coughing and my chest was sore." She paused and tried a laugh, but it was small, frightened. "I took the Tylenol, but it didn't do much."

"Why are you whispering? Can't you talk? Is your throat hurting too?"

"No. Oh, no. It's just that I'm upstairs and Harry is still home. I don't want to scare him, but I have to do *something*." She stopped. "He's leaving for the office soon."

"All right. Now listen carefully. I want you to go to your local doctor and have him X-ray your chest and look you over. Then I want you to arrange to come down here as soon as possible. Tomorrow. Bring the X-rays with you, so we'll be a little ahead of the game and won't have to wait for them. Can you get down here tomorrow, do you think?"

When her voice came, it sounded composed again, but strained. "Well, you'll get tired of me if I come this often," she said. But then, at once, as if she realized that that kind of facetiousness wouldn't do, she added, "Yes, of course I can. I'll fly down tomorrow."

"All right. Come directly to my office and tell my secretary. She'll page me. Will you do that?"

"Yes. Thank you. I'll be there."

"All right. And take the other Tylenol, the one with the codeine in it, tonight." He paused. "And don't worry."

"No. Thank you. I'll see you tomorrow."

He hung up and drew a long breath. How could that have happened so soon? It was her lungs, of course, but why hadn't he spotted that? It had happened too fast. The last time she'd been there, there'd been no sign of anything except the bone activity. The bone scan, of course, didn't show it. And she hadn't had a chest X-ray for four months. They didn't like to do too many when there was no indication. She hadn't mentioned coughing. Well, it was D day now. He flinched. Once the lungs were invaded, there was less and less to do. Surgery, perhaps. He got up abruptly.

"I'll have Mrs. McFarland's file, please, Maxie."

She looked at him and went without a word to the little file storage cabinet where he kept his folders. It was a fat file.

"Maxie, tell Shannon I want to see him immediately and I'm on my way."

As he left, he had to go through the little knot of residents and nurses waiting to go on rounds with him.

"Sorry," he said, as they made way for him, "I'll be a little late. Will you wait, please?"

They looked at each other, surprised, and fell back a little.

He was through and by them then and on his way down the corridor. How could they have missed it? How could it have happened so fast? He reviewed the X-rays and the scans in his head as he walked. The back was clearly involved, but the femur was all right, the pin firmly in place, and there seemed to be nothing else. Oh, God. He imagined the night she had spent, beside her husband probably, but unwilling to wake him. That would be like her.

Shannon was in his office, looking at some pelvic shots.

"Hey, Jason," he said, smiling his broad Irish smile, "what's up with you?"

"Nothing's up with me, Mike, but I'd like you to pull the chest X-rays of Mrs. Harold McFarland for the past year and go over them with me."

"Hmmm-nn . . . high priority?" But something must have stopped him, for he nodded then and went to his files. He came back with two X-rays. "She's had two this year. Wait a minute." He put them up on his screen, switched on the light, and they stood and looked at them.

"Nothing, is there, Mike? Do you see anything in either of them?"

Shannon was silent, staring at them. "No," he said slowly. "They look quite clear, unless you count that little haze in the upper left quadrant. And that's a fairly typical technician's error."

"Is it one of your films?"

"No. It was brought here in her file."

"You mean she's never had a chest X-ray *here*?"

"That's right. These are both from her local hospital lab. They look quite good. The last one's dated four months back. What's the story?"

He looked at Mike Shannon. A good man, pinkish-haired and balding, bluff and maybe too hearty, but he knew his job. "She's got severe chest pain, Mike. She's coming in tomorrow. With a new X-ray."

"Ah, man, I wish you'd let me do the X-rays here. Some of these small-town radiologists can't tell cancer from tennis elbow!"

"Well, I thought it would save time. You know—" his smile was twisted sideways—"patients wait for you for hours sometimes." He remembered the old man, the old *men* he'd seen out in the hall, waiting, waiting.

"Well, it will do that, sure enough, but I don't trust them. I'll see what she brings, and maybe it will do, or maybe I'll do another. All right?"

"Good. Thanks, Mike. This blew up awfully fast, and I don't want to lose this one if I can help it."

"Sure, sure, Jason. Bring her stuff right along."

They both knew such frequent X-rays weren't a good idea, but they also knew it didn't matter in this sort of case. They weren't thinking of developing a tumor in ten years. They had to know what they had *now*.

He went off again with an awareness of Mike Shannon looking speculatively after him. He had to keep calm about this. He was no good to anyone unless he was calm. But the shaking inside him went on like a metronome. He wasn't going to lose her. Not now. Not yet. He would have to do *something*.

hen she got off the plane with her small bag, she was coughing. The stewardess looked at her, smiled, and shrugged as if to say, "Flu season. Too bad!" She smiled and shrugged back. Maybe it was. Maybe it was just pleurisy. Uncle Mel had had pleurisy, she remembered, and he had coughed and groaned and held his chest. He had done just what she felt like. So why was she so sure it was *not* pleurisy? If she cut her thumb these days, she assumed it was cancerous! Even cancer victims occasionally got *other* things wrong with them, didn't they?

The taxi driver heard her and said, "That flu's going around, all right," but then, after she gave him the address of the hospital, he was silent. People didn't usually go to the hospital for flu these days. Cost too much. They got penicillin.

It was strange to be here so fast. Harry had wanted to drive her, of course, but he was in the middle of a case and anyway, she didn't want to drive for four hours. So she had talked him out of coming. She wanted to be a patient, even a crisis patient, who didn't have to act well for anyone. Thank goodness, Ann and Jeff had left before the coughing got so bad. She could see how frightened they would have been, how reassuring she would have had to be. The thought of all that reassurance exhausted her. She wanted to think of herself alone, to cry and stamp her feet and not to have anyone there to hear her. Except maybe Jason, who had undoubtedly heard it all before and with whom she wouldn't need to act.

She checked into admissions. It was the same girl as last time. "Back so soon, Mrs. McFarland? I guess you must like us!"

She smiled. "I guess I must." It didn't hurt much just now, luckily, since she was pumped full of all the Tylenol with codeine tablets she had. And she had survived the trip. It always surprised her to survive a plane trip. That was one good thing about cancer, she thought: it kept you from worrying about other ways of death. She'd always been a white-knuckle flyer who kept a sharp eye on the wings, expecting them to buckle and fall away. And she was always the first to see that little trickle of oil out of the engine and wonder if she should inform the pilot. But this time she'd barely glanced out. After all, if the plane crashed, she wouldn't have to go through the rest of this damn disease. She wouldn't have to take her Nembutal pills. It was almost a disappointment when the plane swooped down and landed with hardly a jar.

"Dr. Darvey phoned and said would you go to his office as soon as you get in."

"Oh. Yes. Thank you." Thank God. She didn't relish the idea of going to that waiting room and waiting for more hours. The girl in his office was a friendly child. She came out of her tiny office and gave her coffee and said she'd let Dr. D. know she was here. Doctor D. She liked that. It was friendly without being intimate. Was that what it was intended to convey? She looked at the girl, back now behind her glass window. A pretty child, surely not more than twenty or so. Did he have anything going with her? How easy it was for doctors! Their patients all idolized them, and their nurses and secretaries were young, and often willing, probably. She got out her pocket mirror and glanced at herself. Too white, and there were little pinched lines around her mouth that she hadn't noticed before. They must have come last night. What a wretched night!

Harry was such a light sleeper that he woke when she turned over. And then his voice, kind, patient, half dead with sleep, "You all right? C'n I get you anything?" And her thanks, her refusals, maybe five times before she could decently get up. Why did she have to hide everything from Harry? Why had she always hidden every mark, every blemish, every ugliness or illness? He had married a beauty, he'd always said with such pride, and over and over remarked on how beautiful she continued to be. What would happen if she stopped being beautiful? If she grew really old and wrinkled and hideous? Would he still care for her? Why was she so afraid of being less than perfect for him? That's what the books call *insecurity*, and it was *her* fault, not his. What she had longed for all their life

together was to have him love her for some unnameable
element in herself, not for her looks. And maybe he
did, but he never expressed that. It was always how
pretty she *still* was, with the ominous undernote that
when she no longer was, he would disappear into the
whirlwind and leave her alone. All in her own head, a
leftover from childhood. Mom and Dad fighting, their
voices rising in rage outside her bedroom door, the tear-
ing sound as Dad ripped things up. He always tore
things when he was mad—cloth, usually, a towel, a curtain—once a brand-new tablecloth. And she, cowering
in her bed, had been sure that any minute they would
run from the house in opposite directions and leave her
alone. The only saving possibility was to be so good, so
amenable, that they would not leave her or throw her
out the window in their anger. She was still being
amenable and good, because if she weren't, everyone
would cease to love her and she would be alone. Now it
was Harry who would throw her out the window if she
ceased to be pretty, who would run away if she was too
much trouble. How idiotic! And how little it mattered
if it were idiotic or not, since she continued to act this
way now out of habit, or fear ingrained too long to be
lost. How strange! It was the same sort of thing she had
done to Ann and Jeff when she had left them! But
surely, since it was only that once, it couldn't be as
lethal to their personalities as her long-fighting parents
had been to her.

She sipped her coffee slowly, trying to relax, the cup
warming her cold hands. She hadn't drunk half of it
when he was there.

"Ah, you're here. Your trip all right?" He stood over
her in his white coat and his eyes were so warm and

worried that she felt a gush of gratitude and love.

"Yes. It wasn't bad." She smiled. "I'm still a bit high on my Tylenol."

"Huh! I don't know anyone else who could get high on Tylenol. Come inside, will you?" He took her not into one of the little examining rooms on the clinic corridor, but into a room just behind his office. It was the same sort of room—the white table, the sink, the metal cabinet—but it was separate.

"You have an examining room all for yourself?" she asked.

"It just happened to be there and it's convenient. Now." He sat her down on the end of the table and looked at her. "What, exactly, hurts?" He took from her hand, gently, the huge brown X-ray envelope she was clutching and put it on the small table.

"My chest," she said. "All of it, I guess. Probably referred pain?" She used the term in a show-off way because it sounded so medical. And then she smiled when he did.

"Referred from where? Show me exactly." He was very quick and businesslike all of a sudden, his thin face watchful and alert as she described what and where and how much and pointed. He asked her to put on a gown, and when she did, he reached under it as she lay on the table and touched her breast. She shivered. He had examined her like that at least a dozen times before, but now she shivered and her nipple, her single, placid nipple, leaped into life and stiffened under his hands. She turned her head away, dying with embarrassment, but he didn't look at her. He looked up as if he were communing with the ceiling and moved his hand away, pushing here and there, probing.

"There?" he asked. "There?" And at last he came to the place under the breastbone where the soreness lay like a sleeping tiger, a little dulled with drink.

"Yes. There," she said, her face turned sideways into the pillow.

"All right. Why don't you put your clothes on now?" he said. "I'll have these X-rays looked at." He looked at her and his mouth, his beautiful, full mouth, twitched a little as though there were something more he wanted to say, something to do.

"Yes. I will." She sat up and looked at him. "It *is* my lungs, isn't it?" she said quietly, but she could hear the tremor in her voice.

"I don't know yet. We'll have to see." And, as if he had no volition, his hand came up and stroked her hair, just once. Then he was gone and she was stuck there, once again, in a white, faceless room, waiting. She dressed and went to the door that opened into his office. No one there. Why not sit out there, find a book or something to read? The secretary was out of her little cubicle. It must be coffee-break time. She came into his office and looked around. His desk was crowded with folders and scraps of memo paper. And there were two photographs. A woman. And a woman with a girl. That would be his wife, of course, and his daughter. He had told her that much. The wife was lovely, she saw at once—and young, younger than he was, not four years older. She had nice features, a pleasant smile, and rather odd blond hair piled up on her head. But she was a pretty woman, a little too plump. The daughter was a sweet-looking girl, also blond, gentle-looking, not frowning and tough like Ann. Dear Ann. These two looked as if nothing on earth had ever hurt them,

as if they lived in a warm cocoon, protected even from chilly breezes. Had he done that to them? Had he made so much security for them? Or was it camera delusion, the camera smile that was put on like "cheese" and told you nothing true. She couldn't know. But she couldn't draw her eyes away from them. They were his family. They knew all about him. They were intimates in the special way that only a lot of years can make. As she and Harry were. Hah! Perhaps it was the same sort of intimacy, a knowledge of sore spots, places not to touch, things not to say, cautions, facades. Perhaps these happy-looking women were the same.

She turned away at last with a sigh. She thought those two were happier than she. They had, at least, this gentle man with the loving eyes to care for them. That was something. She wandered about the room, took some coffee, and came back to the desk. The folders must be patients. And there, with her name on the back spine of the top one, was hers. She looked around guiltily before she picked it up. It was like picking up a secret life, the secret life of her body. Everything was in it. The notes from her other doctors, the treatments, prescriptions, even the things she had said, the complaints: "patient complained of pain in left femur, even without pressure." And the latest entry: "patient telephoned. Severe pain in chest. Advised to have X-ray and return to hospital."

That was all. None of that dramatic stuff like "Prognosis Negative," which Bette Davis sees on her chart and which sends her into a tailspin. What *was* that old movie? Something with that awful actor in it—George Brent. Big, fattish, mustached, expressionless. *Dark Vic-*

tory. That was it. Bette Davis drinks and parties, but finally she marries her doctor and lives peacefully with him for her last few months, waiting to die. And when the time comes, announced neatly by a dimming of her vision—it was a brain tumor, she remembered suddenly—she doesn't tell him. She smiles bravely and sends him off to a medical conference, and then goes upstairs to die. Aaargh! She wasn't able to die like that. The thought struck her suddenly that she *was, really*, going to die, just like that girl, that it wasn't a movie at all, that this sore ache in her chest meant she was actually going to die very soon! How could she believe it? Philosophy was all very well, being a mote in an enormous universe was great, but that was when it was still vague, distanced, uncertain. Now there was this thing in her chest, and it meant that there was not much more time. What could she make of it? How do you die decently, without damaging anyone? Could she do that? She felt herself trembling. She wanted to kick and yell and beat her heels on the floor. It wasn't fair, she howled inside her head. It wasn't *fair*! Even though she knew quite well that nothing in this life is *fair*. It wasn't fair for her neighbor's daughter Anita to weigh 250 pounds and to be homely and full of acne and only eighteen years old. It wasn't fair to be born deaf or blind. It wasn't fair to be killed in a plane crash on your way to your first Pulitzer prize banquet. It wasn't fair to survive four years in Vietnam and then be killed in a car accident your first night home. What was fair in this world?

"Sara?" He was back, his eyebrows drawn so tight over his eyes that she knew what to expect, despite his smile. He sat down beside her.

"It's bad, isn't it?" she asked, and marveled at her calm voice. She even managed, heaven help her, a "small, brave smile."

"It's not good."

"It's in my lungs, isn't it? I guess I always knew it would happen," she said, and suddenly everything in the room swam about her and she was falling into blackness. When she could see again, she found her head down between her knees, and a hand pressing it. She stared at the floor. Her shoes, the tan ones with low heels. His shoes, black, with scuffed toes.

"What is it?" she said, trying to lift her head.

"It's all right," his voice came from above her, the hand releasing her. "You just fainted."

"Fainted? Me? I've never fainted in my life!" She sat up, indignant.

"Well, you just did. How did it feel?"

"Well, interesting, really. Everything just dissolved." She sat back, rubbing her eyes experimentally. They seemed all right, none of that *Dark Victory* dimming. "Why did I do that?"

"I don't know. Maybe I frightened you. Did I?" And his eyes were so nakedly anxious that she reassured him as if he had been Jeff.

"No. It wasn't you. It must have been *it*. I think it's the first time all through this that I've *really* known I was going to die." She looked at him gravely. "Before, it was just *interesting*, somehow. And suddenly it got *real*."

"Well, you're not dead yet," he said, but there was no doctorlike optimism in his voice. There was grimness. He wasn't going to give up on her, she thought, with a wave of joy. He would save her yet. What he didn't

know, he would find out. He would save her and they would wander off into the sunset. And he would love her forever, even though she was old and mutilated and might even lose her hair!

He kept wanting to touch her. But he didn't want, any longer, to touch her as a doctor. That was awkward. Evidently for her, too. There was no escaping her response to his hands, nor the fact that it had made *him* warm too. Thank God for Dr. Teckli. He could do a good physical exam. But it was more than a response to her body, to her erogenous zones. Why did he also keep wanting to touch her hand, to stroke her hair? He was going backward from the modern norm. The thing nowadays was to leap into bed with someone and *then* backtrack to fall in love. Well, he wasn't going to do either—leap into bed with her *or* fall in love with her. He wasn't a callow boy any longer, nor she a nymphet. God knew! The worst of it was that he felt so foolish all the time, and he wasn't used to that. It wasn't as if there hadn't been plenty of willing patients in his life, but always before

they had been a "problem," an awkward situation to evade or overcome. Even the times he had been tempted by really beautiful creatures like Sandra Dunning, he had controlled the itch—and it *had* been largely an itch. A massage parlor could have served the same purpose, and would be in all ways better than a patient. Beth, for all her loveliness, was not a sensual woman. She seemed to like it all right, but she didn't *wallow* in sex the way all men dreamed of. In fact, it often seemed to him that she preferred the aftermath to the main event, like the coziness of après-ski! And she was letting herself go a bit, eating too well, her jawline doubling.

But what *was* this thing with Sara McFarland? It wasn't, surely, just horniness. He had been there, and would surely recognize that. But it wasn't sexless friendship either. It was some odd combination of sex and tenderness, protectiveness and interest, a sort of feeling he might have for a daughter if he were also incestuous. But thinking of Ellen, he saw that that was not right either. There was no incest there, and the tenderness was larger than anything else.

. He shook his head like a bulldog pestered by flies. Why bother to encapsulate it in words? The big thing was to keep her alive, and then they'd see. He stopped in front of Kimutu's door and glanced in. There were two people there, but they looked absorbed in magazines. Alice was at the desk and the inner office door was closed.

"Alice?" he asked quietly. "Is he here?"

"Mmm-nn, yes. But there's a man in there with him. You want to see him?"

"Yes." He glanced at the waiting two. "Could I get a minute in between?"

"Sure. You're the boss." She grinned. Alice looked like a fourteen-year-old in her out-of-date miniskirt that she couldn't or wouldn't give up. She had good legs; he couldn't blame her.

"All right. I'll be in the library. Would you ask him to come in when he's through but before those other two?" He always felt like a dog when he jumped a line like this, but he had no time for waiting today.

The medical library was two doors down, a busy place, humming with doctors and nurses catching up on what they should have learned yesterday. No patients here. The books were all tough and medical, except for one little rack that featured paperbacks by, or about, doctors. He went at once to the oncology stacks and riffed about till he found the latest journal on lung cancer. It was so hard to keep up. But the article he read was no comfort. Once metastasized to the lungs, the chances dropped dramatically. Less than 5 percent survived more than a year. Surgery was the usual procedure, but the results were scarcely more impressive than leaving it alone would have been. There were hormones, of course, estrogen if the patient was premenopausal, androgens if post menopausal. Not much hope, though. Chemotherapy hadn't any answers yet. Sometimes people referred back to Colley's fever technique, an idea more than a hundred years old: giving the body such a high fever by inducing erysipelas that the cancer cells were wiped out. So were the patients a good deal of the time. But they knew that heat was useful. He wondered why nobody seemed to be following that tack now—extremes of heat and then cold, perhaps—to kill the bastards. All you heard of now was immunotherapy, chemotherapy, radiation, and surgery. But

there must be other, completely *different* directions to move! He looked up from the page and stared blankly in front of him. It was so easy in research to get locked into a *type* of investigation. The grants were there, government support was there, so research went that-a-way. That's why Rodmill Hospital was all immunotherapy, and Austen General was all chemotherapy and Parker Memorial was all gung ho to cut out hormones, so they did ovarectomies and adrenalectomies as standard procedure. And now pituitary excisions were coming in. But why not entirely different ways of looking at the bug? Like fever and freezing, or rather, dropping the body temperature drastically, but short of freezing? Or like certain kinds of vitamin or nutritional therapies? Medical schools didn't bother with nutrition except to say what was bad, like sweets for the diabetics (exploded now, anyway) and salt for the hypertensive. They—and *he*—didn't really know what certain diets might do, not as prevention, but as cure. Nobody was doing controlled studies for the NCI on Pauling's vitamin C or on the old Max Gerson diet. Nobody really knew why, for instance, those Georgians in Russia lived to be 140 or more. Was it goat's milk? A low-fat diet? Hard work? Good air? Continuing prestige in the community? Genetics? All of the above?

Damn it, there were so many intangibles, so much they didn't know, so many directions they didn't even explore. He was no medicine man. He believed in finding things out by scientific research, so that you knew, when you had it, *what* you had and *why* and could use your results on everyone. But maybe it wasn't that simple. Maybe each patient was a complex of factors who needed her own particular treatment. Maybe all those

weirdos with their ESP nonsense were for real. Maybe even hypnosis had a place in this. Perhaps even voodoo! Certainly it was true that mental state was important. The depressed and the pessimistic *did* die sooner than the positive thinkers. Giving up emotionally *did* kill people. It was suggested, though not proved, that certain psychological types developed specific types of cancer. So what could one do about all that? That was surely a matter of temperament, not accessible to doctors' exhortations. Could anyone be cured by telling him that every day in every way he was getting better and better? Coué was a nut, after all. And yet, there were people who responded to that sort of thing, just as there were people who responded to faith healers and placebos. The strange thing was that faith and placebos worked less on the bright, the educated, the scientific, who *couldn't* believe, and maybe because they couldn't believe, they died. They died as truly for science as though they had been injected with yellow fever.

"Well, you must have all the answers by now!"

He looked up blankly at Kimutu's smiling face.

"Oh. Sorry, I was woolgathering. I wish I did. Come over here, Seji, will you? I only have a few minutes and I want to talk to you about Mrs. McFarland. You've seen the new X-rays of her chest?" He drew Kimutu into a quieter alcove where they could sit across from each other.

Kimutu stopped smiling. "Yes. It's lousy, isn't it?"

He felt suddenly chilled. Even though he knew it wasn't good, it didn't help to hear Kimutu agree so quickly.

"Do you think you can cut it out? What are the chances?"

Kimutu shook his head so his black hair swung over his glasses. "You know them as well as I do. One in a thousand, maybe less. It's not localized, you know. It's massive in the left lobe and beginning in the right. I could try, of course, but I'm not sure it would be worth the struggle."

When Kimutu talked that way about his beloved knives, it was pretty hopeless. He tended to think you could cut out *anything*. But it did, it *had* worked on some people, a lot more people than the overadvertised Arthur Godfrey.

He looked at Kimutu grimly. "You think it's not worth a try, Seji?"

Kimutu shrugged. "Everything's worth a try. But what about you? Isn't there anything left in your bag of tricks?"

"Not much."

"Maybe Tony has something more by now."

"He would have told me." And he *would* have, gloating in a pseudomodest way that would be all the more irritating. He would check again, but it was too soon for anything new to surface.

"Well, Seji, I'll see. I just wanted your opinion."

Seji's round face looked suddenly grim, too. "Well, there it is, for what it's worth." He paused and looked down at his strong, blunt fingers. "Too bad. She's a nice lady."

So he went to see Tony Qual.

"Hi, Jason, you got trouble? You only stop in here when there's trouble." Tony smiled broadly, but not warmly.

"There isn't much time for social calls, Tony." He felt his hackles rise as always when he talked to Tony.

Surely there was some crassness in the man that turned him off. Or maybe it was just chemistry. They were not organized to like each other. Not that it mattered much. The work was the thing, and Tony was a thorough professional.

"Tony, I've come to about the end of my box for a breast patient with metastases to the bone and now lung. Even the adrenal suppressant isn't working anymore. Kimutu isn't very hopeful about surgery. Have you anything new that might be tried?" He didn't say NCS-42968. He didn't even want to think of that stuff and Laura. Surely there was something else.

Tony frowned, an unusual expression for his usual vast self-confidence. "Well, there's still some stuff on trial runs with the rats, but nothing there we could use yet. There's NCS-four two nine six eight, of course." He paused and went on crossly. "But we're having some trouble with that."

"Yes, I know. The side effects are worse than the disease." He had a vivid image of Laura in his head, hairless, gaunt, nauseated, and, finally, dead.

"Something like that. But we're working on side effects. I think we may get them down by next year."

"Next year is too late. When next year?"

Tony spread his hands, palms up, and raised his eyes to heaven. "Che sarà, sarà," he said. "No way to tell."

His shoulders dropped. He felt tired and blank. All around them were the cages and test tubes of science, and there was nothing here that would help. Maybe next year. Maybe in ten years. But Sara was now.

he sat
in the hospital bed and watched the door. He had asked
her to check into the hospital instead of into Chancery
House so she could be there for tests. Tests! There was
all this enormous paraphernalia, all these machines, and
they all had to be used, so they were always doing
"tests." And the tests, at least for her, always came back
positive. Yes, you have cancer. Yes, your cancer has
spread. Yes, it's in your bones. Yes, it's gotten to your
lungs. Yes, YOU'RE GOING TO DIE.

Everyone *knew* he would die, and nobody *believed* it.
It just wasn't a concept you could domesticate. Surely
everyone in the world who had died had done so in a
state of outraged disbelief. She looked around the room.
Jolly yellow for cheery dying. Well, where and how
would she prefer to do it? The answer was so immedi-

ate that she knew it had always been there. By the sea. She wanted to lie down by the sea in a warm sand dune and watch the waves and die. There were other good ways, of course. Who was that old Roman—or maybe Greek?—who had invited all his friends to a feast, then cut his wrists, and talked and joked with his friends until everything went black? That's not a bad idea, though hard to accomplish nowadays. She didn't have any good, stoic friends who would come! But it *was* a good idea. The worst thing about dying was its lonesomeness. It was a scary thing that everyone had to do by himself. She envied the suicide pact-ers. They, at least, could die wrapped in each other's arms, like the Mayerling pair, or at least the movie version. Harry would never do that. She smiled a thin, wry smile at the thought. He would be sorry when she died, maybe even lost without her for a while. But he loved his life, and it would not occur to him to give it up just because *she* had to. That was a pretty steep price to pay for love, after all. She probably wouldn't pay it either.

She looked at the door again. So now she knew, and she knew *he* would try his best for her, and she knew it wouldn't help, and she knew she would give everything she had to have him with her when it happened. Because she was frightened, and lonely, and there wasn't anyone at home who could help her, or whom she could even tell this to. Harry would be miserable and mute. Ann and Jeff would be terrified and angry, and she could never tell them how terrified and angry *she* was. Being a mother meant mothering, protecting. You didn't lay your miseries on your children, even when they weren't children and wanted to help. Her brother Bill was in the Middle East laying pipeline, and they

had little in common anymore. She watched the door, and its outline wavered from a crisp rectangle to melting ovals as she dozed in and out of consciousness. They were feeding her things that made her drowsy, but her chest felt better.

When he came in, she saw him break the wavy oval of the door and she sat up sharply. There wasn't time for all this drowsiness!

"Hello," she said gladly, and he smiled at her like God. She didn't believe in God, but she knew what he looked like. He looked like Jason Darvey. And she laughed aloud. "I'm so glad to see you!" she said. How could he have doubted it? He came up to the bed and took her hand.

"You're supposed to be asleep," he said, "or at least drowsy. I'm not much of a medicine man if you're so wide-awake!"

"I'm not. I've been dozing for hours. What time is it?"

"Four o'clock. Almost dinner time."

"Do I have to stay in bed?"

"Not really. Do you mind it?"

"No. It's just that I'm so comfortable I could just drift off and die right now, and I'm not ready to!"

"Of course not," he said heartily.

She looked at him. "Oh, come on, don't talk like that. You know there's not much time left. I'm scared, but I can't stand it if *you* get all bluff and phony about it!" She could feel her eyes misting over and her nose getting damp. "You know, Jason . . . may I call you that when there's nobody around?"

He nodded, and his hand tightened on hers.

"You know what I'd really like to do? I'd like to get

out of here and go someplace by the ocean and take my pills. Want to come?" And she smiled up at him, amused at the dream. What joy to have her private doctor with her when it happened!

But he didn't laugh. He looked at her, she thought, oddly.

"That's peculiar," he said, "because I was going to suggest you might like to try Dr. Ramsey's new treatment, and he lives on Tonaco Island in the Virgins."

"Are you serious? I've never been to the Caribbean. What *is* this treatment?" Had he really come up with some crazy new thing—the sort of thing that all cancer patients dream of, the thing that will arrive just in time to save them? Her heart began to batter back and forth so fast that it almost made a noise, and her chest began to ache again.

"Well, it's completely experimental, and what's more, it doesn't have the blessing of the AMA or the FDA. I've been doing some exploring. I've been on the phone to Ramsey and to some of his colleagues back here. And it sounds, well, possible. He's not a quack. He was a reputable research man in Chicago, and he thought he was onto something great. He'd done all the animal tests, but the FDA wouldn't let him start human tests. Well, anyway, the long and short of it is that he left Chicago and went out to the Virgins where there are no restrictions. He's using a derivative of maytansin— that's an African tree bark—but he'd added and changed things so he couldn't get permission to use it in this country. But he has had some interesting successes." His mouth twitched up in the way that made her want to touch the corner of it. "I have to tell you what the options are, though."

"Yes. I'd appreciate that. You remember"—she smiled slightly—"I've always wanted to *know.*"

"I know." He smiled. "I've got all your clippings to prove it. Well, then, here we go."

Nothing he could say could make it sound good. They had tried everything they knew in certain areas. Radiation wouldn't help much in that location. Adriamycin was a possibility, but it had, as she knew, side effects. Tolerable side effects, he thought, but she must know them. He told her about NCS-42968, but he could not make his voice neutral, not with Laura's raddled young face in his memory. Surgery chances were very slim for lung cancer.

"No," she said at last, "none of it sounds very good. Well, what if we leave me alone?"

"Then it gets worse, invades the other lung, and gets more painful."

They stared at each other a moment, absorbing it all, and then, suddenly, she burst into tears. He sat down quickly on the bed beside her and put his arms around her. She cried until she could scarcely breathe, and began to cough. And he held her, softly, gently, as if he would never let go.

"I'm sorry," she gasped at last. "I didn't mean . . ." and she couldn't control her voice anymore, and so lay against his chest, exhausted and at rest as she hadn't been since this gruesome thing had happened to her.

"We'll go to Tonaco Island," he said, almost crooning into her hair. "We'll find the answer. Go ahead and cry, darling Cry."

He thought later, with amazement, how easy it would have been for someone to have seen him with Sara. What would the nurses have thought if they had seen him holding her? And he realized, with the same dumb amazement, that he didn't care at all. It was a remarkable state of mind for a cool, somewhat inhibited character. That, he knew, was what his friends thought of him, and maybe Beth, too. Maybe that was why she was so cool, why he had never been able to heat her. Didn't they say, the psychiatrists, that there was no such thing as a frigid woman—only men who didn't overcome their wives' inhibitions?

He walked through the halls like a stunned ox, because he knew what he was going to do, and it was totally outrageous and unheard of. He was going to run

away with Sara McFarland! Run—that was a laugh. She limped still, and he wasn't all that agile these days. But it didn't matter. He was going to take her away from here and do something he could never even have contemplated before. He was going to try something outside of what he knew and trusted, as unscientific a thing as Philippine faith healing. He felt strange and unlike himself as he walked into his office. It was clinic day, and patients still sat in the waiting room.

"Hello, Mr. Bancroft," he said, "Miss Randovsky." He nodded and smiled his way through the room and into his office. Maxie came in at once, full of news, hands dripping X-rays. Miss Randovsky seemed to be picking up on her CMF. Mrs. Roglin's baby was vomiting too much and now had diarrhea, too. Dr. Britton had set their meeting for tomorrow at ten.

"Yes," he said, "all right. I'll see Miss Randovsky now, and bring the Roglin baby into room six. And Maxie—well, never mind, I'll do it myself."

She looked at him curiously. Did he act odd? Was there something about him that looked as distrait as he felt? "Maxie," he said, "call Dr. Hall and ask for an appointment as soon as possible. Tonight, if he can, or tomorrow morning."

"Yes, Dr. D."

My God, what am I doing? he thought, watching as Maxie put through the call. This was his place, his kingdom. He knew it as he knew his front hall at home. Was he really going to leave it and run away to some crazy, probably futile place with a dying patient? He felt disembodied, not at all the Jason Darvey he was sure of. This was like a zombie that had taken over his limbs and was moving them about. Remarkably, no

one seemed to notice. He talked to Miss Randovsky and felt her neck nodes and she seemed to see nothing new about him. He dispensed information, told nurses what to do, prescribed for the Roglin baby, examined the two new patients, one of whom had melanoma and would be dead soon, the other with Hodgkins that they could *do* something about now. And he *was* useful here, needed here. Slim as the results sometimes seemed, they *did* get results. Only not for Sara. And he loved Sara.

The word jolted him. He was ridiculous, a foolish man caught in the seven-year itch—the twenty-one-year itch would be closer—a middle-aged idiot. He used all the names he could think of, but it didn't make any difference. He wanted to be alone with Sara. He wanted to kiss her, hold her, make her laugh and whimper and cry out with joy. He wanted to watch her laugh, listen to her voice, lie in bed with her, eat dinner with her— all the things any young lover wanted. And they were middle-aged and married, and she was going to die soon and he couldn't help her. He could hold on to her here, for a brief time, but only at the expense of seeing her like Laura, sick and vomiting and in a pain that cried out for hypos, *anything*. But he couldn't do that.

"Dr. D., Dr. Hall says can you come over right after your clinic? He has some work to do and he's staying late." Maxie's voice on the office phone.

"Yes. Thanks, Maxie. I'll be there."

The rest of the day went in a kind of blur. He saw patients, prescribed, sent them here or there for tests, palpated them, listened to their chests, and all the time he was busy making up his speech for Martin Hall.

He was free at last at six o'clock, almost time for his

evening rounds. But he went instead to the office in the old building that Martin had taken over because it was so big. They were prodigal with space in the old days, so even though it was somewhat inconvenient, Martin had chosen its spaciousness and its high ceilings, and now it would take dynamite to dislodge him. He knocked on the old oak door that said Martin Hall, M.D. No title, but everyone who needed to know found out that he was the chief executive of the hospital.

"Come in, Jason, come in. What's on your mind?" Martin sat back in his desk chair and looked at him inquiringly. He was not a man to waste or mince words. Six and a half feet tall, with a shock of rather theatrical gray hair that he had "styled," he didn't suffer fools gladly. But he was a strong executive. He hired and fired with no sign of dismay. Not a warm character, but a respected one. The nurses all but tiptoed when he was around.

"Martin, I have an unusual request." He didn't sit. He was too restless to sit down in the big leather chair beside the desk. That chair always made him feel like a petitioner and today, when he *was*, he didn't want to feel that.

"Oh?" Hall's eyebrows rose slightly. "That sounds ominous. What is it?"

"I want to leave for a few weeks, and I'd like you to get someone to cover for me."

Hall sat forward, frowning. "Leave? Why? Where are you off to?"

"It's a personal matter, Martin, but I do need some time off."

"Are you well?"

He smiled at that. "Yes, of course. If I weren't, I'd

stay right here, wouldn't I? No, it's not my health." He paused. How to make it sound like sense of any kind? "You know," he said, and they both knew it was an evasion, "I haven't taken any time off for six years now, except for the occasional conference or a long weekend here or there."

"I know, Jason. I know. Not that you *couldn't* have, of course, if you'd wanted to."

"Well, Martin, now I want to. What I want is a kind of leave, a sabbatical, if you like, but not that long."

"Jason, you're one of the best men in this hospital. We both know that, and so there's a tendency to keep you grinding away." He sat back and smiled suddenly. "Of course you can go. How on earth could I stop you?"

"By telling me I couldn't come back!" He said that but he didn't mean it. He would have left even then, though he knew it would never be exacted from him.

"Who do you have in mind as a replacement?"

"Dr. Harmon. He's quite capable of taking over, and he knows most of my cases. And, of course, I have several residents, third-year men, who carry a lot of the load right now. But Harmon as chief."

Martin looked at his steepled fingers and over them at the photographs on his desk.

"How's your family?" he asked abruptly. "Beth and Ellen okay?"

"Yes. Fine. Beth's in Martinique with her sister at the moment. And Ellen's at school, of course."

"Oh? You're all alone?" His eyes sharpened, and Jason knew he should never have said that. After all, what did men do when they were alone and free? And was he, for that matter, any different? He had a quick moment of wanting to tell Martin—to tell *someone*—

what he intended, but he couldn't do it. He had never been intimate with Martin Hall, despite their good working relations and the annual staff picnic at Martin's house in the suburbs.

"Just briefly," he said, and smiled as naturally as he could. "Well, do I have your permission?" He used the word like a schoolboy before a housemaster, and they both smiled at that bit of pretense.

Hall got up. He was so tall it was like a skyscraper rising. He reached across the desk and the two men shook hands. "What choice do I have?" Martin asked, with an attempt at humorous pathos. "Only have Harmon get in touch with me as soon as you go. He may need an assist here and there."

"Right. I'll do that."

And then he was walking down the peeling yellow corridor back to his office in the new building, as free as a bird. How fantastic! As easy as that! Why had he never tried it before?

When he came into Sara's room, she was talking on the telephone, a cheerful tone that he could recognize as wifely at ten paces. Beth sounded just like that. Funny he'd never noticed. She looked up, smiled at him, and covered the receiver with her hand. "It's Harry," she said softly. "I'll be with you in a minute." And then she turned back to the phone and said, "Sorry, dear, they're coming in with their testing apparatus again. I'll call you later."

It was a lie, of course, and he was amazed at the ease with which she did it. Were women all such good actors? Or did you have to have a big stake in something before you got so good? After all, he had done quite as good a job on Martin Hall just a few minutes ago.

"How are you feeling?"

"Not too bad, actually. I've begun to think of our article again. That's a good sign, isn't it?"

"Listen, Sara," he said, and he couldn't conceal the urgency in his voice. He felt as though he had to speak fast, like an international spy with a spool of vital microfilm. She sobered at once and reached out her hand to him. He took it but he didn't sit down. "I am arranging for you to be treated by Dr. Ramsey, the one I told you about, on Tonaco Island."

She looked at him. "My God, how do I get there? Do I make plane reservations or what? Does my family come? What do you want me to do?"

And she was so clearly in his hands that he could hardly swallow enough to talk.

"Could you possibly get away *alone*? I have some time off from the hospital, and I could take you there and oversee the treatment." He paused. He couldn't ask her not to tell her family, and surely they would want to be with her when it was obvious that this was an unusual and last-ditch kind of effort. What he was doing, essentially, was asking her to throw over her family and run off with him. There were medical reasons, of course, but he knew quite well that they were not the big thing. Those medical reasons were exactly the same ones that should make her family's attendance so important. He was asking her to go with *him* instead of *them*, perhaps to her death, though they could always be called and be there in four hours if she wanted them.

Her brown eyes looked enormous in her pale face as she sat, her hand in his, considering.

"Can you really leave here? Don't they need you?"

"I'm not indispensable, Sara. I've asked for a leave."

"You *have*? And *got* one?" Her smile was like light-

ning, and she clasped both his hands in hers. "How marvelous!" And then, like a schoolgirl, "I don't know if *I* can get a leave." She looked down at their clasped hands on the sheet. "You know, Jason, this is absolutely crazy, isn't it?"

"Absolutely," he agreed.

"What about your family?"

"Well, they're away at the moment." He couldn't keep his smile from looking guilty until suddenly, with delight, they both began to laugh, thinking of the possibilities.

"I'll tell Harry I have to go for this new treatment. He'll want to come along, but you know, it's awfully hard for him to do. He's all tied up with the court calendar for his cases. I'll tell him you're making all the arrangements. *Are* you?" Her eyes were like stars, if there are such things as shining, brown stars, and they couldn't seem to stop smiling.

"Yes. All you'll have to do is get dressed and take a taxi to the airport and pick up your ticket at the desk. Can you do that?"

"Oh, yes. Yes, of course. When?"

"Tomorrow morning at eight. The plane leaves at nine-thirty." He didn't tell her quite what a fantasy this was—the miles of lies he would have to perpetrate first, the hospital release he would have to sign tonight, the discussion about her with the resident on her case, the arrangements for her plane ticket and his own. He didn't think he should get on the plane at the same time as she did, if possible, because there were always people he knew flying about, though probably not to Barbados, where they would have to change. Perhaps he could have gone openly if he were taking her to another clinic

center, though doctors didn't do that either anymore, any more than they made house calls. If a patient in extremis had to go somewhere, he would *send* her, either in her family's car or in an ambulance, and he would telephone to discuss her treatment. Doctors didn't just fly off into the blue with patients, not unless they were on permanent hire with the Rockefellers or the Kennedys. And for them to go to Tonaco Island was the last straw. Dr. Ramsey was outside the pale of orthodox therapies. Who could believe staid, straight Dr. Darvey would send a patient off to such a place? They'd be far more likely to believe he'd stay and send her down the regular, approved chutes to death. Her face looked more alive than that of anyone he knew. He couldn't imagine it dead like Laura's, etched in stone or ice.

"Oh, how marvelous. Yes, of course I can. I'll have to call home, but I can manage that." She paused suddenly and her face grew somber. "You know, I'm very fond of Harry, but I've never wanted to die with him. Does that sound crazy? Living with him has been fine. We get along very well, but years ago I remember thinking I didn't want to die with him. I couldn't be open and wretched with him. Why don't I feel that way about you?"

"You mean I'm the right man to die with?" He tried to sound indignant, but he knew quite well what she meant. There are people who are quite all right to live with, to eat, drink, and sleep with, even to have children with, and minor problems, but there was too much buildup of facade sometimes. You couldn't be totally open with them. There was always some acting, and when you were dying, you didn't want to have to pretend. Dying was enough of a torment without having to act out a scenario.

"Because I'm used to death and dying—and because I'm going to keep you alive," he said. And then he heard efficient footsteps, and at once, like guilty lovers, they dropped their hands and put on their proper faces.

othing new is easy. To change your pattern in any way is to shift all the connections of your life. Sara told so many lies within the next twenty-four hours that she almost lost track of reality. Harry was more insistent on coming with her than she had anticipated. He could let her go alone to the hospital because he knew it now and just what she would be doing there. To go suddenly to a strange Caribbean island to a new doctor—and to go alone—he couldn't contemplate.

"I can delay the Marcome case," he said. "I just need to push it back on the calendar a week or two. Don't be silly. Of course I'm coming."

"Darling, listen. They're going to put me on the plane here and take me off at the other end. I'll just be

there two weeks, and the treatment involves my spending most of the time in bed. They prefer I don't have visitors during that time. So what would you do?"

"I'd watch you sleep and get a sunburn!"

"Harry. Darling, listen. It's just a simple, straightforward treatment, but it's too new to try here, and there's some problem about getting the drug in. But I'll be perfectly comfortable and taken care of. . . ."

"What do you think Ann and Jeff will think of *that*?"

"My new treatment?"

"No, going for it *alone*!"

For once Harry seemed not to notice the mounting telephone bill. It took twenty minutes to get him to agree that she should go alone, on condition that she called him every night.

The calls to Ann and Jeff were even worse. But she got through them all at last. She went through the whole farce of hospital release with a straight face, though it had always struck her as absurd that sick people had to have a doctor's permission and check out before they could leave. It was like being paroled from prison. But Jason had signed her release, and the adolescent at the desk made no complaint.

Then, at last, she was on the plane. What she was doing was so extraordinary that all her usual reactions were changed. She hadn't once looked out the plane windows to check for oil leaks. She sat in relaxed content, like a kitten after a bowl of cream, her hand clasped loosely in his, flying God knew or cared where. They didn't talk much. Both of them were exhausted from the struggles with people and with their own consciences. Every now and then they rolled their heads sideways and smiled into each other's eyes. She had had

a shot of something or other—she didn't know what—but nothing hurt her. She felt only warmth and a delicious drowsiness. When she thought at all, it was to wonder how she had gotten here, how this man beside her had so wiped out the world.

"Do you know," she said once to Jason, "this reminds me of an old play called *Outward Bound*, where a whole shipload of people are on their way somewhere, and it's really to death, but they don't know it? And you know, Jason, I don't *care*. I feel so—lucky!" She said his name with delight. For now it was hers to say, as he had miraculously become hers. So unexpectedly. How could she have hoped for an event like this; all the years of dry, expected days had drifted down like silt on an ocean floor, and she had expected nothing more. After a certain age, what goes out of life is expectancy. And no matter how good or comfortable or kind, nothing quite makes up for the expectancy of change, of joy, of new love. She'd scarcely realized that before, even when she'd beaten her head back and forth against the pillow—Harry was brushing his teeth in the bathroom, she could hear the buzz of the electric toothbrush—and cried out in her head, It can't be all gone; there must be something more!

The stewardess brought them dinner. They could see that she found them intriguing, this man and woman so clearly middle-aged, so clearly delighting in each other. Nowadays, the big thing was youth, dropping old wives for nymphets. She must think we are on a second honeymoon. And when she looked at him, he smiled as if he had noticed it too.

The food was wonderful: flakes of chicken on biscuit with a kind of pale yellow goo on top, a tiny paper cup

of red and green coleslaw, three strips of asparagus with a dab of cheese melted on top, an ice cream cone of mashed potato. On the side of the tray there was a paper plate with a square of cake with shocking pink icing, and a cup for coffee, and tiny silver containers for salad dressing and salt and sugar and cream. Doll house food. None of it looked at all real, but she was ravenously hungry suddenly, and she ate every crumb, even the papery cake. She hadn't eaten cake for months, so she could be slim, at least. But now, with total abandon, she ate her way through it all like a locust through a cornfield. And asked for more coffee.

He ate, too, but lightly. Mostly he watched her in smiling amusement.

"Don't you dare laugh," she said, chewing. "I'm starved!"

"I know, darling. I *see.*" And he laughed at her, but with such loving eyes that it was like bathing in a warm sea. How had she been so lucky? How could she bear this much happiness? Did she have to get cancer to find this out? How absurd. How priceless! The word "darling" on his lips stopped her in the middle of a gulp of coffee, and she leaned to kiss him, softly, secretly, on the lips. They stared at each other, amazed—at least *she* was amazed. She had never kissed him before! They were certainly not movie lovers!

"Jason, darling," she said, "I've never kissed you until now."

"Yes, you have," he said. "You kissed me when I left you that day at Chancery House. I hardly made it down the stairs!"

"Really? I know I did, and I worried about it all night, but I never thought it mattered to *you.*"

"Hah! What exactly did you think I felt?"

He was so close beside her in the cramped seats that she could feel the warmth of his body, the heat of his face.

"I didn't know. I just felt foolish and embarrassed and wished I hadn't." How little we ever know of what goes on in another head—even the heads we think we know and love. Whatever happens to join us, the real truth of life, human life, anyway, is that we are doomed to be separate. "Isn't it sad," she said, "how we misunderstand each other, how people never really know each other? I can't see how anybody ever falls in love and makes it through to marriage and goes on for years with another person. How did *we* ever get this far? How did *you*? What is your wife like? I saw her picture on your desk. Do you love her?"

He was silent, sipping his coffee, and she wished she hadn't asked that. He might just as fairly ask her about Harry, and she wouldn't know how to answer.

"Never mind," she said quickly. "If you're like me at all, you're a whole ragtag of feelings and it doesn't matter now. What matters now is that we're on this quite outrageous holiday and that we've discovered each other. Isn't it incredible?" And she turned to him with such rapture that he stopped drinking and kissed her again, softly but thoroughly, until a voice over their head said, with scarcely hidden laughter, "Would you like a liqueur?"

They drew away guiltily, but the stewardess's face was all smiling amusement, and they laughed suddenly, including her in.

"Yes, I'd love one," she said. "Cointreau?" and the girl busied herself with her little wagon of bottles and glasses.

"What will you have?" she asked him, feeling as reckless as if she had ordered heroin.

He looked at the array of tiny bottles. "How about a cognac?"

They fingered their glasses until the girl had gone on and then clicked them together.

"Here's to a long and happy life," he said, smiling at her.

"No, that's no good. That's not possible. Here's to *us*, long or short. I'm so happy now I can hardly breathe!"

His brows drew down a little, but he drank to that. She should not have said that, she thought, angry with herself. It brought up the whole awfulness of the future, because, really, they *had* no future, did they, not even if she lived. What could they do, leave their wives, husbands, children, whom they surely loved, run away to some crazy never-never land? They were as close to a never-never land today as was possible in this life. And maybe it was enough. One shouldn't tempt the gods too often. They were jealous gods. It didn't do to be too happy.

"Tell me," she said, "do you like your work?"

"I do today," he said, laughing, the line smoothed out from between his brows.

"Oh, come on, now, I mean it. Tell me how you can bear it. You don't run away with *all* your patients, do you?"

"Not quite all!"

"Well, then . . ."

"Are you interviewing me again?" He leaned and kissed the end of her nose.

"I do want to know, for myself, really. I want to know all about you. You're as strange as a new fish in an aquarium to me. I want to know where you came

from and how you got this way and why you care about me. Is that asking too much?"

"Far too much, but I'll tell you all there is to tell—all I know. I feel as if I've been asleep for years."

"Do you?" She was delighted. "How marvelous. So do I. And that we have somehow waked up together at the same time on a new planet!"

"Ladies and gentlemen, we are arriving over Barbados. Will you please fasten your seatbelts for touchdown in six minutes?"

They couldn't stop smiling at each other, almost grinning.

"How clever they are," she said into his ear, "to be so sure it won't be five minutes or seven."

*I*t's a terrible thing to feel like one long cliché, she thought, especially if you've used words all your life. Why should the most important feelings of life all fall into such trite verbal forms? I love you. I hate you. Haven't we met in another life? I want to know all about you. Flaubert was right when he said, somewhere in *Madame Bovary*, that we make songs for bears to dance to when we want to move the stars. It was true. Our words fall into the same grooves. Happy families have no history and lovers are all alike. They say the same things, see the same things in each other's eyes, dream the same dreams.

The curious, even remarkable thing about it was that knowing it all, seeing it quite clearly as a very old song, seemed to make no difference. I love you is always

fresh. When she looked at him and said the words, she shivered a little, as if she were offering to conquer Rome. And when he said it back to her in a tone of surprise, he looked as though he had just won the Irish Sweepstakes.

They walked out from the plane into the brilliant sunshine of Barbados like people stepping into a new world—a Plymouth Rock with an airstrip and a building surrounded by sharp, fanged cactus and palm trees. The temperature was about eighty-five.

They checked on their flight to Tonaco Island, but they were too late to catch it that day.

"Tonaco has no lights, sir," said the girl at the desk. "If you come in after five, you have to go tomorrow when it's light. Shall I make your reservation for the morning plane?"

They were dismayed for a moment, until she thought, Why not? What difference does it make where we are?

"I guess there's no choice," he said, and he looked at his watch and then, swiftly, at her in a way that chilled her suddenly. Was she supposed to do something? Take something? Was she about to turn into a pumpkin?

"We have made hotel reservations for you for tonight, sir, and the airline will pay your taxi and hotel fees."

"Oh?"

The girl smiled. She was a lovely, dark-skinned girl with blue eye makeup and incredibly long eyelashes. "We are at fault that you are late here, sir," she said, "so it is only fair."

"Well, that sounds fine. Where do we go?"

"There are taxis outside, sir. You give one of them this chit and he will take you." She wrote briskly, and handed him a form.

"Thank you." He nodded, they both smiled at the girl, and they started for the door. She was quite wide-awake now and feeling very well.

Taxi drivers clustered at the door, waiting. Very orderly they were, in a neat line of cabs that took off one after the other without confusion or argument. This, after all, was a British island, and the British were good at organization.

"We want to go," he said, and looked at the paper, "to the Marinaya Hotel."

It was a long trip, almost the length of the island, it seemed, but they enjoyed it all: the flat land with waving green fields of unidentified vegetation; the little dusty villages where the action seemed concentrated in small, open bars; the people walking on the road in brilliant-colored clothes, so close they almost brushed the taxi; the smiles and waves; the times the taxi driver called out greetings or something less friendly in words so fast they couldn't understand them. The cab seat was black leatherette, and it was hot. She felt her skirt sticking to the leather, and a line of sweat came out above her mouth. She certainly hadn't brought the right clothes for the tropics. He was hot, too. His thin, fine-boned face was sheened with sweat, and his hand on hers was moist.

"Do you know," she said, "I didn't think you could sweat!"

He laughed. "Can and do. From temperature—and you." And he looked as pleased with his rhyme as a child.

"No, really," she protested, smiling too, "I thought of you as I used to of my teachers. They had no body functions at all in my mind. I used to try to imagine an old biddy I took history from going to the bathroom.

Impossible. And you were another—all so white and starchy and cool. *Do* you go to the bathroom?"

"This *is* an elevating conversation. But the answer is occasionally. Regularly in leap year."

"Good! That settles *that*. And do you also eat and sleep and belch and fart like real people?"

"Damned if I'll tell you *everything*. Some things have to be hidden for romance to survive!"

"No," she said, "I don't want there to be anything hidden, anything at all. Do you know that after twenty-odd years of marriage, Harry and I still close the bathroom door and get a little embarrassed if we walk in on each other by accident?"

He looked at her soberly. "And do you undress in the dark?"

"Yes. I never used to, but I do now. I can't bring myself to be seen naked. It seems such a horrid travesty."

"A lot of my patients have told me that. And I can understand it. But I don't want *you* to feel it. He paused and looked out the window. "At least, not with *me*."

A wave of heat flooded over her so her face almost dripped with moisture. He meant, then, that they should be lovers. Why had she been so careful not to think of that—to accept the love and the kissing with delight, and to think no further, to try, at least, to block it out. How awful she was! How could she undress before him? He had never seen her really naked, just the bits and pieces that stayed uncovered from the so-carefully-adjusted examination sheets.

"Jason," she said, meaning to say something about this, but all at once she began to cough. She couldn't stop herself. It was like one of those tickles that wouldn't cut off. Her face grew red and her shoulders

shook. And far down she felt a soreness rising into pain.

He held her in his arms for a few moments, and then he reached for his bag, opened it, and took out a hypodermic. "Driver, will you please stop?"

The driver rolled his eyes back at them and pulled up at once.

He took her arm, caught and held it between coughing spasms, and injected something into it. Slowly the coughing stopped. The tickle subsided, leaving only a deep, far-off pain in her chest.

"Oh, Jason," she said in an exhausted whisper, "I'm so sorry."

He pulled her head down on his chest almost fiercely.

"All right, driver. Go on, please."

"Will it always be like that?" she asked cautiously, so as not to start anything. "Will it get worse?"

When she looked up sideways at his face, she was startled. His mouth was drawn up into a grimace of pain, and his eyes were closed tight. He pulled her head down again. The answer had to be yes, or he wouldn't look like that. But he didn't want her to see his face and guess.

"Darling, I'm better now. Let me sit up." She wanted to see him again, but when he released her head and she sat back, that twisted look was gone and he looked at her quite normally. "Jason, we're not going to lie to each other, are we?"

"No," he said, but his voice seemed caught far down in his throat.

"You know what I mean. None of this hearty stuff between us. All right? Agreed?"

"Yes, all right." He looked taut, his jawbones hard as though his teeth were clenched.

"Don't worry, darling," she said. "I don't intend to

ask you every ten minutes. Anyway, I think I know the
answers. This *is* a kind of outside chance, isn't it?"

He looked at her and pulled her hot face against his
moist one. "Yes, but we could be lucky," he said.

The Hotel Marinaya was beautiful. A long drive
lined with palms led up to a Spanish-style house with a
pillared portico dripping bougainvillea. The inside was
cool and dim and floored in red tiles. Their rooms—it
amused her to find that they had two adjoining rooms,
registered in their separate names—had balconies that
looked out over the slow heave of an incredibly blue
sea. There were pots of flowers everywhere, and great,
unlikely plants. There was a faint but audible hum of
insects or birds, she couldn't tell which. The rooms
were dim, with wooden jalousies over the windows.
When she opened them, a great downpour of sun came
in, heating the cool room. She closed most of them
again, but she couldn't resist leaving two open. She
didn't like enclosed places, and would rather be hot and
open than cool and closed in. The bathroom had a leak
somewhere, so the floor tiles were wet, but they were
pretty tiles, green and yellow, with birds on them.

She was combing her windblown hair when a bolt
was shot back and he came in.

"Oh, are you right next door to me? Do we share this
bathroom? Look out, darling, the floor is wet!"

He slithered, caught the sink, and laughed. "I see it
is." And then he held her in his arms, leaning against
the wall, and kissed her. Their faces, their lips, were
warm and moist and their kiss was liquid and perfect.
She had never liked wet kisses, but this was a moisture
that took in their whole bodies, this whole hot, sun-
struck island. They stood there for long minutes, and

when they drew apart at last, it was because she was out of breath and had to breathe.

They moved in silence into her room. When he began to take her clothes off, she felt his hands trembling. She stood quite still, like a child, looking away, ashamed to let him see her, but shivering a little with an ague of desire for him. When he had taken everything off, he picked her up and put her on the bed and looked at her as he undressed. How lean and beautiful he was! A faint line of dark hair led down from his stomach, and his arms and legs were hard-muscled as though he were an athlete instead of a man who spent most of his life in an office.

"I love you," he said into her ear. When he touched her, she quivered. He knew just where to touch her and she shook and looked at him almost in a swoon of pleasure, and hid her face in his neck. He cupped her one breast and fondled it, her nipple rising under his finger like a polished stone. He kissed her in all the places that she felt most wounded, and his lips seemed to find no flaw. When he spread her legs gently at last, she could hardly breathe for the waves of delight washing over her. His penis was slim and stiff and entered her softly, slowly, and his fingers touched her where she wanted them to so she said in a cooing, dovelike voice, "Oh, yes, yes," and didn't even know it. When he moved inside her it was like a river, a strong, fierce river, rising and rising until she couldn't bear it and cried out, "No, no!" but went on moving herself, moving until they both cried out aloud and gasped and held each other tight, tight, hot and moist, with their breasts, hips, legs entwined, still, motionless at last.

When she opened her eyes, the light washed into her,

but it looked dimmer than before. "It's growing dark," she whispered. He mumbled something, his arms tightening around her, and then he opened his eyes. "It's getting late," he said sleepily, smiling at her. "You are my lovely, beloved woman," he said, and closed his eyes, and she knew that somehow, incredibly, unaccountably, it was so.

y the time
they decided they needed dinner, they had made love
again, and they came downstairs at last in that vague,
exhausted state of lovers everywhere. They scarcely
needed to talk; they just smiled sleepily at each other.
Anyone looking at them would have recognized at once
that they had come directly from bed.

The dining room was very Spanish, dark-walled,
with refectory-type tables and straight, carved wood
chairs. Each table had a lantern with a lit candle in it.
There were woven pink mats and elaborately carved
stainless steel cutlery to retain the illusion of Spain
without the cost of true silver. They took their napkins
out of ivory rings—or probably bone—and smiled and
looked at their menus.

There was no one else in the dining room. "Are we too early or too late?" she asked the dark, white-coated boy who poured their water.

"No, no, missus," he said. "The hotel is quiet now. More coming in tomorrow."

"Oh. What time is it?" She had taken off her watch in her room to take a shower and forgotten to put it back. For one so used to noting time, it was odd. She was disembodied without that perpetual counting going on on her wrist.

"Seven-thirty, missus."

"Well, then, that should be all right," she said to Jason, "maybe early for Spain, but it should be all right here. I wonder why it's all so Spanish. Barbados is English, isn't it?"

"I think it's the temperature. Wherever it gets really tropical, there seems to be this Spanish thing. I don't know why."

They talked like that all through dinner, desultorily, casually, but with a kind of Mona Lisa smile on their lips that wouldn't go away, a kind of visible expression of their pleasure and their tiredness. She had not made love to anyone twice like that since she and Harry had been newlyweds. And it had not been like this, a meeting demanding but tender, with a kind of empathy between them that she could hardly believe. His hands were as sure as a surgeon's. He had known exactly where to touch her, what to do. And she had dropped all her inhibitions and responded like a woman on fire. Maybe it was true that a woman was sexually green when she was young. Maybe the old wives' tale that women mature sexually when they are in their thirties and men when they are sixteen was really true. Jason

was not sixteen, nor she thirty, but somehow the ratio was better now than she had ever known it.

"Were you an A student in anatomy?" she asked once during dinner, giggling into her glass of champagne.

He smiled self-consciously, she thought with amusement. "Well, as a matter of fact, I *was!*"

"I thought so. You know, darling, you're quite wonderful for me. Isn't it astonishing? However did I find you?"

"In an examining room—no—in a bedroom of a hospital, throwing up."

"No! You didn't! I don't remember that!"

"Yes. When you had just come out of the anesthesia. I held your head and thought what a beautiful woman you were."

"No woman is beautiful when she's vomiting!" She was indignant that she couldn't remember this, and that he had seen her so.

"Yes, you were."

Her indignation washed away like mist. He was surely the oddest man in the world, so maybe he had not felt the horror of her sickness. Certainly he had not been put off by her one breast.

"I love you," she said softly, leaning toward him, toward the steady light of the candle flame reflected in his eyes.

"You'd better," he said, teasing her. It was extraordinary how much laughter and teasing there was in him. Their doctor-patient encounters had been, on the whole, so sober. Even their mild pleasantries about her clippings or the article had not shown this side of him.

He reached across and took her hand in his thin, strong fingers. "You're about to say that we must have

met somewhere in another life. And so we did!" And they both laughed, because once again the trite and the cliché had become simply true. Another absurdity about the world.

"I'm all ready," she said, "to believe that early to bed and early to rise make a man healthy, wealthy, and wise, and that birds of a feather flock together and that a stitch in time saves nine."

"In surgery, they tell me, it often *does*."

She drew back a little, reminded that he was a doctor, *her* doctor, and that she was dying. A chilly breeze seemed to blow through the wide-open jalousies and flicker the glass-enclosed candles. He saw it at once.

"All maxims are true," he said, "including this one. Pride goeth before a fall, and a penny saved is a penny earned, and I love you." And he lifted his glass to her and drank. She looked at his dark, slightly graying hair, curling near his temples, and thought, as she had every hour for days now, How is this possible? How can I be so lucky?

When they had finished dinner and risen to leave, there was a bustle at the door and two parties of people came in with much noise and irritable talk. They had missed their plane connection too, and they were angry. They announced this to each other fiercely, condemning the airline, calling down anathema on the entire feckless Caribbean, making a disaster out of this lovely, peaceful dining room with its glow of candles and the warm breath of flowers.

They hurried a little to get out of the room and outdoors. The hotel garden shone in the rising light of a half moon. Moonlight lay on the garden pool and, beyond it, on the sea. A strange bird was singing an elaborate whistling song.

"Now seems it rich to die
When thou art pouring out thy heart
In such an ecstasy."

"Who said that?"

"Keats. I haven't got it quite right. How terrible for him to know he was dying when he was so young and so in love!"

"No," he said, "it seemed to him 'rich.' Maybe we're all wrong. Maybe we should all die at our peak of experience, die young."

"Not me," she said. "I would have to die middle-aged, at *my* peak experience." She leaned to kiss his cheek. "Why is it, Jason, so hard to accept death? Why does it always seem so unnatural, so unfair? I feel that too—more than ever now, I think—but it's so silly. After all, since everyone—and everything—dies, shouldn't we, by now, have come to absorb the idea into ourselves, to accept it? Why are we just as far as ever from doing that? Maybe *further* than they were in ancient times, when people were always dying visibly."

"I don't know. I've seen a lot of death, and it still seems to me the enemy. It makes me grind my teeth and snarl." And he told her about Laura.

She moved closer to him, so their hips moved together in one slow motion. "That *is* awful. Maybe it's because she suffered so. Would you have felt that way if she had just taken her shots and fallen asleep?"

"I don't know." He was quiet a moment, looking up at the moon. "Yes. You're right. I wouldn't have felt half so bad. To die is to be wiped out, and, as you say, everything in the world dies. But to die in agony and ugliness is something else. There's no excuse for that, for doing that to ourselves. Laura made me ashamed to

be a doctor. I wondered what the hell I was up to, why I didn't leave her alone. She made me realize we have, sometimes, to agree to death simply, and not fight and make more anguish. Funny, I didn't know I felt like that. Most of the time I've thought my patients—and everybody else—ought to fight back, '*not* go gentle into that good night.' "

"Oh, darling," she said, "that's so much what I feel like. I'm so glad you do, too. That's what Dr. Kimutu must feel, too, I think. That's why suicide seems reasonable to him. That's why he told me how many pills to take."

"Ah, you and your goddamn pills!" He swung her around to face him. "You're not to take any pills without my say-so, do you hear? I'll tell you when it's time to die!"

She laughed at his fierce expression. "Yessir," she said. "What a bundle of contradictions you are! I thought you'd just said you believed in accepting death *simply* when it was inevitable! And anyway, am I not entitled to decisions about my own body? Where were you during all those battles about abortion and women's rights?"

He pulled her to him so she felt the strong, angry beat of his heart against her. "I know. Who said I was logical? But you just remember. I'll tell you when—and if. Agreed?"

She looked up into his shadowed face. "Agreed. But you've got to promise you won't hang around making me do a Laura just because you won't give up. Will you?"

He was silent. A birdcall and the *slurr* of the sea on the shore below were the only sounds. The garden was

dim under the moonlight, making fantastic plant shadows. The lit-up house behind them looked like a ship at sea.

"All right," he said at last. "I promise."

r. Ramsey was
a huge, fat, angry man. His mustache quivered when he
spoke as though there were some volcanic eruption
going on down below. He looked hot and cross even
when he was talking to a colleague, thought Jason Darvey, so how does he act to patients? He followed Dr.
Ramsey on his clinic rounds, curious to see, and was astonished. With his patients, somehow the volcano subsided. He became calm, gentle, even soothing. When
they came back to his office he sank down in his chair,
the frown back on his big, fleshy face, as if it had re-
grown itself.

"You have a number of terminal cases here," Jason
began, and the man's eyes suddenly shot forth lightning.

"I don't use that word!" he said. "We are all termi-

nal. Some of these will live because they want to so desperately, and because of my treatment. And some will die because *nothing* will save them—at least, nothing *yet*." It was a small concession to the great world of research going on in all the cancer centers in the world. Suddenly, he leaned back, looked at Jason sharply, and smiled. It was like a mountain caving in.

"I'm sorry," he said. "You didn't come here to fight with me. I mustn't be like those preachers who give angry sermons about absenteeism to the people who *do* come to church. It's just that I get very tired of my role as a 'quack' and I get very furious sometimes to be *here*."

"It's a very nice 'here,' though, you must admit," said Jason. "If it has to be exile, you could have done much worse."

Tonaco was a tropical dream. They had driven across it to get to the clinic. There were great mountains in the middle, with plantations of cocoa and nutmeg trees, jungly areas where they had leaned out of the windows to see brilliant parrots flit from tree to tree. Then the road wound down the flank of the mountain through little villages of tiny houses, where every dooryard had an avocado or a grapefruit tree and oleanders blossomed everywhere. And finally, they had come to the town on the seashore, where old red-brick buildings climbed the hills around a fine harbor full of fishing boats. The clinic was already famous on the island, so when he asked directions, there was much pointing and flashing of white teeth in dark faces. When he had left Sara at the hotel, she had walked out onto their balcony with a sigh of pleasure and sat down to look at the sea. He didn't like to leave her alone, not even for the short time of this visit, but he wasn't going to take her to the clinic

before he saw the place and talked to Dr. Ramsey in person. It was a relief, after this long, crazy trip, to find that the clinic looked professional, and that Dr. Ramsey—he was certainly a fanatic—was not a quack. At least not in *his* sense of the word: a phony who sold fake medical knowledge for money.

Telephone conversation hadn't prepared him for Dr. Ramsey. The man was a great mountain of flesh, and he smiled rarely, but he talked with furious energy. He had no small talk—never bothered to ask how his trip had been, whether he had a good hotel, what he thought of the island. He plunged at once into a description of his method. It was flattering that he knew some of Jason's articles, but essentially, what he was doing absorbed him to the point where other treatments than his own were merely glanced at.

Now, in his cool office with the venetian blinds slatted tight against the sun, he described what he was doing, and why.

"What I have," he said, "is a maytansin derivative that kills cancer cells without damaging other cells." He paused, aware that he was claiming the cure all the world was seeking, and then shrugged his huge shoulders. "Well, without damaging *many* of them. And also without the toxic side effects that are so damaging with drugs like CMF, platinum, or Adriamycin. What's the good of treating people so they would rather be dead than be treated?" He looked angry again, and Jason had a flashing, vivid memory of Mrs. Croghan and of Laura before they had died. Nothing would make him send Sara through that unless he were sure of a cure. "Cure" —the word was never used in oncology. The most any of them would say was "a long remission." Well, what

was "long"? It might be worth some hell for five years, or three, maybe even for one. But for a few weeks? A month? To *him* it would be worthwhile to keep her alive even an extra day, but it was not himself he had to consider. And suddenly he was horribly frightened. He had promised Sara he would tell her when it was time for her to die, but how could he do that? How could he have made such a stupid promise? He could only do that when it was so hopeless and she was in such torment that *he* couldn't bear to see her. And that was *his* problem, a judgment for *him*. How could he make it for her?

"Yes," he said now to Dr. Ramsey, "I agree. We do too much damage. That's why I'm here with my patient. You have seen her records and her X-rays. She's had almost all we could give her except the most drastic surgery. And she didn't want that. What do you think?"

Dr. Ramsey looked at him keenly, and his ragged mustache twitched. He wanted, Jason was sure, to ask what his relation with Sara was, why he had brought her here. Very few patients could have arrived with their private oncologists in tow. But he didn't say anything. Perhaps he thought it was irrelevant. Perhaps he thought it would emerge later. For whatever reason, he went on to talk solely of Sara's case, as impersonally as if she had dropped from the moon into his clinic for observation.

"The lungs look bad," he said, "but you know that or you wouldn't be here. I think, myself, that it has gone too far for surgery. But we *may* be able to do something. Here is what I propose." And he spent the next half hour outlining a series of treatments and tests and

checks. "If there is no improvement in two weeks, it is likely that I can't help her."

"Two weeks! Surely that's not enough time!"

"It's enough time to tell. It won't be enough for a remission, but it will be long enough to see if she is going to respond. Not everyone responds, you know, not even to *me*." He said this heavily, and Jason could guess that he had lost patients he was still suffering over.

"Does she have to be here?"

"Would she prefer to be an outpatient?"

"Yes, she would." He hadn't asked her, but she would surely rather live at the hotel with him than here in the clinic. Unless she had to be monitored very closely, and even so, *he* could do that.

"Well, there's no need for her to be here. She will come in every morning for injections, and the rest of the time she can do what she wants. There's one side effect only: sleepiness. She may be drowsy, so she shouldn't drive."

"No. I'll see she doesn't."

The huge man heaved himself up out of his chair. "Well, then," he said, "you will bring her in tomorrow at ten?"

"Yes. Thank you." He held out his hand and it was engulfed in Dr. Ramsey's huge, clammy fist. The man ought to lose weight or he would be dead himself before very long. Or maybe not. How little we all know, he thought, and how good it was to admit it to himself. He went out into the brilliant sun glare of the marketplace.

When he got back to the hotel, she wasn't in their room. He had a moment of sheer panic. Was it all too much for her? Had she taken those damn Nembutals? Where had she gone? Surely, he thought savagely, as he

went down the dim hall and out the back way to the beach, surely she wouldn't give up before she had tried this treatment! No, he was sure of that. She was not a suicidal type, she said, and he knew it was so. Her vitality was too intense. She wasn't a depressive person.

So where was she? He hurried down the path that led to the beach. It was an old-fashioned hotel, Victorian, really, with turrets and round rooms, quite incongruous in this climate. But they had both fallen for it, over the local Hilton, which looked, further down the beach, like a fugitive from Miami Beach.

He looked away from the Hilton. There were few people on the beach, but far down he saw one stooping and rising as though she were picking flowers. That had to be Sara. She was a shell collector. He started down the beach, but stopped halfway to take off his sand-filled shoes. The sun beat down like a hammer, though it was already four in the afternoon. It was too hot for her to have gone so far. And when he got a little closer, he saw that she was standing up, looking toward him and holding her chest.

Oh, God, she's gone too far. She doesn't know how weak she is. How can I keep her quiet without telling her how bad it is? He slowed down, waved, smiled. And she waved back and held up something he couldn't see. Some perfection of shelldom, no doubt. His own chest felt sore as he approached her and heard that she was coughing.

"Darling, what are you doing way down here?" He came and stood before her and held her in his arms, his shoes, tied together, banging against his back.

But she couldn't answer. She leaned against him, coughing, coughing as if her chest would explode.

"Here," he said. "Sit down and swallow. Swallow as

hard and as often as you can." It was a nonsense remedy, not a doctor's, but he didn't have his bag, and maybe he could psych her out of that shattering cough.

She sat and did exactly what he told her, like an obedient child who has perfect faith in her father. And, for no reason, it worked. Talk about placebo effects! Her coughing slowed, and as she gulped and swallowed, she began at last to gasp instead of cough.

"There!" she said in triumph, still gasping for breath. "You're marvelous!" And she leaned against him, her head against his chest, still swallowing hard.

He must have been holding her too tightly, because all at once she wriggled a little in his grasp and moved away and turned to face him.

"Jason," she said, and his name still sounded strange and lyrical from her lips, "I'm all right now. How did you find me?"

"I guessed, and there you were. I figured you'd walk away from the Hilton!"

She laughed. "Isn't it crazy to build a place like that *here*? Our place is so much nicer. Well, what did you find out?"

"It looks good. You start tomorrow. I rather liked Dr. Ramsey, though he may surprise you."

"How long will it take? I must call and tell Harry tonight."

Harry? For a moment he couldn't think who that was. And then he thought of all those people back there somewhere over the horizon, all those people who waited and wondered—Harry and Jeff and Ann, and soon Beth and Ellen, and Martin Hall, and Maxie—all of them came and sat on his back like some vast mountain of responsibility. Something had to be done about

them. They hadn't—quite—disappeared off the face of the earth.

"It will take at least two weeks to tell, maybe more." He couldn't bring himself to say that in two weeks they would *know*. It seemed so final a date. And anyhow, he didn't see how Dr. Ramsey could be really certain so soon. But it would do as a date to give all those people back home. Curious that he could think of them as "all those people" when he so loved Ellen and Beth was still dear to him—wasn't she? He felt now as though nothing existed but this little island and this woman. He neither wanted to nor could think of those others.

"Well, I'll say that, I guess." She looked at him and her eyes crinkled up with laughter. "I feel wonderful—full of lies and wickedness—and I don't care. Two weeks here sounds like a million years if we can spend it together; and I can make up stories all the way to hell and back. Isn't it terrible?"

"Terrible," he said, but he couldn't laugh. It was too possible it might be to hell and back.

"Don't be so solemn," she said. "If we're going to do a deathwatch, let's at least make it a jolly Irish wake!" and she pressed her cheek against him and turned to kiss him. "I'll tell Harry I'm staying at this great hotel and that I'm having daily treatments and that I must keep very quiet and not be disturbed and nobody must come. And I won't say you're here at all, shall I?"

He pondered that. Actually, there was no one who knew where he was, neither at the hospital nor at home. Beth would be away for a couple of weeks or so, and Ellen was back at school. As far as anyone knew, he was on a trip somewhere. And when Beth came back, he could call and tell her he was at a meeting, or some-

thing. She wouldn't believe a holiday, probably. But if it were a conference, she might call some of their friends, or even Maxie, to find out where. Unless he called first and told her when, exactly, he would be back. It was all so complicated that it made his head ache, unless it was the sun.

"You're worried, darling, aren't you?" Her voice was suddenly sober. "You shouldn't be here. It must have been terribly hard for you to get away. And what about your wife?"

"Never mind," he said. "I'll call her when she gets back. It's all right. Besides," he looked into her serious, questioning eyes and felt his heart wrench with awful premonitions. "Besides," he said, "we'll get divorces. We'll get married, shall we?"

"Oh, Jason," she said, and her eyes were lit and luminous in the lowering sunlight, "we can't, but what a lovely thing to say!"

W*hat I hate* is being so ugly for you!" she said, a passion of anger in her voice. She stood naked before the long mirror in their room. They had been in bed all afternoon, the big, lazy, useless fan creaking round and round above them. And now, on the way back from the bathroom, she had stopped, held by her own image. "Why must people get old and ugly? Why can't we go on just as we were when we were twenty and then be wiped out suddenly? The world is so badly organized!"

"Darling, you know you're not ugly. You can see that. The one breast is the only visible flaw—and that doesn't matter to me at all. Half my life is lived with one-breasted women!" His laugh, she thought, was a little bitter.

"How awful for you!" she said. "And here's another."

She couldn't stop looking at herself. At home she had rarely found the time or the will to look so long. If it weren't for the breast, it wouldn't be too bad. She hadn't, at least, gotten too fat. There was still a waistline where it should be. So many women of her age were all of a piece, straight up and down, wearing overblouses all the time to hide it. She hadn't *that* to worry about at least. But there *was* that thin white scar running up her belly, and the little one on her hip where they'd put the pin in. And her face! Crinkle marks around the eyes, little lines at the corners of her mouth, a new, tannish mole on her cheek that would probably grow into a big, black thing, given time. But it probably wouldn't be given time.

"Do I have to reassure you again? I'm getting awfully worn-out!" he said, spread-eagled on the bed, laughing at her.

"I hate being older than you," she said, still looking in the mirror. "Do you know that bit in, I think, *Hamlet*, where he holds a skull and says, 'Paint you ever so thickly, to this favor you must come at last!'?" She turned to him and smiled. "You know what's a nice thought? When I'm dead, my skeleton won't show that I had only one breast. It almost pays to die!"

"Come here," he said. "You're too full of graveyard humor today."

When she came, he pulled her down gently, but even so, she began to cough again. She turned away, sitting up on the edge of the bed in the dim room. She had never coughed like this in her life—a thick, racking cough that came from way down and seemed to bruise her chest. And when it came, she couldn't stop.

"Wait," he said, and got up quickly for his bag.

There was some wonderful thing he gave her that stopped the coughing. He stood, naked and beautiful before her, the hypo in his hand.

"You look like a ministering angel," she said when she could speak, and put her arms around his naked waist and pulled him close. He was as slim in the middle as a Hermes statue. So different from Harry, who was getting a little paunch.

"Oh, dear," she said drearily, remembering, "I have to call Harry."

"Yes, I suppose you must. Shall I tell you what to say?"

"Oh, yes, darling, do. Tell me something dense and medical that will stall off questions. I don't think I can stand many questions without cracking up."

When she called—and by some miracle, the call went through—she heard his voice, from eight hundred miles away, as clear as ice. "Sara! How are you, dear? Are you all right?"

"Yes," she said, "I'm doing fine." She had put on a robe, and so had Jason, as if, by tacit agreement, they would be soberly decent when they talked to their mates.

Then she told him the words Jason had given her and written down on paper for her, because who could remember such stuff? "I have to stay very quiet and not go about too much. So I sit in the garden and read. It's lovely here, Harry—all sun and flowers—and the temperature is eighty-three!"

"Hah! It's twenty-seven here! Shall I come down?"

"No, dear, I think better not. They want me to do nothing much but eat and sleep and get these shots. What's going on there? How are the children?"

"Worried about you, mainly. Ann calls, I swear, every night! What her phone bill is going to be, God knows! And Jeff, too. He's just finished his midterms. Says, of course, he's flunked everything."

She laughed. He seemed, in that phrase, so near. "Of course. When he says that, I know he's done fine. It's only when he thinks he's made a killing that he fails. I *do* miss them so." And hearing about them, she did. She missed them all. Only she was a little glad to be missing them. She didn't think she could stand their dear, apprehensive faces.

"Well, if you're all right, I'd better sign off. I just wanted to hear your voice."

There he was again, one of his quickie long-distance calls. But now, for once, she didn't want him to talk on.

"I'll write to the kids. Tell them not to worry. Good-bye, dear."

"All right. Do you need anything?"

She laughed. "Well, my clothes are winter-weight, but I've bought a couple of things here. I guess I don't need any more." She thought for a moment of asking for books, but that would be too difficult, and probably they wouldn't arrive before she left. "Good-bye, dear. Take care."

When she'd hung up, she turned slowly. Jason was standing out on the balcony, pretending not to hear.

"Well, did I do all right? Would you have believed me? Would you have guessed your sick wife was standing a few feet from her lover? Could you tell from my voice?"

She saw that, in some conscientious fold of his brain, she had shocked him. "I know, darling. I sound as hard-boiled as any whore. But I'm not. I'm not. I just *can't*

feel evil about you. I love you so much, darling, that whatever we do seems to me right and perfect and I can't possibly be wicked. I wouldn't hurt them for anything, but what else can I call you to *myself* but 'lover'? You are my first lover, and I love having a lover. I'm an abandoned woman and I don't care, unless *you* do." She was afraid, suddenly, of going too far. He had a strong bump of reserve and formality, and it came out sometimes when she least expected it. But she couldn't be conventional about him, and he must *know* that. If she could undress before him and make love in such uninhibited ways, it was hopeless to try to behave "properly." Hopeless.

"I'm an old fuddy-duddy," he said, holding her. "You *do* startle me sometimes, but it's because I'm not used to abandoned women." He laughed and pulled her close. "But I'm getting used to this one. And I love it."

When she came
to the clinic the next morning, she saw a long, low white building smothered in oleander and passionflowers. Bougainvillea festooned the door. Even the inside smelled unmedical. It didn't *smell* like the hospital at home. It smelled like hot wood and flowers, with perhaps just a faint touch of Clorox. The procedure was the only thing that was similar. Here, too, was a waiting room full of people, and a series of doors through which white-uniformed nurses popped like rabbits.

She signed in at the nurse's desk and then went to sit with Jason. "Do you feel at home?" she whispered.

"More flowers than I'm used to, but otherwise yes."

The patients, however, seemed to her different. They were tanned, but they seemed more desperate. A middle-aged woman with legs like tree trunks held a

handkerchief to her throat, hiding most of her face except her eyes, which looked like the darting eyes of a
frightened ferret. There was a girl with her mother,
talking rapidly to a young man whose leg had been am-
putated above the knee. The girl looked quite normal,
except that she was very careful to keep her arms covered, pulling down her long sleeves every few minutes
as though they hid a shameful secret. A bald old man
sat deep in his chair and looked at nobody. He seemed
asleep, but every few minutes he would jerk awake and
say, quite loudly, "It's no use at all, no use, no use!"
There were two women sitting together, both knitting
and looking like cozy grandmothers, except that they
were telling each other the history of their treatments,
interrupting each other without seeming to notice, talking fast, with a feverish intensity, as though some detail
of importance might get away from them.

They said nothing for a few minutes, taking it in, and
then Jason said softly, "Is it always like this?"

He didn't particularize, but she knew at once what he
meant. Was there always this mixture of fear and des-
peration? Was this *his* waiting room, too?

"Not quite," she whispered back. "Your patients
seem to me less frightened, more hopeful. *Should* they
be?"

He shook his head. "Not necessarily. But I think
maybe they come here as a last resort." Then he looked
at her quickly, his hand on the seat between them moving to clasp hers. She knew he was sorry to have said
that. It made her own case a last resort, too.

"Never mind," she said, smiling at him. "I know that
anyway. You're not to be hearty, remember?"

"Yes." But he looked unhappy. It was a strange thing

for him to be sitting in a waiting room like this. It was the other side of what he was used to.

When she went into the examining room, he came along. Doctor Ramsey was an enormous fat man who could scarcely waddle. Physician, heal thyself, she thought in dismay, watching him engulf the tiny room.

"For today, Mrs. McFarland, I will give you your first shot, and you will take it very easy. Don't play tennis or run." His tattered mustache jerked, and she realized he was smiling.

"That will be no change," she said, smiling back. "I haven't hit a ball in three years. Can I swim?"

"Today I think not. Till we see." He didn't say see what, but she could guess. Till he saw whether she collapsed with an allergic reaction, or fell asleep in the water, or, as Ann might say, turned into a pumpkin.

"All right. Thank you."

"I'll see you tomorrow," he said, and was out of the room with the speed of light, moving as fast and as unexpectedly as a bull elephant.

"Do I do that?" Jason asked as they went out.

"Exactly that." She grinned at him. "This fast-disappearance act must be the signature of oncologists everywhere. You're all afraid your patients will ask you big, substantive questions!"

His arm tightened about her shoulders, and he laughed. "We're not so dumb, are we? We're not going to get stuck with questions we can't answer!"

"I know." She was silent, enjoying the feel of his arm about her in the busy morning street, but thinking of those questions: Am I about to die? Is there any hope for me, doctor? Can I really die when the sun is so bright and the market so busy?

The clinic street led right into the marketplace, a

wonderful crammed area where tiny open-air buses waited for passengers and people sat on the ground in front of a heap of lemons and were in business. They strolled through the market, looking. He bought her a big straw hat so she wouldn't get too much sun. They stopped in front of a stand full of huge, distorted brown tubers. "What are they?" she asked the wrinkled old woman sitting beside it.

"Them ground provisions, lady. You want some?"

"Oh, I'm sorry, no. I have no kitchen here, but I've never seen anything like them."

"That all right, we got heaps of stuff they ain't got in Noo Yawk." And she laughed hugely, her face shining with goodwill.

They smiled back at her and went on, stepping carefully around piles of plantains and mangoes on the ground. There was a stand that sold drinks of a deadly-looking shocking-pink color.

"Should we try that?" she challenged.

"God, no," he said. "It looks murderous." And just then two small boys came up, took a paper cupful apiece, and swigged it down.

"*They're* not scared," she said rebelliously. Whatever could it matter at this point? she thought. Why couldn't she try everything in the world? Dying was a kind of freedom, wasn't it? Nothing to lose.

"Please," he said, drawing her away. "They're used to it. But there's no point in getting dysentery on top of your own problems. It's damned unpleasant."

"Jason! Have you had dysentery?" She looked at him in surprise.

"Sure. I've had lots of stuff. Did you think I'd spent my forty-three years in my office?"

"No, of course not. No, I'm wrong. I guess that's ex-

actly what I did think. You've got to tell me the story of your life, darling. I don't know *anything* about you!"

He rescued her from falling down a deep hole in the pavement, and laughed. "I've had a wildly checkered career," he said.

"Where did you have dysentery?"

"In Vietnam."

"My God, you were there?"

"Yep. Field hospital. A regular 'M*A*S*H' team. Only our nurses were mostly pretty homely. And everybody got dysentery, which tended to take the starch out of our sexual enterprise."

She looked at him in wonder. "Why shouldn't I have guessed that?" she said. "I must have thought you sprang out of the ashes like a phoenix. How strange! You know, forty-three years is a long time for me to catch up on. Where will you start? You were born . . . ?"

They went to a waterside restaurant for lunch and sat looking out at the busy harbor boats. Everyone in the place was so cheerful that she felt suddenly perfectly well and normal, just like everyone else. She ate her flying fish with zest and got all sorts of questions answered. The waiter liked them. They laughed a lot and watched little boys jumping in and out of a banana boat, and drank an interesting drink made with island rum and coconut juice.

"You look great," he said to her once, and smiled with what she could see was great relief. And she realized how hard this would be on him. It's the worst thing in the world to have to watch the agony of someone you love. The Nazis had figured that out when they squeezed information out of parents by torturing their

children. She thought of Ann's tight, anxious face, and of Jeff's embarrassed hugs. It was good that they were not at home to see her fall apart, if she was going to. And Harry, for that matter. He was so good and gentle with her, but what would he do when she couldn't smile anymore, what would happen when she started to scream? What would happen if this didn't work and she had to go home again?

"What are you thinking about?" he asked. "You've gotten so quiet all at once. Can't you take a compliment?" And there was Jason Darvey, across the table from her in this strange place, the light from the sun-rippled water waving over his face.

"I keep thinking how lucky I am to have you. *Do* I have you?"

"You sure do. I can't see how you did it, but here I am, a Prisoner of Love!" He squeezed her hand across the table. Then he grew serious. "But that wasn't what you were thinking. I want to know *really*. You weren't looking happy or lucky when I asked. What *was* it?"

"I was thinking of Jeff and Ann. Do you know, when I was home last, I promised them I wasn't going to die, at least not without a pitched battle? That was a stupid thing to do!"

"Why was it? You *are* putting up a pitched battle, aren't you? And you *are* going to win it!"

"What a flaming optimist you are, Jason! I wish you weren't. Because if you were a pessimist, I might be more of an optimist, just out of sheer cussedness!"

"All right. You're going to die. So is everybody. Do you need to dwell on it? I've had patients who thought they were dying and who lived on while their parents died and their young friends got killed in car accidents

and their doctors fell over with heart disease. Who can predict anything? Don't waste time on it, love." He looked at her with a kind of fierce anxiety. "I had a wonderful old Jewish patient once who kept telling *me* I shouldn't worry. 'Enjoy, enjoy,' he kept telling me."

"All right, darling. Just one thing, and then we don't have to talk about it again. I'm a little frightened of dying alone. Will you . . . will you stay with me while I do it?" His face looked so dark that she smiled and added, "It's not really my thing, and you've had so much more experience!"

"Flattery again?" He looked out over the water that laughed and sparkled in the sunlight. "Yes, I'll be with you. Don't worry."

he first few days were like a honeymoon—not like his own, which seemed to retreat when he tried to recapture it—but like the ideal honeymoons in movies. They went each morning for her shot, and then, free as air, they wandered. The sunny little town was beautiful. They were always discovering new hilly side streets with baskets of flowers fastened to the bricks of the houses, or sudden little open piazzas with benches and shiny green lemon trees.

"It's like Spain," she said, delighted, as they sat down in a tiny square. "Have you been everywhere in the world, Jason?"

"Not *everywhere*, but lots of places."

"I haven't. I've only been to England and to southern Spain. It was so exciting I thought I'd like to spend a

year in every country in the world. Where have you been?"

"Well, in England, Scotland, Wales, Denmark . . . France, Spain, Italy, Greece, once in Turkey for a week . . . in Vietnam, in Java, just briefly in Bali. . . ."

"My God," she whispered, looking at him almost with awe. "You must feel at home—or at least *recognizing*—almost everywhere. Tell me, where did you like best?"

It was a child's question, but it was the kind of question that made him think about his experience as he rarely did. He had traveled and enjoyed it, but he had tucked it away without much thought. Sara's favorite phrase—*one* of them—seemed to be that "the unexamined life is not worth living," and her questions made him examine it, almost for the first time. It was eerie, but also stimulating, because she would not be dismissed, as a child might, with some vague generality.

"Where did I like best?" He stared dreamily across their sunny piazza. "Well, aside from right here, now" —she made a little face to egg him on—"I think maybe England . . . and Greece."

"Why?"

Well, now, why had he said that? "Funny, I've never thought I'd pick those two before. England seems to me very special. I like the English—they're tough and funny—and I can talk the language, and the country is so dense with history that you trip over it. You can't turn a corner but someone has written a book about it or been crowned there or written *Hamlet*." He sat silent, holding her hand and thinking over what he had just said. "I like the sense of a rich past, and also of a decent people living actively in the present on top of that past." He laughed. "Does that make any sense?"

"Oh, Jason, exact sense. I loved England too. And I think for those same reasons. What about Greece?"

"Greece is like that, too," he said in surprise. It was a discovery he had not been aware of before. "I can't talk the language, but I have the same sense of people living on a rich midden of history, and doing it with toughness and humor in the present. Odd. There are ruins everywhere, and they're very proud of them, but they're alive *now*, too. I once asked a man on the street to direct me to a museum. He turned out to speak some English, and he *took* me to the museum and spent half a day in it showing me things and wound up arguing about American baseball." He smiled at her. "Do you know, we are still friends and write to each other occasionally?"

Her smile was radiant. "That's *it*," she exclaimed. "That *should* be what travel is all about, but it rarely is. Everyone talks about 'getting to know the people,' but really they only get to know the hotel managers and the taxi drivers, and you can hardly call that knowing. It's not easy to get past the stereotypes!"

They looked at the people in the piazza. There were two small boys sitting on the edge of the fountain with their feet in the water, pushing each other like small boys anywhere. And there was a wizened black man who watched them with what seemed a disapproving eye, until one of the boys slipped in up to his waist. Then, suddenly, he laughed aloud, his pink gums like a bright gash in his face. "You watch that, fella, maybe he gone drown!" He was teasing, but he sat up alertly watching, as if he had to take care of that child, just in case. And, smiling at the boys, a woman with a basket of green stuff on her head walked by on her way to the market.

"That's how women carry things in Greece, too," he whispered to her. "Look what it does to their walk!"

"Do you suppose I could learn that sway if I carried a book on my head for a few days?"

"It would probably take years to look like that."

"Well, I could perhaps get rid of my waddle!"

"You don't waddle!" He was indignant. "I wouldn't be here with a woman who waddled!"

"Oh, so *that* was the touchstone!" she said, and they laughed.

They kept talking, and laughing, and it reminded him of that wonderful year at Cambridge when he had read so voraciously. Now, it seemed, he couldn't get enough talk. Wherever they went, the dialogue went on. When they went for a swim and lay on the beach, cocooned in sun and hot sand, they touched each other, and talked. She wanted to know everything about him, and he had never realized there was this much to know.

She turned her face toward him once, a bit of dried sand on her nose, and asked, "What are you afraid of?"

"Afraid of?" He was a man, wasn't he? He had been brought up to be afraid of nothing—or at least not to show it when he was. And he had tamped down fear so much that he had almost killed it. He was, of course, afraid of disaster for his daughter, but he knew she didn't mean that. She wanted something more particular, about *him*, not the universals like fear of death or worry about his loved ones.

Thinking it over, he said at last, with a laugh that he, himself, felt to be shy, "I'm afraid of spiders."

She didn't laugh at that. She raised herself on one elbow and looked at him. Her face was getting tan. But she was quite serious. "Spiders? Yes. I can understand

that, even though I don't mind them. I'm afraid of snakes, crawly things. And please, spare me Freud! Do you know *why* spiders scare you?"

He couldn't remember why, or what had started it. He only remembered that once he had decided to turn their cellar into a recreation room and had started work on it when he discovered the place was full of spiders. They hung on webs in the corners. They dropped down from the ceiling. He had rushed up the steps, and gotten a carpenter to do the job. He'd never told Beth why, after he'd made so much of his ability to do the job, he had given it up so fast. He had pleaded other work to do. He told Sara that, and she nodded seriously. "Yes. I don't see why people are so ashamed of being afraid. We all *are*. What else scares you?"

"Well, besides the usual things—like being in an accident where I get paralyzed for life—I seem to be afraid of some pretty silly things."

"Like what?"

"Like lightning storms." He shrugged more deeply into the sand beside her.

"Oh, that's interesting! Do you know my mother saved me from that one? She used to send me out in the rain to play, even when it was lightning and thundering. She told me years later, when I was grown-up, that she was terrified of storms, but she wasn't going to let *me* be!" She laughed affectionately. "I wonder what she'd have done if I *had* been struck by lightning!"

He sat up abruptly. "Did she really do that? Do you know, it is just what I've done with Ellen! Beth thinks I'm crazy, but I used to send Ellen out to play in the rain too. I was determined she shouldn't be afraid of things—of anything at all."

She smiled up at him. "And I suppose she's like me—not afraid of storms, but afraid of something else my mother didn't even anticipate. Everyone seems to have something to fear in this best of all possible worlds!"

"Come and swim," he said, feeling suddenly merry and relieved, as though some ancient burden of pretense had been lifted from him. "Are you afraid of sharks?"

"Terrified!"

"Well, I'm not, so stick close to me and I'll fight them off."

And he did.

They went out in a glass-bottomed boat once because she so loved the ocean and had never seen a reef outside of television.

"Do you know what my ambition is?" she asked that day.

"What?"

"To be a crew member of Jacques Cousteau's boat. Or to go around the world on a great yacht and write articles about it for the *National Geographic*."

"Well, why not? You write, and you surely love beachcombing!"

"Yes. Why ever don't we do the things we want to do, Jason? Well, *you* do, I know, but most people don't. Writing is an awfully lonely job. And really, I'd rather be a jolly member of a yacht crew investigating sea turtles or an archaeologist digging up ancient ruins somewhere. It would be lovely to have a dozen lives and time to try out all kinds of tastes."

"I know I'm lucky, liking what I do, but you know, darling, there *are* other things I'd love, too!"

"Like what?"

He laughed. "I'd like to be a famous novelist or a very rich man with time to travel and loaf, and build beautiful houses everywhere."

"Huh. Being a novelist's not much, unless, maybe, you're Dostoevsky." She paused dreamily. "Poor, unhappy man. I wonder if the really great geniuses *know* they're great and feel compensated for all that's wrong with their lives. Wagner must have felt that, he was such an egotist. But do you suppose Bach did? Or Shakespeare? Or Leonardo?" She stared down into the limpid green water beneath her shoes. "Oh, look!" she cried out, so loudly that the boatman laughed and nodded. "Oh, Jason, *look*!" Because there below the glass was another world, strange and wonderful to them both. Flotillas of small, bright darting fish swam down there. A head poked out of waving grasses. Once a huge, solemn grouper passed by, mouthing up at them with great jaws.

"Oh, Jason," she said again and again, breathless with delight. "Oh, *look*!"

He had never been in a glass-bottomed boat before, and it was all a wonder to him, too. When they returned to shore at last, they were both dazed with heat and excitement. And then they made love in their dim, shadowy room, and were dazed with pleasure.

It was a wonderful week. It might have been anyone's honeymoon except for the dark warnings that filled him with concealed alarm.

 *he grew more* breathless every day, and could not even kiss him for long without twisting her head away to gulp in air. Climbing the few steps to their room made her wheeze so that she had to stop, and he could hear the air move in and out of her lungs. And she coughed—more now than when they'd first arrived. She tried to keep it from him, but at night, when he was asleep beside her, he had twice waked up in terror remembered from childhood, alone, with Sara up and leaning out of the window, a towel clasped to her mouth, trying to cough without waking him. It was like the old nineteenth-century horror stories about tuberculosis, only it was, he knew, nothing so benign. Strange that he could wish tuberculosis on his lovely Sara! Because now they could deal with tuberculosis, and her trouble was so much more deadly.

"Sara," he said, feeling his own body wracked by that suppressed coughing, "Sara, darling, please don't do that. Don't *not* cough!"

"I hate to wake you," she said when she could talk. "I've never been able to wake people up on purpose. Harry is such a light sleeper that I've spent years creeping out of bed, dressing in the dark, closing doors inch by inch, and it never worked anyhow." She laughed tiredly. "He always woke up anyhow, and I'd hear his voice after half an hour of creeping around, 'What's the matter?' It's the same with the kids. When they tell me they want me to wake them, I never can. They look so peaceful, I feel as though I'm hiking them back to so much worry and unhappiness."

That was what she was, he thought, holding her in his arms, a woman so tuned to others that she protected even their midnight breathing! Only she could not protect her own, not from him. The coughing worried him, and the tiredness. It was what he had expected from her X-rays, but he had so hoped that here she would, by some miracle, grow well before his eyes. He gave her injections to soothe the pain in her chest, but she had less and less energy. Once when they were making love she gave a cry of pain so that he pulled sharply away from her.

"What is it, darling? Am I hurting you?"

"No, not you," she gasped. "It's my stupid leg. I have a charley horse!" And he laughed, or tried to, rubbing her leg briskly to take the cramp out. Even the ordinary postures of love were a problem now. He was afraid to hurt her, and he grew so cautious that she laughed at him.

"Really, Jason, you mustn't treat me like a china doll!

I'll yell if I'm hurt." And she looked at him with such love that he couldn't bear it, and turned to hide his face in her hair.

"All right," he said. "You yell. Let's not hide things from each other. I want you to tell me just how you feel and when things hurt."

"Yes. All right." She pressed her hand against her chest. "All right, my genius, my chest hurts." She spoke teasingly, but he could see the spurt of panic in her eyes.

He got out of bed, naked, and went for his bag. He was having to give her stronger doses of Demerol now. It wasn't good. And he began to feel her own panic. Maybe he had made a mistake, a fatal mistake. Maybe he should have kept her in his own hospital and made Kimutu try surgery after all. Maybe, even, he should have let Tony Qual try his NCS-42968. Not everyone reacts in the same way. Sara was not Laura, after all.

On the tenth day, when he went to telephone Beth, who should just have arrived home from that other island barely over the horizon, he had almost decided to bring her back.

Beth's voice sounded so unfamiliar that he thought, at first, it was someone else—a friend—the cleaning lady.

"Jocko," she said at last, when he was so still, "what's the matter? Where *are* you?"

He had rehearsed just what he would say, but he could hardly get it out. "Nothing's the matter," he said brightly, forcing himself. "I'm at a meeting in Bermuda. How was Martinique? Did you find a house?"

"Oh, did we ever! Wait till you see it! It's up on a bluff over the water, with a terrace you won't believe. It *hangs* over the water like a ship, Jase. We've got to go

down soon so I can show you. When are you coming home?"

She had asked nothing about Bermuda! She was so used to his endless trips that she had become incurious. He might have been in Kabul or in Singapore instead of on an island not far from her.

"Soon, Beth. I'm awfully tired. I thought maybe I'd take a little boat trip through the islands for a couple of days when the meetings are over. Would you mind?"

"Oh, Jase!" She pouted over the phone. "I *miss* you, and it's awfully quiet around here. Oh, go on, honey, I guess it's only fair after *my* trip. My, did we *eat*!"

"How's Ellen?" He couldn't believe her loneliness was for him. He didn't believe he mattered to her so much anymore. Maybe he was wrong. He'd been wrong so much about Beth, and surely now he was wrong to think she felt nothing deeply. At least for him. And he felt so reamed out, so open, so fragile. It would be good if she didn't feel much, but it wasn't fair to assume it was true.

Wild horses couldn't take him from Sara now, but he felt so tired, so emotionally taut, that he couldn't deal with futures. Later, he thought, later, when we get back home, there'll be time to tell her. He would have to tell her, of course. He knew now, without question, that he wanted to live with Sara, and that meant such upheavals in their lives that he couldn't contemplate it. Nor could he contemplate her death.

"Give her my love," he said, when she had regaled him with all of her last telephone conversation with Ellen. Ellen was what worried him most. She was such a loving child. How would she take the news that her parents no longer loved each other? She was a college

girl now; maybe she would have grown sufficiently independent that it would matter less. But he could see her face, lit up by a campfire, laughing, holding out to him the first charred marshmallow on a stick. It was *like* her to give him the first. Oh, God!

When he hung up at last, leaving the precise time of his return still vague, he was wet with strain. Even on his worst days at the hospital he had never felt so drawn-out, like a hot wire pulled too thin. When all he wanted in the world was to walk about in the sun here forever with Sara, a Sara grown strong and well, a Sara full of laughter, showing him a shell, quoting a poem, kissing his ear.

But she wasn't well. She only tried to be, for *him*. And he knew it, and refused to know it. He opened a drawer once, and, rummaging for some Kleenex, he found her bottle of Nembutal capsules, a small bottle, but full to the top. He looked at it with anger—her goddamn bottle of pills!—and put it in his pocket. But later, when she was dressing, she opened the drawer for something and grew suddenly rigid.

"Where is my pill bottle?" she asked in a frozen voice.

"Oh, you and your pills," he said, startled by her voice but cross too. "I threw them out!"

"You didn't! Jason, you didn't! You had no right. They're *mine*!"

She was suddenly a fury. She ran at him and hit him on the chest, screaming with rage. "You go and find them. Get them back! Jason, don't you dare!" And she hit him till he caught her hands.

"Darling! All right. I just mean you don't need them. I wish you'd stop carting them around. Sara!"

She stopped as suddenly as she'd begun and held out her hand imperiously. "Give them to me!"

Shamefaced as a child who has stolen candy, he dredged them out of his pocket and gave them to her. She might have been a heroin addict from the fierceness of her demand.

"All right." She put them in her pocket. "Don't *do* that to me, Jason. I count on them. Don't you see?" She turned to him at last, almost herself again. "I'm like Linus with his security blanket. I *need* them, Jason."

"Yes, all right, darling." He held her gently till the trembling in her body stopped. "I'm sorry. But you don't need them, love. You've got me, remember? I'll shoot you if you like!"

"Oh, Jason, I wish you would sometimes." She looked up at him tiredly, the rage washed right out of her. "Darling, tell me something, will you?"

"Anything in the world." Relief poured over him like a warm bath. He had never seen her angry. He was ready to tell her anything.

"Here, sit down a minute, will you?" She pulled him down beside her on the bed. "It's something I want to know, and nobody will tell me. Ready?" She looked at him now with the humorous quirk of a smile that he had first loved about her. "Tell me *how* people die of barbiturate overdoses!"

"What do you mean, *how*?"

"Just that. You always read about people dying of overdoses, but nobody ever says *exactly* what happens. I read somewhere that you could drown in your vomit." She shivered. "Is it true?"

"It's conceivable, but unlikely, and anyway, you wouldn't know it." He tried to sound calm, judicial.

"Why? Tell me *exactly*!"

Oh, God. He didn't *know exactly*. You couldn't until you did it. But he could tell her medically what hap-

pened. "All your body functions slow down, like when you're asleep, only more so. Your organs cease to function. Your breathing slows down. As far as the person is concerned, he just falls asleep, like from an ordinary sleeping pill. Only he doesn't wake up. Is that what you wanted to know?"

Her eyes were riveted on him. "Is it really like that? That doesn't sound so bad. Is it better than cyanide?"

"Good God, Sara!"

She told him about her friend who had killed herself that way. "It was very fast," she said thoughtfully, "but I don't know if it hurt. Does Nembutal hurt?" She looked at him like a child who is afraid of the dentist.

He held her in his arms and they sat there on the bed, rocking together. "No," he said, "it doesn't hurt. It's like falling asleep."

She was silent a moment. "You know what else I'm scared of, Jason?"

"What?"

She gave a small, embarrassed laugh. "I'm afraid of being buried alive. Suppose I were dead from an overdose, just *suppose*," she added hurriedly, looking at his face, "and suppose I wasn't *really* dead. Suppose I was just in a sort of coma, and they buried me and then I woke up." Her whole body shuddered in his arms. "I keep thinking of ways for them to be *sure* I'm dead. Like couldn't you stick a needle through me from ear to ear? Or through my heart? I wouldn't mind that. As long as I don't get buried alive. That's always terrified me!"

"Oh, Sara!" His body felt molten, fitted into hers so it could not be pried away.

"If I wrote that I want to be cremated, would it happen?" She paused, her head against his neck. And then

she looked up and kissed his cheek and laughed. "It's really a terrible dilemma, darling. I like the idea of being buried in a nice churchyard, with people walking through and reading my long-winded stone aloud. But I'm not fond of the notion of being buried alive. So there's cremation. But then my kids would have no nice place to go and be sad. You can't properly be sad over an urn on the mantelpiece!"

"Sara, do we have to be so morbid?"

"Darling, I'm not morbid! I'm just being practical, and telling you the things on my mind. I thought you wanted me to tell you what I thought!"

He put her face up and began to kiss it, small, warm kisses that covered her cheeks and forehead and went on down her nose to her mouth. "Yes, darling. I'm sorry. I just can hardly stand thinking of you in terms of *arrangements. I'm* too morbid, I guess."

She wriggled and pushed him down on the bed and lay on top of him so that her one breast pressed against him. "I know," she whispered in his ear, "I'm a brute . . ." But she wasn't giving in completely. "It's just that dying is pretty scary, and you have so many answers for the things I've always been scared of. *Please* don't get angry when I ask you, darling. I'm planning to live forever, really, but just in case, I need to know these things."

"All right," he said, trying, and failing, to sound as didactic as he had with his nurse trainees. "If you want to know the best way, it's for me to give you a shot of Demerol that will put you to sleep. Like when you had Jeff, remember? You said you fell asleep and when you woke up, he was born. Well, then, while you're asleep, I could give you an overdose of morphine and that

would be all there was to it." He said it calmly, but his heart beat against her so frenetically that she lifted herself up and looked at him.

"But then they'd find out, wouldn't they? I mean, if they did an autopsy and found me full of morphine, you'd be had up for murder. Wouldn't you?"

"Oh, Sara, for God's sake, don't worry about *that*. All I want is for you not to worry about anything, and to get well and to go off with me!"

"Into the sunset?" She laughed. "You want a movie ending, don't you, darling?" Then she relaxed and lay beside him, wiggling into the contours of his body so they fitted like spoons.

When the telephone rang they both leaped.

Sara, on her feet in the dark, was saying, "Oh, where's the damn light? I can't find the telephone!" It shrilled again.

"Wait!" he said tensely. "Don't answer it. It's *my* room!"

She found the switch, and the light glared on.

"No," she said. "Jason, it's *my* room!"

He looked around blankly, his hair all tousled from the bed. "Yes. Okay, yes. It's yours!"

She picked up the phone on its fourth ring.

"Darling! Did I wake you? I'm sorry!"

"Oh, Harry, of course not. I was in bed but not asleep." She looked at the clock. "It's only ten o'clock. But you scared me. Is anything wrong?"

He laughed. "No, no. I just wanted to tell you I've gotten my ticket and I'll be there day after tomorrow around eleven o'clock."

"Harry! What for? I can come back myself!" She could think of nothing reasonable to say.

"I know that, but my case is over—I won, by the way—and I could use a few days off, so why not?" He paused. "Can you stand having this beat-up old husband around to bring you home?"

"Don't be silly, darling. It would be lovely. It just seems like an awfully long and expensive trip to take for just a few days."

He laughed. "Come on, Sara. It's only money!"

He was teasing her. It was what she always said when he was upset about the cost of something. It always infuriated him.

She had run out of arguments. "Well, all right, dear," she said as brightly as she could manage. "It will be good to see you."

She turned to Jason. "He's coming," she said numbly. "I couldn't seem to think of what to say to keep him there. Oh, Jason!" She walked fast around the end of the bed and hugged him fiercely.

He held her tightly. "Darling," he said into her hair, "it was bound to happen. I don't know how we got *this* much time."

She pulled away from him and looked up into his face. "You mean it's all over, don't you?"

"Sara, my love, it's not over. It never *will* be over. But we probably *do* have to go back and get ourselves and our families sorted out. We can continue the treatment at the hospital. I'll get what we need from Dr. Ramsey. . . ."

"But can you? I thought it was illegal. . . ."

"Oh, it's not illegal in itself. It's just illegal to use it on people. But no one has to know I'm using it on you. You'll be at the hospital or in Chancery House and I'll give you the daily shot."

She looked at him with sad amazement. Had she

made this pillar of honest medical practice into a felon?

"Well," she said, "if you do that, you'll have to get the stuff and leave tomorrow. Then, when Harry gets here, you'll be gone, and all I'll have to do will be to keep him from talking to Dr. Ramsey and finding out you were here!" She burrowed her head into his chest and felt, already, the seeds of exhaustion welling up inside her. It was all so complicated.

When they got back into bed, they were both too tired and grim to use their last night as proper lovers. She had her back to him, and they lay nested together, but he could feel, in the darkness, the bend of her elbow that told him she had her hand pressed to her chest.

he next morning she told Jason that she wanted to see Dr. Ramsey alone.

"Why?" he asked, suspicion pouring through him.

She smiled impishly. "Because he's my *doctor*, darling, and there are things I have to talk to him about without *laymen* in the room."

"Sara!" What did she want to ask Dr. Ramsey—more questions about dying, being cremated, being buried alive? He'd never answer her. It was all he could do himself to discuss such stuff with her.

"Please, dear, indulge me! Do you know we haven't been out of each other's sight since we got here?"

"Is that bad?"

"No. It's been heavenly. You know that. But there *are* a few personal matters a female needs to do alone. Try for a minute and you'll think of some!"

They were at the door of the clinic by this time. He looked at her. She had bought a light sundress and she'd gotten some tan. She had quite lovely shoulders. But she was thinner. He could see by the bones in her neck and a certain tautness in her cheeks that surely hadn't been there before. And she wouldn't let him see her weight. It wasn't working. Dear God, it *had* to work!

"All right," he said. "Throw me over like an old shoe!"

She made a noise like a giggle, but it turned into a cough. She turned quickly, coughing, and went inside.

He looked after her a minute and then turned back toward the market. It wasn't true that there was anything female she wanted to talk about. She had told him all there was to tell about that. What did she really want to ask Dr. Ramsey? Obviously, just one thing, the big thing. She must want to ask him if the treatment could be working; she must want to tell him what she wouldn't tell Jason, that she felt worse and that she was in pain. She'd tried hard to conceal it these last few days, but he knew she was in more pain than she told him, even when she took some Tylenol or furtively took the codeine tablets he had gotten for her. He knew what she took. He counted the tablets whenever he could be alone in the little bathroom.

The market was humming with life this morning. It was Friday and people were doing their weekend marketing. He had to pick his way carefully to avoid stepping on some eighty-year-old entrepreneur sitting on the ground, or to pass two tied but twitchy goats held by a little girl. There were a number of Americans and English people walking purposefully around, followed by native taxi men with loaded baskets. The buses stood there, mostly empty, with mottoes emblazoned

across their backs that told everyone where they
went. True Love and Love Me Tender and Don't Step
on Me and You're My Thing. He and Sara had climbed
on True Love last week, waited for it to fill, and then
been treated to a ride that covered half the island,
stopping at houses so small they barely showed through
their flowering vines. It had been delightful. A man had
come to them at one stop with a great abalone shell and
he had bought it for her. All the way back she had held
it close, exclaiming over its pearly sheen, listened to it
and pretended to hear a storm coming. A good day, that
had been. He shook his head irritably at himself. He
was beginning to tot up the good moments as if they
were over. Maybe they were, but he wasn't giving up
yet. Not by a mile. Not if he had to try NCS-42968
and a Philippine faith healer! What about psychology,
anyway? Cancer patients were supposed to be so re-
sponsive to emotional trauma. Why wasn't the opposite
equally true? Why didn't being happy make them
better—surely Sara had been happy with him here! He
couldn't be mistaken about that. And yet, in spite of it,
she had grown worse; she was weaker and in more pain.
There was no use denying that. It seemed clear that the
tumor had taken over her lungs and was invading her
chest wall.

He sat restlessly in their favorite little piazza with the
fountain. What would Dr. Ramsey tell her? He didn't
know the man very well. He could easily tell her the
wrong things. He, Jason, knew the things she was
afraid of, but how could he trust this fat man to know
where to stop with her, what to avoid? He got up and
walked back toward the clinic. The street was crowded
and cheerful and he felt sore and gray.

When he went into the clinic, there was the usual

crowded waiting room, which seemed never to empty out. She wasn't there, so she must be inside with Dr. Ramsey. He sat down in a corner to wait, growing more and more uneasy as the minutes went by. When he had been there twenty minutes or so, he could stand it no longer. He got up, and just then the inner door opened and a man came out. He looked at the man blankly and then went up to the desk.

"Is Mrs. McFarland in with the doctor?" he asked the girl.

"Mrs. McFarland? Oh, no. She left. She's been and gone."

"Oh? How long ago?" She mustn't have stayed very long. He had lingered too long in the piazza.

"Oh, I don't know, maybe half an hour or so."

"Did she say where . . ." He paused, looking at the girl's blank expression. "Well, thank you," he said. "Now will you please tell Dr. Ramsey that Dr. Darvey must talk to him right away."

That made her more doubtful than ever. "He's awfully busy," she said, and glanced around the waiting room.

"Yes, I know. Tell him it's urgent." He wasn't one to jump queues, but this was no time for niceties. He would pull rank if he had to. He had to know what Dr. Ramsey had told her.

"Yes, sir," she said, and went into the back corridor.

She was gone what seemed a long time, but when she came out she beckoned to him. "You go on in," she said disapprovingly.

Dr. Ramsey was waiting for him in the long corridor.

"Come to my office, doctor," he said, and led the way, his great bulk almost touching the wall on either side.

When he had settled himself in a chair clearly built for him, he looked at Jason with his habitual expression of anger.

"Well?" he said.

"I want to know your prognosis for Mrs. Mc-Farland," Jason said as impersonally as possible. "And also whether you have told her what it is." He was aware as soon as he had said it that the second question implied the answer to the first, but it didn't matter now.

"She is a relative of yours?" asked Dr. Ramsey.

"Yes," he said. "As you know from our first conversation, there was not much left to do in traditional therapies. You *did* say you would have a prognosis in two weeks. It is almost that now."

"Yes." The big man looked angrier than ever, and it came to Jason all of a sudden that Dr. Ramsey's anger was like his own, a kind of constant, molten frustration with this plague of a disease.

"I'm afraid I have no good news for you." Dr. Ramsey looked down heavily at his desk. "It seems that she is not responding to treatment as I had hoped. I took another X-ray this morning and I have just looked at it. The other lung is involved."

Jason drew in his breath sharply. "Does she know?"

Dr. Ramsey looked up at him and then away at a calendar on the far wall. "She asked very specifically," he said. "She didn't seem like a patient to fool. I told her it didn't look promising but that I would try to vary the dose and we would see."

"Have you done that before?"

"Of course." He was silent a moment. "But it has not improved matters much. I have worked out optimum dosages, and that is what she has been getting. I doubt if any variation would help much."

He nodded. More would probably be too toxic for her to handle. He sat there like a lump, unable either to speak or to get up.

"I am very sorry," Dr. Ramsey said. "But you are an oncologist. You know these things." His heavy head swung like an embattled elephant's to stare at Jason. "It's a beastly enemy we fight," he said.

"Yes. Would you mind if I looked at the new X-ray?"

"Of course not. I have it right here." He pulled it out of a long cabinet, stuck it up on his viewing screen, and stood beside Jason.

There was no mistake. Both lungs were involved, and perhaps the breastbone. The tumors were white fingers against the dark background. It was clear surgery was impossible. So there was just NCS-42968 now—if it was not too late even for that.

Neither of them spoke as they looked.

"Thank you," Jason said at last, and turned to go.

Dr. Ramsey was silent until he had reached the door. "I'm sorry," he said then. "She is a nice lady."

It was what Kimutu had said, almost exactly. She is a nice lady.

hen she came out
into the sun she felt queer and disembodied, and for a
few minutes she seemed to see everything with a sun
halo around it. She gripped her bag hard and walked as
fast and as firmly as she could because she didn't want
to faint, and she had to get home before Jason did.

It was true, then. It didn't seem possible that here, in
this warm, friendly island full of burgeoning fruit, she
could be going to die. The sidewalk was full of people,
tourists buying little carved boats and tortoiseshell
combs, a group of young men on the corner laughing
and slapping each other. If they existed, how could she
not? She was having trouble breathing, but she couldn't
tell whether it was the cancer or the frightened racing of
her heart. Last night she had seen blood on her Kleenex
when she had coughed. She slowed down a little to

catch her breath, but there was no question of what was to come next and there wasn't any time. Jason would not leave her alone for more than minutes at a time, and she had to do it alone. He wouldn't really let her do it. Or if he did, he would be too wrecked to contemplate. She thought with sudden wonder that that old movie *Dark Victory* was true after all. What you had to do, you had to do finally alone. You couldn't put that on anyone else, surely on no one you loved.

The hotel was dark and cool as she came out of the glare. She said hello to Mr. Harcourt, the proprietor, who was fussing with some bottles in the bar. At dinner last night, Jason had bought sparkling burgundy, which she loved, but which showed she was no drinker. Drinkers liked tougher stuff than that sweet bubbly. But Jason liked it too. Would she really not have another dinner with Jason? She walked faster and her face was full of tears. She mustn't cry because it stopped up her throat and made her cough. And when she coughed it felt as though her chest would rip apart. She hadn't told Jason how bad it was, that ripping sensation in her chest that was so frightening. When she'd coughed up that blood she had gone quickly to the bathroom and flushed it down the drain, as guiltily as though it were a crime she'd committed. She should have told him, but she couldn't, any more than she could have told Harry or Ann or Jeff. Oh, God. She went up to their room, thinking of the children. What should she say? What could she do so they would not think she was deserting them?

She took a tablet out on the balcony and began to write, without thinking too much, because she couldn't think of anything huge or permanent to say.

Dearest Ann, she wrote, and her eyes filled with tears so she couldn't see the page. *I know I promised I wouldn't leave you, but sometimes you can't help yourself. My treatment hasn't worked, darling, and I really can't seem to face more months of this. It's in my lungs now, and there's nothing anyone can do. But I want you to know how very much I love you and to ask you to forgive me for all the things I've done wrong. This is a very beautiful island, and I shall go very easily. You know me, I've* checked! *I'm writing to Jeff and Daddy too. I don't have any profundities to offer. Life has been really very good to me. I couldn't have had a better family, so I feel terribly lucky. And since everything dies, I don't see as I have any complaint. Don't be angry with me, darling. I just couldn't bear to go on any longer and this is a beautiful place to end up. All the love there is, darling, Mom.*

She tore the page off the block quickly and started another to Jeff. It wasn't very original, she thought sadly, but then, all there really is to say at the end is love and good-bye. The letter to Harry was harder. She told him that Dr. Darvey had been here to visit her on his holiday and had stayed a few days. She didn't say what had been between them, because it would be too painful altogether, but she had to explain why he was here. If he guessed, that couldn't be helped. A wave of feeling engulfed her as she wrote, and all sorts of memories of their life together came back to spill onto the page in jerky little phrases. She felt so mean to be doing this to them at such a distance, and the longing to see them once more almost overwhelmed her. But it wasn't any good. It wouldn't be a matter of seeing them once more, but of going back and dying by inches under their miserable eyes. No. That wouldn't do.

When she'd finished, she put the letters in envelopes

and sealed them and put them in the drawer with their names on them. And then she had another thought. She wrote a note to whom it might concern. She wrote that she was committing suicide because she was dying of cancer and was in pain. She said she had saved her sleeping pills and was taking them, and nobody was to blame. She looked at that bleak little note for a minute and shivered, but she had to protect Jason from any trouble later. Was there anything else she should put? Something like "While of sound mind . . . ?" Well, this was probably enough. She began to cough and her chest seemed to be on fire. When she had put the letters in the drawer, she took the bottle of Nembutal pills and a glass of water and went out with them to sit on the balcony. She didn't know how long they took to act. And she wanted Jason to be with her. She hadn't enough resolution to be totally alone. But she had to take them before he came, or he would stop her. He wasn't ready to give in, she knew, but *she* was. It would be a tricky maneuver to take them just in time.

From the balcony that looked over the garden and the beach, she could also see the side of the drive and watch for him. She sat there as taut as a string, trying not to cough because it hurt too much. She hadn't long to wait. He never left her for long, she thought with a great surge of love. There he was now, coming quickly along the side of the house.

Quickly now. Quickly. She opened the bottle and began to stuff the pills into her mouth. She felt as though she must choke on them, tiny as they were, but she drank hard and forced them down. Thirty—more than thirty—she had forgotten how many there were in the bottle, but she took them all.

When Jason came in, she had thrown the glass over the parapet into the shrubbery below and put the empty bottle in her pocket. She felt terrified, but also exhilarated, like a motorcycle racer who has just committed himself to leaping the Grand Canyon.

"Sara! Where have you been? I've been looking for you and waiting in Dr. Ramsey's office for ages. I thought you were still with him!" He couldn't hide the knitting of his forehead. He must have talked to the doctor. He must know.

"I got done early," she said gaily. "Darling, let's go down on the beach. Will you?"

He glanced at his watch. "Now? It's almost lunch-time."

"Yes, right now. I've been sitting here for ages, and I'm just dying to go for a walk on the beach. Do you mind a late lunch?"

"Of course not, darling. Sure. Let's go."

What a love he was. Surely he knew by now that it was hopeless. But he held her arm, smiling at her, and they went downstairs and through the back garden onto the beach. The sun was almost overhead and when he glanced up he said, "You've forgotten your hat. Wait and I'll get it."

"Don't bother, darling," she said as calmly as she could, but panicky because she didn't know how long the pills took.

"I'll just be a minute. You'll get sunstroke in this heat!"

He was off. She laughed suddenly to herself. Sunstroke, indeed!

But he was back almost at once with the big straw hat he had bought her on their first day. He perched it on her head.

"There," he said. "Now you look like a real islander instead of a mad dog or an Englishman."

"Thanks, darling. Let's go now."

She led the way onto the beach so quickly that he said, "Hey, wait a minute!"

But she couldn't wait because she didn't know about the time. They walked down the beach, she slightly ahead in her anxiety. They went past the last house and onto the barren, deserted part of the beach where she liked to go for shells. There was a sort of dune there where they had sat sometimes when she was tired, watching the water. She wanted to go there.

When they had reached their favorite spot, she sat down suddenly, feeling rather odd, as though her legs had turned into cooked spaghetti. There was no one on the beach at all. No mad dogs. No Englishmen. Just the sun on waves that creamed and broke unendingly before them.

"Jason," she said, holding his hand hard and looking up at him from the shadow of her hat. "Darling, I've done it. I've taken my pills!"

"Sara!" He leaped to his feet, so fierce and desperate that she was frightened. "You didn't! You must come back right away. You *didn't*!"

"Jason, my dear love, *please*. I couldn't possibly make it back down that beach again. And besides, it's the only thing that makes any sense now. Darling, please sit down with me. *Please*. I shouldn't put you through this, but I'm not very strong-minded. I'm getting a little groggy, I think, but I'm sort of scared, too."

"Sara, we've got to get those damn pills out of you. How many did you take?"

"All of them."

"Oh, God. How do you feel?" He was distraught. She could see that his whole face was clenched with strain.

"Jason, please sit down with me. You told me you'd stay with me at the end, and I *need* you. I've written notes to everyone and another one to say it's my own doing and nobody's fault." She looked at him anxiously. "Do you think that will do? It will be an awful mess for you, I know, love, but I don't want there to be any police trouble. I've told Harry you're down here for a holiday and have been to see me. That will explain your being here. And you could say you just found me on the beach when you came out for a walk, couldn't you? Oh, Jason, will it be all right for you?" Her words seemed to be getting slurred, and she took and held his hand, hard.

He didn't move for a minute, and then he sat down by her and took her in his arms and rocked her. "Sara," he said, "Sara." And she realized vaguely that he was crying. Something wet fell on her head.

"Look, darling, how beautiful it is. . . ." She sat in his arms looking out toward the water. The waves crested in funny ways, differently in different places. Just a little way from them there were some ledgy rocks and the waves leaped and broke on them. Again and again they rolled and broke with a lovely little *plop* noise. "Really, Jason, it's not so bad. It's nice here with the water coming in and you with me. I don't really mind anymore. . . ."

He had never felt such despair. He held her in his lap and she looked out at the water. It was so clever of her to have gotten them down this far. He couldn't carry her back all that way, certainly not in time to do any

good. And anyway, she was right. It was what made sense now. *She* knew it. But he didn't care about what made sense. He didn't care for a minute about what she might have to endure. He was only anguished and despairing because *he* would lose her. He felt selfish and hateful and raw with grief and anger. It had been bad enough with his father, but this was worse than anything that had ever happened to him.

"Jason," she said, looking up at him sideways, her straw hat tilted out against his chest. "I feel fine now. Nothing hurts at all. Is that the way it happens?" She smiled up at him. "I feel warm and a little numb."

His arms clasped her convulsively. He wanted to run down the shore, scream for help, drag her along through the sand. "Yes, darling," he said instead. "That's good. Nothing will hurt you. I promise." He said it as if she were frightened, but she didn't sound frightened now. Her voice was very soft.

"Mmmnn. I like to watch the waves. They're so endless they make living and dying sort of natural . . . foreverness, just like the sea." But her voice had gotten dimmer, as though she couldn't force any volume into it. I could make her walk, he thought in despair. I could make her vomit.

"Jason?" she said. "Jason? I love you." And then she said nothing for a while. They sat and watched a tiny fishing boat way out. Waves broke on the shore, apple green water marbled with foam. Tiny sandpipers ran in and out through the shallows. And then he knew he was alone.